Praise for Georgia Beers

The Shape of You

"I know I always say this about Georgia Beers's books, but there is no one that writes first kisses like her. They are hot, steamy and all too much!"—*Les Rêveur*

The Shape of You "catches you right in the feels and does not let go. It is a must for every person out there who has struggled with self-esteem, questioned their judgment, and settled for a less than perfect but safe lover. If you've ever been convinced you have to trade passion for emotional safety, this book is for you."—*Writing While Distracted*

Blend

"Georgia Beers hits all the right notes with this romance set in a wine bar…A low-angst read, it still delivers a story rich in heart-rending moments before the characters get their happy ever after. A well-crafted novel, *Blend* is a marvelous way to spend an evening curled up with a large glass of your favorite vintage."—*Writing While Distracted*

"The leads are very likeable and the supporting characters are also well developed. A really enjoyable novel, and one that leaves the reader longing for a glass of wine!"—*Melina Bickard, Librarian, Waterloo Library (UK)*

"*Blend* is a fantastic book with lovable but realistic characters, slow build-up sizzling romance, and an expertly crafted plot. The book is a perfect blend (pun intended) of wit, humour, romance, and conflict that keeps the reader turning pages and wanting more."—*Lez Review Books*

Georgia Beers "develops characters that are interesting, dynamic, and, well, hot…You know a book is good, first, when you don't want to put it down. Second, you know it's damn good when you're reading it and thinking, I'm totally going to read this one again. Great read and absolutely a 5-star romance."- *Th̶ ̶P̶*

"Author Georgia Beers delivers another satisfying contemporary romance, full of humor, delicious aggravation, and a home for the heart at the end of the emotional journey."—*Omnivore Bibliosaur*

"This is a lovely romantic story with relatable characters that have depth and chemistry. A charming easy story that kept me reading until the end. Very enjoyable."—*Kat Adams, Bookseller, QBD (Australia)*

"Ms. Beers has a knack for creating characters that feel like real people, with families and pets and backstories and all the general messiness of life."—*Llama Reads Books*

"On paper these two should not work but they do, they really do! And the connection is palpable. You can feel the chemistry—it radiated off the page...I don't think I'm exaggerating when I say Georgia Beers writes the best kisses in lesbian fiction."—*Les Rêveur*

"*Blend* has that classic Georgia Beers feel to it, while giving us another unique setting to enjoy. The pacing is excellent and the chemistry between Piper and Lindsay is palpable."—*The Lesbian Review*

Right Here, Right Now

"The angst was written well, but not overpoweringly so, just enough for you to have the heart-sinking moment of 'will they make it,' and then you realize they have to because they are made for each other." —*Les Reveur*

Right Here, Right Now "is full of humor (yep, I laughed out loud), romance, and kick-ass characters!"—*Illustrious Illusions*

"[A] successful and entertaining queer romance novel. The main characters are appealing, and the situations they deal with are realistic and well-managed. I would recommend this book to anyone who enjoys a good queer romance novel, and particularly one grounded in real world situations."—*Books at the End of the Alphabet*

"*Right Here Right Now* is a slow-burning sweet romance between two very different women. Lacey is an accountant who lives her life to a plan, is predictable and does not like change. Enter Alicia, a marketing and design executive who is the complete opposite. Nevertheless they click...The connection is sexy, emotional and very hot."—*Kitty Kat's Book Review Blog*

By the Author

Turning the Page

Thy Neighbor's Wife

Too Close to Touch

Fresh Tracks

Mine

Finding Home

Starting from Scratch

96 Hours

Slices of Life

Snow Globe

Olive Oil & White Bread

Zero Visibility

A Little Bit of Spice

Rescued Heart

Run to You

Dare to Stay

What Matters Most

Right Here, Right Now

Blend

The Shape of You

Calendar Girl

The Do-Over

Visit us at www.boldstrokesbooks.com

THE DO-OVER

by
Georgia Beers

2019

CREDITS
EDITOR: LYNDA SANDOVAL
PRODUCTION DESIGN: STACIA SEAMAN
COVER DESIGN BY ANN MCMAN

Acknowledgments

I can't recall now what got me thinking about two people who went to high school together meeting up again fifteen years later as the adults they grew into and getting to know each other, but it stuck with me for quite some time. High school was hard for me, as it is for most teenagers. I was a good student, but I was not popular. My parents divorced, and I had to change schools for my senior year. Add to that a years-long struggle with my sexuality, and yeah…not a fun time for me. While I consider myself a fairly well-adjusted adult and have gone to a couple of class reunions, there isn't enough money in the world to get me to actually go back to high school.

That being said, I wanted to show a second chance. A chance to right the wrongs done to others. A chance to talk about the things that were terrifying at the time. A chance to show (and discover) what good people we turned out to be. I hope you enjoy the journey.

Thank you to everybody at Bold Strokes Books for continuing to make the publishing process easier than I ever expect it to be. This is a good place to be as a writer.

Thank you to my editor, Lynda Sandoval, who is like my writing makeup: she finds the blemishes and imperfections, teaches me how to fix them, and makes me look better than I actually do.

Thank you to my author friends who do what I do, who understand when I feel like I haven't a clue how to write a book, and who cheer for me when I actually do just that. I'm so glad to have you guys in my corner and I'm doubly glad to be in yours. Also, thanks to my non-writing friends and family, whose support means just as much. I couldn't do any of this without you.

Finally, I am forever grateful to my amazing readers who lift me up when I need it and keep me going when I'm stalled. Thank you doesn't seem like enough.

CHAPTER ONE

"That's not how Danny did it."

Easton Evans sat at her desk and held the gaze of Brandi White—a mere one-tenth of the sales staff that hated her—and tipped her head slightly to the side. "Well, this is how I do it."

"What difference does it make?" Brandi was the ballsiest of the group, and that made her an excellent salesperson. It also made her unafraid to push back against the new management that had been installed when Hart Commodities had taken over the smaller company and made several changes. This was a tight-knit firm, so when the six managers were let go in the buyout, the staff had been understandably upset. It seemed to Easton that her portion of that staff—the sales force—had decided to vent its frustrations by making her as miserable as possible.

Easton took a deep breath and willed herself to stay calm, to not get defensive. She did her best to keep a neutral tone as she slowly explained. "It makes a difference because my bosses want the sales reports by Wednesday at noon." It wasn't her fault the apparently godlike Danny had been laid off, but she also knew the staff needed somebody to put the blame on, and as their new boss, she fit the bill nicely. But she'd been taking their muffled—and not-so-muffled—comments for over a month now, and frankly, she was getting a little tired of it. "Listen, Brandi, nobody likes change. I get that. But I still need the sales reports in by noon on Wednesdays."

"End of day Friday worked just fine when Danny was here."

"I don't care," Easton snapped, her patience fraying. "I'm not Danny."

"Yeah, no kidding."

This was going nowhere, would continue to go nowhere, and Easton was annoyed that she'd let her frustration show. Wishing she hadn't let Brandi see how much she'd gotten under her skin—but unable to keep from poking the inside of her cheek with her tongue anyway—Easton lowered her voice, hardened it. "Sales reports are due by noon on Wednesdays. End of discussion."

Brandi glared back at her for a few seconds that felt like an hour to Easton. A stand-off. Damn, the woman had a backbone of titanium. Holding eye contact with her wasn't easy, but Easton managed not to look away. Finally, three hours later (not really, but it felt like it), Brandi turned on her heel and left without another word. Easton let out a breath, irritated that she'd been holding it at all.

Her staff hated her. That was a fact. They'd loved Danny... and honestly, he sounded like a great guy. Easton had no idea how buyouts were done. She'd worked for Hart for five years, and this was a promotion for her. She'd gone from account executive to senior account executive to sales manager, but this was the first time she'd actually changed locations, started over in a brand-new setting with brand-new people. She was a good salesperson. She knew her stuff. She also knew, deep down, that she was a good manager as well, but this was messing with her confidence. Having a staff that disliked her intensely was new for her, and she wasn't handling it as well as she'd like.

There were six employees like Easton. Six managers who'd been brought in from various branches of Hart Commodities to take over the departments of this new branch. Sales, marketing, customer service, HR, traffic, and vendor. Those were the management titles, and all of them had been brought in from other locations across the region. They had a management meeting set up for that afternoon, and Easton was anxious to see if any of her fellow managers were having the same continuing issues with their staff.

Allowing herself a moment or two of peace, Easton melted into her ergonomic chair and slowly exhaled. This was the first time she'd ever had an actual office, complete with a door and a window. She'd always been in a cubicle, even as the senior account executive. This was a definite step up, and when she took a moment and allowed it, she felt a warm sense of pride in the way she'd moved up in the company.

Her office wasn't big, but it was perfect. She had a nice desk made of a light wood (oak, maybe?) and a great chair. Behind her was a matching credenza where she'd made things a bit homier by adding a plant and several framed photos, mostly of Emma. Two chairs for visitors sat angled in front of the desk, upholstered with maroon vinyl (Brandi hadn't sat in either of them, as standing—an attempt to keep the upper hand?—was her habit, Easton had noticed). A large abstract painting in pleasant, earthy colors hung on the wall opposite Easton, and she often studied it when she was trying to wind down or destress.

Like now. *God, Brandi White can needle me like nobody ever has.*

Her body jerked slightly when her cell phone rang, she was so lost in her own thoughts. A glance at the screen told her who it was, and a warm and happy wave of relief washed over her.

"Hey, stranger," she said with a smile, as she answered. She stood, crossed the office, and shut the door with a quiet click.

"My *girl*," came the voice of Shondra Carletti. "Why have I not heard from you? Are you too important to talk to us little people anymore?"

"You will never be little people to me. You know that." Easton dropped back down into her chair, felt her entire body relax at the sound of her best friend's voice. Under her desk, she kicked off her heels, if only for a short time. "You have no idea how much I needed to hear from you today."

"Last I checked, phone lines run both ways, baby girl. And did you break your texting fingers since I saw you last?"

"I know, I know. But I have been so busy over here, it's ridiculous. Between learning how this place has been running and deflecting the hateful glares of my new staff and dealing with Emma—is there such a thing as the terrible sevens?—I've just been buried under my life. I'm so sorry. My God, I've missed you."

"Sounds to me like you need one of Shondra's margarita nights."

"Yeah, I need, like, six of Shondra's margarita nights. In a row."

It was amazing how the world just seemed to right itself whenever Easton talked to Shondra. Easton was an extrovert and had many friends; she always had, even in high school. But there was something about this particular friendship with Shondra that steadied her like no other in her life. And Easton had the same effect on Shondra, despite her being five years younger. They'd discussed it more than once, settling on the conclusion that, for whatever reason, the universe meant them to be friends, and who were they to argue?

By the time Easton hung up fifteen minutes later, she'd set up dinner at Shondra's on Saturday night. "Bring Emma. I'll have my niece come over to watch the little ones so we can just chat. Tony's got a poker night with the guys." The idea of an evening of visiting, joking, and Shondra's margaritas was heavenly enough to make Easton feel almost relaxed as she jotted notes about some things she needed to bring up at the manager meeting that afternoon.

Almost.

When the Xavier Company had been purchased by Hart Commodities, there had been dozens of changes. First had been the huge sign on the building that lit up green at night, replaced by the well-known blue-and-red Hart logo. Easton had felt a pang of sympathy for the Xavier employees who had been there from the beginning, as the Xavier sign was taken down in the middle of the workday when anybody could step outside and watch. Next, and sorely needed, had been the complete remodeling of the large conference room. Extremely dated, it had contained a long, pockmarked table that was probably older than Easton herself and shockingly uncomfortable chairs with beige fabric upholstery that was so worn it was nearly threadbare. One of the first lessons she'd learned when coming to work for Hart was that making a fabulous first impression was key. You couldn't do that with a conference room that looked like it had come straight out of the seventies. So, the room had been gutted, then remade in the image of a highly successful and modern American company. Blue-gray paint on the walls; deep slate carpet on the floor; sleek new furniture with lots of black and glass and chrome; a sidebar for food, coffee, water.

It was impressive.

Easton thought so every time she walked in, even after working there for over a month. She nodded to the other managers around the table and took a seat. A few minutes later, Richard Joplin, their regional manager who Easton mentally referred to as the manager of the managers, entered the room and they got down to business.

By the time forty-five minutes had gone by, they were deep into a discussion about the negative responses of the employees.

"You all know this is not a surprise, right?" Richard stood at the head of the conference table and looked around the room with dark eyes that seemed to take in everything, seemed to actually *see* each of the managers present. Easton had only met him a handful of times, but she liked him. Liked his wisdom, liked that he was business-minded but also seemed to understand people. "Xavier was successful and good to its employees. It only makes sense that they're all feeling a little betrayed and battered. It's only been five weeks. We need to give them some time." He picked up the tablet he'd brought with him. "That being said..." He left the sentence dangling as he scrolled. "We've had some complaints."

Groans went around the table. Rolled eyes. Scoffs. Shaking heads. Sighs of exasperation.

Richard held up a placating hand. "I know. I get it. And again, this is to be expected. Every one of you has received at least two grievances from your staff. Some of you, more."

His gaze didn't stay on any one person, and Easton wondered how many she had. She braced.

Instead of rattling off some of those complaints, though, he clicked off the tablet and set it back on the table before taking a seat and folding his hands neatly in front of him. "So, here's what we're going to do." All the while, the eye contact remained, and he moved it slowly around the table. "We're going to send you all to a conflict resolution class."

This time, they weren't groans. They were gasps of surprise, of annoyance, of anger.

"You're kidding," said Kim Banks, the customer service manager, her cheeks blooming red.

"I'm not." Richard's voice remained calm and matter-of-fact. He waited them out, sitting quietly while they looked from one face to the next, grumbling their displeasure. While Easton wasn't thrilled with the idea, she was willing to hear the explanation, which came once everybody had calmed down. "None of this is to reflect poorly on you. Not a single one of you would have been promoted to your current positions if we thought there'd be any issues. Granted, personality clashes happen, and there could conceivably be some at play here. But sending you all to this class is a show of good faith to the one hundred fifty employees we've taken on here. They were promised a smooth transition, and we want to make sure to keep our word."

"What about them?" asked Henry Deets, the traffic manager, pushing his glasses up his nose with a finger. "I mean, it's not just us. You said so yourself."

Richard nodded. "They'll be handled as well. We've got some things in place." He glanced at the HR manager, and Easton realized they'd probably discussed it. Had to. "You've each been emailed the time and location of a conflict resolution class. I've put you all in the same one, figuring you can help each other out, talk about common issues. It takes place in the evening, which is an inconvenience, I know, but you'll all be paid for your time. Once you pass the class, the instructor will send us the paperwork and you'll be all set. Then we'll have a company-wide meeting to let everybody know the steps we've taken."

Each of them was on his or her phone, scrolling to the email, muttering. Richard gave them a moment before asking if there were questions. Then he ended the meeting.

The rest of the afternoon went by in a blur of phone calls, emails, and side-eyes from a couple of her staff, and it wasn't until she was in her car and on her way to pick up Emma from after-school day care that she had time to actually think about what had transpired.

"Conflict resolution, huh?" she said aloud as she sat at a red light and rolled it around in her brain. Despite the fact that it would be inconvenient and time consuming for the managers, it would show the Xavier-now-Hart employees that their new bosses were listening. It was a smart move in an attempt to promote harmony between the new and old factions of the company. Easton got that. It didn't thrill her, but she understood the motive behind it. She would go. She would listen. She would pass. And that would be that. She'd only given the email a quick glance, but she saw that it was a six-week course, one hour for six Wednesday nights starting next week. And she'd get paid. Wednesday through Saturday morning were Emma's days with her father, so at least Easton wouldn't need to find a sitter.

She parked in the Denby Day Care parking lot and got out, pulling her light jacket tighter around her and wishing she'd worn the heavier one. The weather in late April was hit or miss, and today, she'd missed.

"Mommy!" The cry that Easton lived for. A seven-year-old blond torpedo shot across the room and wrapped its arms around her thighs. Easton squatted, took her daughter's face in her hands, pushed her hair out of the way so she could see those huge blue eyes. "Hi, baby," she said, and kissed Emma's forehead. "I missed you." She said it every day. Every day, it was true.

"Look!" Nearly everything Emma said sounded like it had an exclamation point on the end, and she held up a piece of red construction paper with some other colors glued to it.

"Did you make that?" Easton asked as she took it and scrutinized it like an art dealer.

Emma nodded vigorously as one of the day care aides approached them with a smile. "Hi, Mrs. Evans," she said warmly.

"It's Ms. Evans." Easton smiled as she corrected the aide for what felt like the millionth time. "But call me Easton. Please."

"Can I have a word with you before you go?"

"Sure," Easton replied with a nod, and told Emma to get her things together.

"Let's go in here." The aide led her into an empty office and closed the door behind them.

Oh, this can't be good. Easton kept smiling.

As soon as Easton opened the front door of her house, Emma blew past her, dropping all her kid crap on the floor as she did, and was through the kitchen heading toward the family room where all her toys were.

"Um, no. Get back here, young lady." When there was no response, she raised the volume. "Right now, Emma!" Easton was not a woman accustomed to raising her voice. It wasn't done in her family (probably because nobody talked about anything emotional…at all) and it simply wasn't something she had experience with.

Until Emma was able to walk.

It started slowly, maybe raising the volume a notch or two here and there. And then Emma turned four and it went up another notch. At five, Easton wondered if all kids instantly went deaf, as Emma didn't even turn to look at her most of the time. And seven?

God. Seven was killing her.

"Emma Catherine Douglas, come here, please." Easton rolled her eyes and muttered, "Yeah, because asking nicely will make all the difference."

It seemed like another ten minutes went by and Easton had to force herself not to chase Emma down instead. Shondra was always on her about that. "Don't give her the power. You're the mom here. You're the boss." Easy to hear. Hard to enact. Finally, Emma came trudging back to the entryway, casually brushing the hot pink mane on one of her My Little Ponies.

"What is going on with you?" Easton asked, her voice calmer.

Emma continued to brush as she lifted one small shoulder in a half shrug.

Easton squatted to be on the same level. "Sweetie." She put her hand gently over Emma's brushing hand to get her attention and waited until Emma's big blue eyes met hers. "You're a big girl now, and you know how to share toys. You can't be snatching them out of other kids' hands. You can't be mean like that. You know better."

"I don't like her," Emma said, so softly Easton barely heard.

"Who?"

"Millie."

"Is that the other girl?"

Emma nodded, working the pout hard by sticking out her bottom lip.

"Why don't you like her?"

Emma looked off into the room as if searching for the right words. "'Cuz she thinks she's better than everybody. She's always talking about her stuff, how her toys are better than the stupid ones there."

Easton rolled her lips in, not wanting to smile at the tone of grave injustice Emma was using. Instead, she nodded with understanding.

"So, I told her to go play with her own toys then." Emma went back to brushing her pony.

"And you took the one she had."

Emma gave one very satisfied nod.

"Emma." When she kept her focus on the toy, Easton gently took her chin and turned her face to look at her. "You know that was wrong.

Don't you?" Using her best Mom Look of Intensity (TM Shondra), she waited.

Emma finally sighed. "Yeah."

"And you're not going to do it again?"

"Ugh! *Fine.*" Emma groaned then, making it sound like Easton had asked her to eat nothing but vegetables for a week. Without waiting for more discussion, she turned on her little heel and stalked back toward the family room.

Easton stood up with a sigh. Being a parent was the single most rewarding and frustrating thing she'd ever taken on in life, and she often wondered exactly how badly she was destined to screw up her daughter. The fear of every parent on the planet, she'd discovered.

"All mothers think like that, honey," Shondra would say. And she would know, being slightly older than Easton and with three kids of her own. But knowing all mothers felt the same way didn't make feeling it any easier.

Shaking the thought away for the time being, she took off her lightweight jacket and hung it in the coat closet. Soon she wouldn't need it. It was still a bit cool, but May was this weekend and then summer would be on them before they knew it: Easton's favorite season. She sifted through the pile of mail as she fantasized about the upcoming months. She loved being warm. Loved the sunshine. Loved lounging by the pool (which had been a requirement when she bought the house last fall). Loved—

Easton swallowed hard as she stared at the big white envelope in her hand. The one with the names of four attorneys in the return address corner. She knew what it was, didn't need to open it. Knew she should be happy about it, happy to have the failed chapter of her life finally done and over with, but... Tears welled up in her eyes and a lump of emotion sat solidly in her throat, despite her efforts to swallow it down.

Her divorce was final.

"Mommy, can I have Goldfish?" Emma's words died as she stopped in front of Easton. "Are you okay?" she asked softly.

Easton nodded, pulled herself together. "Yes. Absolutely. Mommy's fine. You want Goldfish?"

Emma looked unconvinced, but nodded anyway, her eyes carefully tracking Easton's movements, watching her face. Easton could feel it even when she wasn't looking. She might be in her terrible sevens, but Emma had always been a very emotionally tuned-in kid. She worried about Easton, and Easton knew it. And hated it. She didn't want to add more stress to her child's life than she already had.

"One bowl of Goldfish crackers, coming up," Easton said, with forced enthusiasm. She sniffed, mentally shook herself, then held her hand out to Emma and marched with her into the kitchen.

Closing that chapter. Time to start a new one.

That was her mantra. She used it all the time, said it aloud and in her head. But starting a new chapter was easier said than done.

It was also terrifying.

CHAPTER TWO

"Hidey ho!" Bella Hunt called out as she walked through the front door of her friend's town house. The smell of burnt toast immediately assaulted her nostrils—a good way to be sure she was in the right place.

"Nobody says 'hidey ho' but hobbits and leprechauns, Bells. And you're small, but not that small." Amy Steinberg smiled and wrapped her arms around Bella. Lowering her voice, she added, "Heather's busy scorching the eggs. Be nice."

Bella shook her head with a grin as she took off her jacket and tossed it on Heather's overstuffed couch. "Who burns eggs?" she whispered as she followed Amy back to the kitchen.

"Really? Have you met our friend Heather? Sweet, funny, thinks she can cook?"

Louder, Bella said, "Hey, you!" as Heather Simmons came into view. "What's cookin'?"

"Omelets. Hungry?" Heather smiled at Bella, her face a portrait of endless hope, her black apron telling everybody God's honest truth with its screen-printed words: Dinner's Ready When the Smoke Alarm Goes Off.

"Starving," Bella said, and kissed Heather on the cheek, trying not to look at the devastation in the frying pan Heather manned. "I brought bagels." She held up a bag and stifled a laugh as Amy mouthed a silent "Thank God."

These were her best friends, and not a day went by when Bella didn't thank her lucky stars for them. They'd met in college, had all been on the same floor their freshman year, all with roommates they didn't really click with. Once they realized they shared the same psychology major, they'd decided to get a suite together their sophomore year, and the three of them had been the best of friends ever since. They'd seen each other through everything: job changes, deaths, breakups. Their lives were busy—Bella worked at a corporate wellness center, Heather was a social worker, and Amy, a school counselor—but they had brunch together every Sunday they could, and their group text was constantly active.

Amy handed Bella a champagne flute filled with the lovely orange shade of a mimosa, then touched her own glass to it with a pretty clink.

They worked as a team, removing plates and silverware from cabinets and drawers, each of them knowing mostly where everything was in one another's kitchens. Amy chatted about one of her students as they set Heather's small kitchen table and Bella put the bagels on a plate, arranged two kinds of cream cheese around it.

"I thought you were making omelets," Amy commented, as Heather scooped what could only have been considered scrambled eggs onto her plate.

"Shut up and eat," was Heather's response.

"Yes, ma'am," Amy said as she glanced at Bella, who was grinning.

"There's cheese and green peppers and onions," Heather said, defending her case. "All your favorite things. Eat it."

Bella laughed. "Wow, somebody needs more coffee."

"No, I need more alcohol." Heather grabbed the third flute and sipped, punctuating it with an exaggerated "Ahhhh!" of satisfaction.

They sat down to eat, and Heather brought up a family she'd been dealing with that involved a father dealing drugs and a mother working herself to the bone, how heartbreaking the situation was. Bella never said so, but the clients Heather'd just described were the very reason she hadn't gone into social work. She didn't think she could handle it, the emotional toll it would take on her. Heather didn't look nearly as tough as she was. Bella thought she looked a bit like a '50s housewife with her ash blond hair cut to chin length, her plump build, her penchant for floral dresses, and her perpetual smile. She was instantly likable. Endlessly optimistic and cheerful. Bella had no idea how she did it, given what she saw every day. But when you were in a bad mood or felt you'd lost hope for all humanity, spending an hour with Heather was the cure. She was the opposite of sadness and frustration, and she always had plenty of good things to say about anybody and everybody. Which was not to say she was a pushover. Far from it. Amy, a little more descriptive than necessary sometimes, liked to say Heather could put a person's balls in a vise, turn the crank, and smile sweetly the whole time she was doing it. Bottom line was simply that Heather was the kind of person Bella wanted to be when she grew up: sweet, kind, tough as nails.

The three of them talked. All the time. About everything, good and bad, especially when it came to their work. Bounced things off each other. Everybody always remained nameless in their conversations—clients, patients, and the like—but the three women found it endlessly helpful to get the thoughts and opinions of the other two. Often, new angles or perceptions were discovered in their discussions.

"What about you?" Amy asked as she pointed to Bella with a fork.

Bella shrugged as she forked some well-done egg into her mouth. It didn't taste bad at all if she didn't eat the blackened parts. "The usual. Nothing much to report since our last brunch." She swallowed, then recalled something. "Oh! I'm doing a conflict resolution class starting on Wednesday."

"Your first one," Amy said.

Bella nodded.

"Do you know who's in it?" Heather asked.

"We were hired by a big company. Hart something. They're sending us their entire management team, I think."

"Wow." Amy sipped her mimosa. "They must be having issues if all their managers need conflict resolution."

"Not necessarily," Bella told her. "From what I understand, they've just merged with another company. A lot of times, according to my supervisor, corporate businesses will send their people to classes like mine just as a…" She searched for the right word. "Like a refresher-type thing. You know?"

"Night class?" Amy asked.

Bella wrinkled her nose. "Yeah, which I'm not thrilled about. But it's only for six weeks. I'll live." She spread cream cheese on a bagel and said, "Truth is, I'm a little nervous."

Amy and Heather scoffed at the same time, which made the trio laugh. "That's ridiculous," Heather offered.

"I've never taught this before."

Amy waved her off. "Heather's right. Don't be ridiculous. You're gonna be great. You're trained to run it, right?"

"You've probably memorized all the information. I've met you." Heather shot her a grin and Bella had to return it because Heather was right: she'd read every single thing she could find on the subject of conflict resolution, going so far as to search her old laptop and find a paper she'd written in grad school on the topic. She was more than ready.

"You're right," she said. "I know what I'm doing. I think I'm just nervous in general."

"I get that," Amy offered. "Standing in front of a group is different from dealing with somebody one-on-one. Is it a big class?"

Bella shook her head as she chewed. "Six."

Amy made a sound like *pfft*. "No biggie, then. You got this."

"You do," Heather agreed and started to stand. "More eggs?"

"No!" Bella and Amy said together, more forcefully than necessary.

Heather squinted at them as she slowly lowered herself back onto her chair. "You guys are subtle."

❖

"Okay, girls, I know dinner's a little early, and I'm sorry about that. But Mama's got to teach a class tonight, remember? So, we need to move it along. All right?"

Lucy looked up at Bella as she chewed. Slowly. Like she had all the time in the world. Ethel, on the other hand, had done a terrific impression of a vacuum cleaner and was now doing her best to lick the paint off her ceramic bowl.

"Come on, Ethel. Outside." Bella slid the back door open just as her cell rang from the kitchen counter. "Hey, Mom," she said as she answered, leaned against the counter next to Lucy, who was *maybe* almost finished.

"Hi, sweetie. What's new?"

"Not a lot." Bella put the phone on speaker and set it down so she could gather her things together. "I'm teaching a class tonight and I'm trying to get Lucy to eat a little faster than she would if she lived her life in slow motion. *Which she does.*" She leaned down and said the last three words closer to her dog. Who blinked at her, unimpressed, and moved not one iota faster.

"I will not have you spreading lies about my granddoggies," her mother teased. "Grandma loves you, Lucy-bear."

Bella rolled her eyes good-naturedly as Lucy finally finished her dinner and sauntered toward the back door. "No, no. Take your time, Luce. Don't mind me. It's not like I have anything in life besides you." She slid the door open and let Lucy out into the small backyard.

"I almost FaceTimed you," her mother said.

Bella laughed. "Not until you figure out where the camera lens is on your phone. Last time, I talked to your forehead for twenty minutes."

Her mother chuckled, a sound that surprised most people with its huskiness, given that Michelle Hunt could only be described as petite. "I only have a few minutes tonight, so you lucked out."

"Working?" Bella's mom had been waitressing at the same diner for more than twenty years. It was exhausting, thankless work, but she had regulars who loved her, considered her part of their routine. She would never think to inconvenience them by taking time off or changing her hours.

"I'm on my break. Got about ten minutes left."

"Mom, you have more than enough seniority to request only the day shift. I hate you working at night."

"I make better tips for dinner than I do for lunch. You know that." Michelle's voice was light, cheerful, like it always was, despite the fact that they'd had this same conversation a million times.

"I know." Bella kept her sigh as quiet as she could. "How's Dad?"

"He's good. Strained his back a little bit the other day helping to lift something at work, so he's taking it easy tonight on the couch."

"Has he been taking his meds?" Bella's father had been on pills for arthritis for as long as she could remember, but he didn't always take them like he was supposed to. Because he was a stubborn, stubborn man.

"He's been pretty good about it." Translation: not always.

"I'll call this weekend and get on him."

"When will we see you?" Her mother's voice held a hint of wistfulness that never failed to make Bella feel guilty for not visiting more often.

"Soon, Ma. Soon. The girls and I could use a road trip."

"Good. I have a couple of steak bones in the freezer I stole from the diner."

Bella grinned. It wasn't the first time her mother had snagged steak bones from a customer's plate and saved them for Bella's dogs. "You're a good grandma."

They chatted a bit longer before Michelle had to get back to her customers. As with so many people, Bella's perceptions had grown and changed around her parents as she became an adult. When she'd been young, part of her was embarrassed by them and their working-class jobs. They'd never had much money. Bella's clothes were often from thrift stores, which was horribly embarrassing when she was a teenager. Now she was still embarrassed, but with herself for being so self-centered as a kid. Now she admired her parents for how hard they'd worked to give her what she needed. No, she'd never had designer clothes, and she was still paying off the student loans she'd had to take out as she put herself through college, but she understood that her parents had loved her more than anything, had done their best to keep her fed with a roof over her head and a mom and dad who adored her. Now she wanted to protect them from so much hard work, always had to remind herself that her mother was an adult, an intelligent woman who could make her own decisions about what shifts she preferred to work. The biggest realization that comes with being an adult is understanding that your parents are merely human. It took Bella a while to get there.

Both dogs stood at the back door looking in wistfully, like children peeking in a store window. Children with barrel chests and the huge square heads of pit bull mixes, but children just the same. Bella grinned at them and let them in. Ethel went right for the toy basket, as was her after-dinner routine, and pulled out a tennis ball. Lucy headed to her bed in the corner of the living room, as was *her* after-dinner routine, and curled up to watch Tennis Ball being played.

"Okay, but this has to be quick, E. I have to leave in, like, twenty minutes." The way her small house was laid out, if she sat on the floor at the end of the living room, there was a straight shot across the room and down the hall to the front door. Not super long, but long enough for Ethel to get a little jog in as she chased the ball. Bella grabbed a folder out of her bag so she could take a quick look at her notes for tonight, then plopped down in her usual seat on the floor and tossed the ball down the hallway. Lucy watched Ethel lope after it, then trot back with it in her mouth, her head turning as if she was watching a tennis match. Bella opened the folder as Ethel dropped the ball in her lap.

They went on like this for a while, until Bella was satisfied that she was fully prepared for the class. Before she closed the folder, she glanced at the list of expected attendees and one name caught her eye, made her do a double take.

Easton Evans.

"Noooo," she said softly, drawing out the word as Ethel whined and nudged her with a nose. "Can't be the same person. What are the chances?" She tossed the ball without looking, squinted at the paper. Easton Evans was not a common name, but still. The last time Bella had seen the Easton she was thinking about was fifteen years ago and about three hundred miles away. "Can't be her." Bella shook her head with certainty and closed the folder. Ethel was back with the ball that was now a little wet and squishy, and Bella grabbed her head with both hands, lovingly ruffled the short fur and floppy ears. "Just a coincidence, right, E?"

Giving the ball one more toss, Bella pushed herself to her feet. "Has to be."

CHAPTER THREE

Framerton High, 2003

Changing schools was awful enough, but doing so in the middle of the school year, junior year, was beyond horrendous. Izzy didn't have a ton of friends at her old school, as she was quiet and shy and kept to herself. But there were a few. When that school closed—some budgetary thing she didn't really understand—all the students were split up and integrated into different schools in the area. Izzy had ended up at Framerton High. Which felt *huge*, like she'd been dropped in the middle of the ocean with no idea which direction she was supposed to swim to next.

She'd found her locker and it had opened on the first try; that was a relief. But now she had to figure out how to get to her lit class. She knew it was in room 217b, but beyond that, she was lost. Standing in the middle of the hall with her books clasped tightly to her chest, she felt a subtle panic start to build. It began in the pit of her stomach and worked its way out, like an octopus reaching its tentacles to all her organs, squeezing them one by one. Perspiration broke out across her forehead just as she was jostled from behind.

"Nice outfit," the jostler said, her tone snide. She shot Izzy a look of condescending pity over her shoulder as she continued down the hall and stopped at a locker thirty or forty feet away. She was tall and had chestnut brown hair that was expertly (and Izzy would bet expensively) highlighted, and at first glance, she'd probably be considered pretty, but her expression was cold. Icy. Her smile didn't reach her eyes.

Izzy swallowed and looked down at her clothes. There was no

way that girl could know they were from Goodwill. Was there? There were three other students at the locker where she stood. Two guys, both with dark hair and the broad-shouldered build of football players, laughing and swearing loudly. And another girl...a girl Izzy couldn't pull her eyes from, even when she tried. She was blond and Izzy could see her enormous blue eyes even from this distance, how they were lined with black. A weird feeling curled in Izzy's stomach, a flutter of sorts. A tickle, but a tight one, like a coiled snake waiting to strike, and as she watched the blond girl throw her head back and laugh, Izzy's mouth went dry.

What is happening?

Izzy's panic only grew as she watched them, not wanting to stare but filled with the desire and wistfulness she'd almost grown used to, it was such a common emotion in her arsenal. That longing to have what she didn't—money, friends, status—to be what she wasn't—pretty, popular, charismatic. It had started with junior high...that slice of school when kids were no longer friends with everybody. When they started to break off into groups. Cliques. When labels appeared out of nowhere, and suddenly everybody had a descriptor. Jock. Geek. Goth. Artsy. Nerd. At least at her old school, she had a handful of other nerd friends because they'd started out together, but now? The other dozen kids that had also been transferred into Framerton had labels that differed from Izzy's. They were kids she barely knew, not friends, so she was on her own here.

The budding panic was still there, and in the next instant, all four of those kids were looking her way.

"Jesus, stare much?" the jostler said, loudly enough for others in the hall to hear and also look in Izzy's direction, and a few snickered.

Shit. Now she'd done it.

As she yanked her gaze from the foursome, she was horrified to feel her eyes well with tears. The panic bloomed large, exploding like a firework, churning her stomach and threatening to expel the toast and peanut butter she'd had for breakfast. Yeah, that was all she needed: to throw up in the middle of the hall. Or burst into tears. Or both. That'd seal her fate completely for the next two years.

There were so many kids in that hall, so many looking her way, and Izzy was only certain of one thing: she'd never felt so utterly alone in her life.

❖

Not for the first time in her life, Easton was confused by her own emotions. The notification of the completion of her divorce had thrown her for an unexpected loop and she was having trouble understanding why.

The first thing she'd done was text Shondra, who'd done her best to comfort her. *It's a big deal*, she'd typed. *It's the end of a major part of your life. There are feelings around that. Big ones. It's okay to feel them.*

But it's not a surprise, Easton had explained back. *I wanted this.* That's what she had trouble swallowing. She'd wanted it. She'd been the one to ask for a divorce. If it had been up to Connor, they'd be doing their best to work things out, but Easton knew that would never happen. Not if she was going to be truly happy.

So why did that simple piece of mail fill her eyes with tears and her heart with sadness?

Easton pulled into a spot at the Hallman Wellness Center and shifted into Park. She was actively fighting the urge to cry when her phone rang and a check of the screen on the dashboard told her it was Dr. Stephen Evans. Her grandfather. Relief flooded through her and she hit the green button.

"Hi, Grandpa," she said, then cleared her throat.

"Hey there, Buttercup. What's wrong?" His voice was soft and kind and made it easy to understand why his patients were so comfortable with him. Easton could picture him, seventy-six years old but looking a good fifteen years younger than that, his thick silver hair probably a little too long, his purple stethoscope hanging around his neck. His blue eyes were magnetic, the color stunning and the warmth in them almost surprising.

"How do you do that?" Easton asked, with a self-deprecating laugh.

"I know you," he answered simply. "You okay?"

Grandpa Evans was one of the only people in Easton's life that she talked to. *Really* talked to. She wasn't sure how a man born in the early 1940s could so completely understand his granddaughter who was born in the mid-1980s, but he did. He *got* her. She discussed nearly everything with him. He was the first one she'd told when she realized medical school wasn't her thing (much to the dismay of her parents). He knew she was pregnant before she'd even told her husband. He was the first person (and still one of the only people) who knew why she'd left her marriage. He *got* her.

"My divorce is final."

"Oh, Buttercup, I'm sorry. That's a hard one."

"But why? Why is it hard? It's what I wanted. It's what I asked for. I don't have the right to be sad about it now."

"Says who?" Easton could hear the rustling of fabric, the groan of a chair, and knew her grandfather was sitting back at his desk. She could picture it clearly in her mind. She'd even bet he'd just taken off his glasses. "It doesn't matter who ends a partnership or why. It's still the end of a big part of your life. I know for some people in dire situations, it can be a relief. And I know that for you, it was the right decision. That doesn't mean you're not allowed to mourn. To grieve."

"Mourning." The proverbial light bulb went on in Easton's head. "That's what I'm doing, that's what this is. I'm grieving the loss of my marriage."

"Of course you are. It only makes sense. And it's okay to do that. You know that, yes?"

Maybe he and Shondra were right. Maybe it was just the final slamming of the book on her marriage that she was having a hard time swallowing. *And that's okay.*

"I don't know why I don't just call you in the first place," she said, with a chuckle. "You always make me feel better."

"I don't know why you don't either." Grandpa's laugh matched hers. "How's everything else? Work? Emma? I've got four more minutes. Give me the abridged version."

Easton did. She told him about Emma's school issues—*"She's a smart girl, she'll learn the lesson."* She told him about her staff—*"They just need time."* She ended with the fact that she was in the parking lot, about to head in to her first conflict resolution class, to which Grandpa groaned.

"You don't need that class. You do just fine."

"I know. They sent all of us, though. A good faith gesture, they said."

"Bah. That's new-agey crap." But his voice was light, and Easton could hear the humor. "I'll be interested to hear how it goes."

"I'll keep you posted."

"Last patient of the day is here, Buttercup. Gotta run. Come visit sometime soon."

Easton promised she would, then they said their goodbyes and she hung up.

She turned the car off and sat there for several moments, stared out the windshield. While she felt better after talking to her grandfather— she always did—the melancholy from before he called seeped back in slowly. This was not where she'd expected to be at thirty three, that was true. When she'd married Connor, she'd convinced herself that was it. That was her life, how it was going to be. Just like her parents wanted for her. Expected of her. She'd failed them by not following in their medical footsteps, she'd be damned if she'd fail them by messing up her marriage as well. What was that saying? The road to hell and all that? She sighed heavily. Starting over with her seven-year-old daughter had never been part of the plan.

And now this. Conflict resolution. She didn't need to be here. Grandpa knew it. She knew it, and her bosses knew it. But her job was important to her, so she would do what was asked of her, even if it meant giving up Wednesday evenings for six weeks. With a resigned sigh, she yanked open her car door, grabbed her purse, and headed into the two-story brick office building.

From the outside, the Hallman Wellness Center looked like any average brick-and-mortar office building. Very standard. Very ordinary. Inside, however, was a different story.

The lobby was softly lit and carpeted (newly, judging by the smell) in a pleasingly warm burgundy. The waiting area was small but its furniture soft and inviting: overstuffed chairs and love seats around a square table that boasted various magazines and a vase of fresh red and white carnations. The air smelled like home—the aroma of cinnamon and nutmeg almost masking the new carpet smell and coming from… somewhere Easton couldn't pinpoint. As it was after hours, there was nobody at the front desk, but a black standing sign indicated in white letters that the conflict resolution class was being held in room 106. Which was to Easton's left, according to the arrow.

A smattering of people was still working, sitting at various desks or in offices, pecking away at keyboards or chatting on phones. Easton walked down the hallway until she found room 106. Four of her coworkers were already present and she grimaced inwardly, glad she wasn't the last to arrive.

Rather than a classroom setting, which was what Easton had envisioned, the room held a desk in one corner and a large, round table with eight chairs. She headed that way and took the chair next to Paul Antonassio, who was their vendor manager and, of all people, *really* didn't need to be there, as he didn't have a staff. As if he read her mind, he smiled and shrugged at her as she sat, his face clearly saying, "What can you do?"

A glance up told Easton the woman running the class, who stood near the desk in the corner of the room, was slight in build, probably no older than Easton herself, and stunningly pretty. Brunette hair that fell just to her shoulders in easy waves, eyes that seemed dark, but it was hard to tell from a distance, high cheekbones and a gentle jawline. She was dressed in business casual attire: dark blue dress pants and a pink button-down top, the sleeves rolled halfway up her forearms.

Also, she was looking right at Easton, her expression hard to read, but definitely not screaming "open and friendly."

"Hi," Easton said, adding a little wave of apology. "Sorry, do I need to check in or anything?"

The woman shook her head. "You're Ms. Evans?" She consulted a paper on the desk.

"Easton, yes."

The woman gave a nod but said nothing more, kept her eyes on the desk.

Kim Banks, customer service manager, was the last one to arrive, whooshing into the room like she'd been blown in by a heavy wind at exactly 7:00 p.m.

"All right," the brunette said, and took a seat in one of the two remaining chairs. She smiled warmly, set down some papers on the table in front of her, and crossed her legs. "My name is Bella Hunt and I'll be running this conflict resolution group for the next six weeks. Every Wednesday, seven p.m., right here. If you have to miss one, you can tell me, but just know that I have to let your boss"—she consulted the paper—"Mr. Joplin know. Not that I'm tattling on you, but you need all six classes in order to be passed. Understood?" Nods and murmurs went around the table. "Good. Okay." Bella Hunt sat forward and folded her hands on top of the stack of papers.

Easton watched as she spoke, liked the calming quality of her voice, found herself sitting up a little straighter.

"Now, I know that, for the most part, conflict resolution sounds like it has some violence attached to it. I'm guessing you're not all beating up your employees?"

"Not because we don't want to," muttered Henry Deets, their traffic manager. Henry was no-nonsense and organized and did not take kindly to having his abilities challenged or criticized.

The others chuckled, as did Bella.

"I know the story behind your company," she told them, moving her eyes from one manager to the next but skipping over Easton. "And let me assure you that this is a very common practice for new managers of established staff. There's almost always strife, ill feelings. The established staff often feel like they've been betrayed, so they resist warming to new management. My point being: none of this is unusual. You guys are not special." She said the last line with a wink of sarcasm and teasing. "So, what we'll do is talk through some scenarios, do a little role-playing, and generally just be open about some of the issues you find yourselves dealing with. I'll help you with ways to best handle them without causing more hard feelings or resentment. Sound good?"

More nods and murmurs and they got started.

The hour went by quickly, and for that Easton was grateful. They talked a bit, did a little role-playing. Easton was never called on to participate, but she didn't really care. Next time. Oddly, Bella Hunt barely made eye contact with her the entire sixty minutes. She didn't exactly ignore her, but she hardly looked her way.

Oh, well. Easton wasn't going to worry about that. Six weeks from now, she'd never see the woman again. Which was too bad because she really was pretty. It had been a while since a woman had caught Easton's attention so easily.

Internally chuckling at herself, Easton collected her things and left, walking with Paul down the hallway to the parking lot.

"Well, that was fun," he said, only a hint of sarcasm in his tone.

"It went fast. That's a good thing."

"She seems like she knows her stuff. Ms. Hunt."

Easton nodded, saving her opinion for now.

"You having a lot of trouble with your staff?" Their cars were parked next to each other and they talked over the top of Easton's.

"You know, the last guy they had, they loved. That's the issue. They're really good salespeople. They meet their quotas. They just miss the other guy. I get it. I can't fix it, but I get it." She shrugged. She really did understand. Which didn't make it easier to deal with the people like Brandi White, who showed how much she missed her old boss by acting out like an angry schoolkid.

Speaking of angry schoolkids... Easton got in her car and plugged in her phone, then dialed Connor while she was thinking about it. He'd been out of town for work and just got home that morning. He answered on the first ring.

"Hey." His voice was warm, like always.

"Hey. She doing okay?"

"Just finishing up a snack."

"So, she had an issue at after-care while you were away." She told Connor what the aide had said, about her chat with Emma once they got home. "I'm not sure she heard any of it, honestly. Maybe you can talk to her about it, too?"

"Absolutely. I think one of her books is about sharing. I'll use that as her bedtime story tonight. That'll be my segue."

Easton couldn't help but smile. "Perfect."

A beat of silence went by before Connor said, voice soft, "Did you get it?"

"Yeah." They were both quiet.

"So, it's official." There was a sadness in his voice that Easton was actually getting used to, and it broke her heart a little bit each time. Connor cleared his throat and Easton could picture him giving himself a shake, running his open hand over the head that he'd been shaving since he was twenty-eight and accepted that he was going to lose his hair. "Okay. I'll make sure I have a little talk with Emma tonight."

"I'd appreciate it, thanks. I feel like I'm on her all the time, and I don't want to be that mom."

"Yeah, I had one of those. Not fun."

"Exactly."

They said their goodbyes, and Easton ended the call with a bit of a heavy heart. Most of the time, she was confident that splitting from Connor was the best decision she'd ever made. Most of the time, she felt free and excited to start her new life. Finally. To be herself, be who she was. But once in a while, like today, she missed her old life. She missed her house. She missed her life as one half of a whole. She missed the steadiness of having a partner who knew her and loved her, quirks and all. Easton and Connor had known each other since the seventh grade. He knew everything about her. Her emotions, her oddities, what she loved, what she couldn't stand, what made her laugh and what made her cry. The idea of "training" somebody new was more than a little daunting.

Sometimes, especially when she was lonely, she just wanted to go home.

Taking in a deep, slow breath, Easton did her best to center herself. Then she shifted her car into Drive and headed home to her empty house, mixed feelings about that rolling through her head.

❖

"Son of a bitch," Bella whispered to herself, in the now empty classroom. "It's her. It's actually her."

Easton fucking Evans. In the flesh. Bella couldn't believe it. How was it possible that she'd run three hundred miles from her town, from her high school, specifically to get away and start fresh with new people, and fucking Easton Evans showed up in her class? How was that possible? How in the world had that happened? What were the damn chances? And how on earth was it fair that she was still that fucking beautiful? Weren't the popular kids in high school supposed to be the ones who ended up bald and out of shape a decade or two later? Because that had certainly not happened to Easton.

Bella sat at the corner desk like she was in a trance. At this time of night, the building would still be populated; there was a yoga class in the basement and a bereavement group on the second floor. But Bella's floor was quiet. She stared off into space, slowly and subtly shaking her head in utter disbelief.

Easton fucking Evans.

Here. In Bella's new world.

Seriously? *Seriously, life?*

The best part—*sarcasm*—was that Easton had obviously not recognized her. And while part of her was insulted, a bigger part wasn't surprised. Bella wasn't even close to the person she'd been fifteen years ago. Not in appearance. Not in personality. Not at all. She'd been a late bloomer. A *very* late bloomer. So while she couldn't blame Easton for not remembering her, she still wanted to. Because it solidified who Easton was in Bella's head. Who she *still* was: self-centered and unaware of the world around her.

But maybe it was better that she didn't. This way, they wouldn't have to struggle through any small talk or feigned pleasantries or act excited and happy to see each other as if they were at a class reunion. So, that was a relief.

Bella sighed loudly. She was a licensed mental health counselor, and as such, she knew in her head that her assumptions about Easton Evans were just that: assumptions. But the seventeen-year-old in her had very strong memories, and very strong feelings about those very strong memories and cutting Easton any slack or giving her any benefit of the doubt at all was very difficult for that gawky, confused teenager who still lived inside her.

Determined to focus on her job, she turned to her laptop and called up her evaluation sheet. She'd constructed it herself, and it allowed her to keep track of her conflict resolution attendees, let her follow which of them needed to work on what. It was only the first class for this bunch from Hart Commodities, so it was early yet. Plus, they'd only had time for one exercise, but she could already tell that both Kim and Henry were going to need a bit of direction. Bella hated to admit that Easton had handled things well, but she had.

We'll see how things progress, she thought, as she snapped the laptop closed and gathered her belongings. As she flipped off the light in the room and headed down the hall, the whole situation hit her once more like a smack and she shook her head.

"Easton fucking Evans. Unbelievable."

This was going to be interesting.

CHAPTER FOUR

Saturday's weather was gorgeous. May was here, and Easton loved what that meant: spring and then summer. God, she lived for summer. She knew a lot of people who loved spring, loved the sense of renewal, the sense of that clean slate fresh start, the colors of the daffodils and crocuses poking their heads up through the dirt as if peeking to see if the coast was clear, if winter was finally gone. Not Easton. She wished they could push right past all the new growth crap and right into the heart of summer. Sunshine and heat and tank tops. Her jam.

"Emma, be careful, please," she called out to what she was reasonably sure were deaf ears as she watched her daughter swinging from the monkey bars on the playground, visions of bruised muscles and broken bones assaulting her mother's constantly worrying brain.

"She's fine." That was Connor's standard response whenever Emma worried her. It was his way of keeping Easton from letting herself coast into a panic. She worried a lot and he was very level and even. They'd made a nice blend in that respect.

"Did you talk to her about the sharing thing?" Easton asked now, as Emma dropped from the bars and ran toward the spot where the black edging separated the rubberized playground area from the green grass of the rest of the park.

"I did and I asked the aide both Thursday and Friday if she'd done any better. They said there'd been no incidents."

Easton let a snort escape. "No incidents. Makes her sound like a criminal."

"Right?"

They sat together on the park bench, watching their daughter play, just like old times. If a stranger looked at them, they'd have no idea the two of them had recently finalized their divorce. They appeared to be just like any other average, good-looking, young couple watching their child on the playground.

Easton was always very aware of that, for some reason.

"You're heading to Shondra's tonight?" Connor asked, yanking Easton from her daydreaming.

She gave a nod. "Margarita night," she said, with a smile.

Connor grinned back. "If you see Tony, tell him I said hey. I owe him a text."

"I will."

When she turned back to her daughter, she was surprised to see her well outside the playground area. She seemed to be holding something bright yellow—a tennis ball?—and a dog with an enormous head and a thick barrel-chested body was running toward her at a full sprint. Easton gasped, and Connor followed her gaze. "Oh, shit," he said, as he jumped up from the bench, Easton right behind him. "Emma!"

"Oh, God," Easton breathed out as they ran toward their daughter, horrifying visions of her being mauled by the dog clouding her head, the huge animal probably double Emma's weight, easily able to take her down. Before they got to her, though, she and Connor both stopped in their tracks.

The dog sat in front of Emma, head cocked to one side, short tail wagging and huge pink tongue lolling out one side of its mouth. Easton and Connor walked briskly up to their daughter just in time to hear her giggle and say, "Nice doggie." She patted the dog on the head and handed over the tennis ball.

Easton squatted down and grabbed Emma, trying to be subtle about the fear that had been coursing through her veins not ten seconds ago, the remnants that still were, and hugged her. "Sweetie, what have we talked about when it comes to strange dogs?"

The dog still sat. It had dropped the tennis ball and seemed to watch them with amusement.

"Ethel, come."

The voice was firm, but not angry. It was also vaguely familiar. Easton looked up and into the eyes of the pretty woman who ran her conflict resolution class. Bella, right?

Easton stood as the dog picked up its tennis ball and met Bella on her approach. She could tell the exact moment Bella recognized her, as her eyes seemed to shutter a bit.

"Hi," Easton said, injecting some cheer into her voice, hoping it overshadowed the worry that had almost drowned her. "Bella, right?"

"Yes," Bella said, as the dog sat next to her feet and she laid a hand on its enormous square head. "Easton." It wasn't a question, it was a statement. Bella remembered her.

"Right." Easton mirrored Bella's stance by laying a hand on Emma's blond head. She turned to Connor. "Bella teaches the conflict resolution class I'm in for work." Looking back Bella's way and trying not to get lost in the gorgeous hazel of her eyes, now clear as can be, she explained, "This is my daughter, Emma. And my—" She hesitated, never having had to introduce Connor since their split.

"I'm her ex-husband. Connor Douglas. Nice to meet you." Connor held out a hand and Bella shook it. "I have to admit, your dog gave us a bit of a scare." He kept his voice light, but his eyes were serious, and Easton wanted to hug him for broaching the subject.

"She just looks intimidating," Bella said. Was there an edge to her voice? "She's a good girl with a very gentle nature. She wouldn't hurt a fly. I'd never let her off the leash in a public place if I didn't trust her." As if proving her point, Ethel licked the small hand Emma held out to her and Emma giggled.

"Pit bull?" Connor asked, venturing to pet the dog himself now.

"She's a mix. Some pit bull, yes. A few other things."

"Rescue?" Connor knelt down, and Ethel dropped, rolled, and showed him her belly. Bella watched him. Easton watched Bella. Her serious demeanor didn't take away from her attractiveness. Even in her casual clothes—jeans, a purple shirt, and a gray hoodie, hanging unzipped—Easton would've noticed her; she was a definite head-turner. The dark hair was back in a ponytail today, still wavy, and her cheeks were rosy from the activity. She looked fresh and outdoorsy.

"Yes. I have her sister at home. I rescued them at the same time, but she doesn't enjoy the park as much." Bella's whole face softened as she talked about her dogs. It brought a small smile to Easton's lips.

"No?" Connor looked up at her.

"She's probably lounging on my couch, remote in hand, watching Animal Planet."

Connor laughed, he and Emma both on the ground now, playing with Ethel, who was loving every minute of it, judging by the wagging of her tail and the giant doggie grin on her face.

"She's smiling at me," Emma said, then slipped into another fit of giggles as Ethel licked her face. "I want a dog."

"Of course you do," Easton said. When she looked up, Bella was looking at her. Intently. Something sizzled between them then. Easton wasn't sure what to make of it, but it was definitely there. Something undeniable zipped from one of them to the other and back, and Easton felt like somebody had just run a fingernail gently up her spine as goose bumps broke out across her arms. She hoped nobody noticed.

"You know," Connor said. "Maybe if you're good and you keep remembering what your mom and I have talked to you about, we can think about getting one this summer."

"Really?" Emma squealed with delight as Easton was hit with instant mixed emotions. Happiness and joy at seeing her daughter so ecstatic. Irritation and a little jealousy that Daddy would be the hero in this scenario. In that moment, Easton realized this was how it would always be as one half of a divorced couple of parents: endless competition. Oh, she knew she could do her best to avoid it, to not let things devolve to that. But it would, at least to a degree. It was inevitable. And a bummer.

"Are you two ready?" Easton asked, for lack of any other course of action. She had the irrepressible urge to stop the activity, to stop standing where Bella could look at her, to stop feeling the weird mix of emotions that suddenly coursed through her.

"Aw, Mom," Emma said.

"Aw, Mom," Connor echoed.

One corner of Bella's mouth lifted in a super-cute half grin. Easton forcibly pulled her gaze away.

"I've got some things to get done today."

They bid goodbye to Bella, and Easton had to force herself not to watch her throw the ball for Ethel, not watch the gentle back and forth of her hips as she walked away. The swinging of her ponytail from one side to the other.

Connor wiped the spring grass off his jeans. "She seems nice," he said, as Emma ran back toward the playground.

"Mm-hmm."

"And she's *really* cute." He bumped Easton with a shoulder. "Gonna check it out?"

That pulled Easton back to the present. She blinked rapidly. "What? No. Oh my God. No. What are you talking about?" *Shut up, Easton,* her brain shrieked at her. *Before you become a prime example of the lady doth protest too much!*

Connor held up his hands like she'd pointed a gun at him. "What? All I said was she's cute. You don't think so?"

Easton looked at him then, looked into the eyes of the man she'd vowed to stay married to until death parted them, and saw nothing but genuine curiosity and maybe a tiny hint of sadness. She forced herself to shrug. "I don't know. I guess?"

"Let me help you," he said as they strolled back toward the playground. "She's definitely cute. There's no guessing necessary. Whether she plays on your team, however..." He held up a hand, palm up. "That's up to you to find out."

With no idea how to respond—seriously, what's the right answer when your ex-husband suggests a woman you might be interested in?—Easton went with simplicity. "She's teaching the class I'm in."

Connor gave a snort of a laugh. "Please. You're a grown woman, not a high school kid. There's no seedy underbelly there."

"True."

As Connor called to Emma and headed toward her, Easton spared a glance over her shoulder. In the distance, she could see Bella. She was throwing the ball, sending Ethel bounding after it. When the dog returned, Bella dropped into a squat and lavished attention on her, repeated the whole thing again. And then Bella looked her way.

The distance was too far to be sure Bella was looking at her, but Easton swore she could feel it. Could feel the heat, the weight of Bella's eyes. It washed over her, through her, and settled low in her body.

Easton swallowed. Hard.

"Ready?" Connor's voice shocked her back to reality and she forced a neutral expression onto her face.

"Yep. You have her backpack?"

"In the car." Connor grabbed Emma by the hand and they headed toward the parking lot.

It took every ounce of energy Easton had not to look back again.

❖

Bella waved from her seat in the restaurant when she saw Amy come through the door.

"Hey, you," Amy said on approach. Her long, dark hair was pulled back in a loose, low ponytail and a fedora topped her head. On many, it would've looked silly. On Amy, it was perfect. Stylish. Trendy. She kissed Bella's cheek and then took the seat across from her at the little round table for two. "Sorry I'm late."

"Please. You're always late. It's your thing."

Amy didn't deny it. "Also, Sky? Who decides on some of these restaurant names? Sky? Really? Are clouds going to float by while we eat? Pretentious." She set her bag down, picked up a menu. "So. How was your week? I meant to text you, but my week has been crazy." Her large brown eyes widened as she had a thought. "Oh! How'd the class go?"

The waitress stopped by and took Amy's order of an extra-dirty martini. Bella preferred something a little safer, so ordered the house cabernet.

"My class had an interesting development," Bella began.

"Tell me." Amy propped her elbows on the table and her chin in her hands, all ears.

"A girl from my high school is in it."

Amy's thick, dark brows met at the top of her nose. "What? Didn't you go to school, like, on the other side of the state?"

"I did."

"That's a hell of a coincidence."

"Right?"

Their drinks arrived then, and they placed their food orders.

"And you remembered her?" Amy sipped her martini, made a sound that was somewhere between pain and pleasure. "Were you friends?"

Bella's chuckle came out more sarcastic than she intended. "Yes, I remembered her and no, we were not friends."

"Oh, I see. Enemies?"

"She'd have had to see me for me to be her enemy."

Amy nodded in understanding. "Got it. Did she remember you?"

"Not even a little. I am a brand-new person to her. And then today at the park, I ran into her again. Her and her ex-husband, who also went to high school with me and who also didn't remember me." This time, her laugh was genuine. So, Easton Evans, head cheerleader, had married Connor Douglas, quarterback of the football team. God, could the two of them be more of a cliché? And apparently, time had only been good to Easton because Connor was now bald and definitely no longer built like a star football player. Bella didn't like the fact that she took some vague satisfaction from that.

"Did you remind them who you are?"

"What for?" Bella lifted one shoulder in a half-shrug.

Amy tipped her head from one side to the other. "Yeah, I guess it doesn't matter, huh? How long is the class?"

"Six weeks." Bella reached across the table and took Amy's glass, brought it to her lips.

"You always hate it," Amy warned.

Bella sipped. Made a face as the blend of vodka and vermouth burned a path down her throat. Amy was right. She slid the glass back and stuck out her tongue. "Blech."

"Every time." Amy shook her head, but her eyes held affection for Bella.

"How go things with Ms. Southwest?" Bella asked as their food arrived.

"Eh, that's fizzled."

"Really? Hadn't it been, like, two months? That was a record for you." Bella was only half teasing, as Amy wasn't known for the longevity of her relationships—and Bella used that term loosely. Ms. Southwest had been a flight attendant whose schedule was unpredictable. Bella hadn't been optimistic but was interested in seeing how Amy handled it. Apparently, she'd decided not to handle it at all. "Is there another on deck, just in case?"

"Oh, you're hilarious." Amy mock-glared at her.

"I try."

"I'll have you know, I am very happy to be on my own right now. Contentedly single."

"Excuse me? Who are you and what have you done with my good friend Amy?" Amy always, *always* had a girl on deck for when the current girl inevitably fell by the wayside for whatever (unreasonable) reason. Bella made a mental note to call Heather later and see if she had any new information that Amy was being stingy with.

Amy leaned forward, lowered her voice. "Listen, Bells, I understand that you're a little jealous here. But you had your chance to snap me up in college, remember, and now you're like my sister. This"—she ran an open hand in a circle, encompassing her own body— "is now a no-fly zone for you. You blew it."

"I did." Bella feigned a sigh. "Forever penalized for being a late bloomer."

"Late bloomer." Amy snorted. "You were practically a no-show. Twenty years old. Ridiculous."

"Just because I didn't know, right out of the womb, that I was gay like some people at this table…"

"Baby, I was born this way." They laughed, then Amy lifted her glass. "To the gay Jew and the late bloomer." They touched their glasses together with a loud ting.

Bella's heart swelled with love. She adored Amy. There was no doubt about it. They say you never forget your first, but she'd been lucky enough to stay best friends with hers, and she knew that was rare. Between Amy and Heather, Bella had all the love and support she could possibly ask for.

"I wish Heather was here," she said wistfully.

"Same."

"I don't like when she's got late visits."

"God, same."

Heather's social work job periodically called for her to do home visits, not always in the best neighborhoods. The night calls worried both Amy and Bella, though Heather was constantly reassuring them she'd be fine.

Tougher than she looks, Bella reminded herself once again.

The rest of their dinner was spent catching up on everyday things. Spending time with Amy was always fun for Bella, and by the time they parted, her face hurt from laughing so much.

When she was back home later that night, Bella lounged in bed watching TV, her legs bookended immobile by dogs, and her brain took her back to the park, to the moment she saw the little girl with Ethel's tennis ball. Seriously, what were the chances she'd end up being Easton's daughter? What was the universe trying to do to her lately?

She always bristled when somebody instantly assumed either Ethel or Lucy was a vicious attack dog, because the exact opposite was true. Ethel wouldn't know *how* to hurt somebody, especially a child. She loved kids. She guarded them, acted as protector. Sometimes, Bella wished she had one just so Ethel could have a tiny playmate to watch over.

To Connor's credit, he'd realized his assumption was wrong and got right down on the grass to play with Ethel and Easton's daughter. Emma, right?

Easton's daughter.

Bella wasn't sure why that was an unexpected tidbit, but it was. Easton had a little girl that looked just like her, all blond hair and blue eyes and beauty. From what Bella had seen, she seemed outgoing and friendly, a nice kid. Well, nice to Ethel, at least. That was all that really mattered to Bella.

Or so she tried to tell herself, despite the memories of Easton that her brain tossed at her then. Clad in jeans, a white V-neck T-shirt, and an olive-green jacket, she'd looked fresh and inviting. Open, approachable. Things she'd never seemed in the past, at least not to Bella. And the therapist part of Bella's mind scolded her then. Reminded her that judging Easton on her high school persona wasn't fair fifteen years after the fact, but still, Bella couldn't seem to help herself. Her memories of teenage Easton were a jumble…and not much of that jumble was pleasant.

Giving her head a firm shake, she did her best to dislodge the thoughts of Easton Evans that had been crowding her head lately and focus on the *Real Housewives* on her TV screen across the room.

She wasn't even mildly successful.

CHAPTER FIVE

Shondra and Tony Carletti lived in a cul-de-sac on the east side of town. The neighborhood wasn't new, but it was neat and tidy and inhabited by a close-knit group of families that looked out for each other's houses and kids. It was the kind of place Easton always thought she'd wanted with Connor...until she'd married him, and years had gone by and she'd realized that wasn't what she'd wanted at all.

Still, she loved visiting, loved the warm, welcoming feel of the house, the company. Easton turned her car into the driveway just as Tony was coming out the door that led from the open garage into the house.

"Hey there, you beautiful girls," he said by way of greeting as Easton and Emma got out of the car. He was tall and broad-shouldered, with dark hair he slicked back. His oxford was open at the neck, cross on a gold chain glimmering in the setting sun. Connor always joked that he looked like he'd walked directly off the set of *The Sopranos,* still in costume and makeup. Which was an absolutely accurate description.

"Off to win all your friends' money?" Easton asked, as she reached up to hug him.

"More like give them all *my* money," he said, with good-natured scoff.

"I'll keep my fingers crossed for you."

"Hi, Uncle Tony." Emma held out her arms so Tony could lift her up and give her a giant bear hug, complete with loud groaning to go with his gentle squeeze.

"You're going to get too big to do that eventually," Easton warned her.

"Not possible," Tony responded, growling playfully into Emma's neck and making her giggle before setting her back down. "Have fun tonight." He strolled down the driveway and across the cul-de-sac to the house right across from his.

"Long commute," Easton called to him. "You'd better watch your drinking for the ride home." Grabbing the bowl of salsa she'd made that afternoon from the car, she followed Emma, who'd already let herself into the house and had most likely hurried off to play with the Carletti kids.

"There's my girl," Shondra said as Easton entered the kitchen and was wrapped in her arms before she had a chance to set anything down. Shondra was a big hugger and Easton loved how safe she felt in her arms. She smelled like coconut oil, warm and earthy, her hair swathed in a brightly colored scarf, her dark skin glowing, her enormous brown eyes catching every little thing around her. Shondra was a unique personality, and she radiated love and openness almost tangibly. Whenever Easton spent time with her, she was reminded how lucky she was to have her as a friend. "It's so good to see you." After a final squeeze, she let Easton go and took the bowl from her hands.

"Ready for a cocktail?" Shondra asked, indicating the blender on the counter filled with a lime-green liquid.

"Am I ever."

By the time they were into their second margaritas, Easton and Shondra were parked in the backyard around the fire pit. The sun had set and the air had grown chilly, but the fire gave off just enough heat to keep them outside, blankets over their legs, breathing in the fresh, almost-summer air. Their chairs were close together but angled slightly so each woman had her feet up on the hearth, crossed at the ankles, mirror images of one another.

This was where Easton was most comfortable lately. Her own house was lovely, and she was growing to love it, but it was still somewhat new. Work was also new, so her office wasn't as familiar yet as her old one had been. Shondra's place, however, was steady and solid, as if carved into a mountain that would always be there, always be the same. From the very first visit, she'd felt calm and loved in the Carletti home. It was good for her soul to be there, and she expressed that by dropping her head back against her chair and letting go of a contented sigh.

"How's your life, baby girl?" Shondra asked quietly. "Tell me more. I feel like I need to catch up."

Easton took a deep breath. "Well, work has been...interesting."

"Details."

"My staff hates me." Easton held up a hand before Shondra could contradict her. "Which I get. It's not necessarily me they hate. They just miss their old boss and they're still resentful of me being there instead of him. I can understand that, and I'm pretty sure it'll ease up with time." She took a sip of her margarita—a little salty, a little sweet—and continued. "But to make them all feel better, the higher-ups decided to send all the managers to a conflict resolution class."

"Seriously?"

With a nod, Easton explained, "It actually makes sense. It's a show of good faith to the employees who were there before the merger. It's the new owners telling them they're valued. So, I do understand."

"I hear a but in there."

"*But...*" Easton rolled her head so she was facing Shondra and grinned. "I wish it wasn't me who had to give up six of my Wednesday evenings in order to boost their little egos." She immediately squeezed her eyes shut in regret. "That was snarky. I take it back."

"No need to take it back. You can be snarky on Shondra's Margarita Nights. That's what they're for. The more snark the better."

"Oh, good. Then allow me to continue with my snark when I say that the teacher seems a little bit bitchy. A little bit bitchy and a lot hot."

When Shondra Carletti laughed, she *laughed*. A big, husky belly laugh that came from somewhere deep inside her body. She did that now, let it loose, and her laughter always made Easton join in, so they laughed together for a moment before calming down. "Hot, huh?"

"God, yes." Okay, the margaritas had definitely hit, and Easton was saying way more than she normally would. But screw it, it was Shondra, the one person who knew all her secrets. "Maybe it's the slight bitchiness that makes her hot?"

"I was just going to ask that," Shondra said, slapping at Easton's leg.

"I mean, maybe?"

"Again, I'll need details."

It felt good to admit it. Easton had allowed herself to think of Bella Hunt as "pretty" and "attractive," but the fact of the matter, the thing she'd been avoiding in her mind, was that Bella was fucking hot and she turned Easton on in a big way. "I guess there's that whole cliché about the more unapproachable, the more attractive, right? The being attracted to the standoffish person *because* she's standoffish?"

"She's standoffish?"

"A little, yeah." Easton relayed the story of earlier that day, meeting up with Connor at the park so he could hand off Emma, and running into Bella and her dog. "She didn't say a whole lot. I mean, I don't really know her..."

"She's just fun to look at." Shondra completed Easton's thought before Easton realized that was exactly what she was thinking.

"God, yes. And then Connor asked me if I was going to 'check that out.'" Easton made air quotes with her fingers to emphasize how she felt about that. "Which was so weird."

"I bet."

"I can find my own dates, thank you. I don't need my ex-husband trying to fix me up."

Shondra was quiet for a beat before saying gently, "Maybe that was his way of showing you that he's okay with your new life?" She phrased it as a question on purpose, Easton was sure. It was a little less pushy that way.

Easton took it in, let the words sit in her head while she sipped her margarita. "I suppose that's possible. Maybe."

"He's a good guy, E. Give him the benefit of the doubt."

"I know. You're right."

"Speaking of dating, any news on that front?"

Easton scoffed. "When would I have time? I've got a full-time job, a seven-year-old, and now a night class."

Shondra snort-laughed in sarcastic response. "Bitch, please."

Easton gasped, feigned horror. "*Excuse* me?"

"What, do you think anybody who's ever dated has had a free and clear schedule? No jobs, no kids, no extracurricular activities? Just," she mimicked Easton from earlier and made air quotes, "time for dating?"

"Gah! I know. I know." Easton covered her eyes with one hand and made a sound similar to a growl. "I hate when you're right."

"Then you must hate me always." Shondra pushed playfully at Easton's leg with a foot. "Seriously, though. Is this hot instructor of yours gay? Maybe you should see if you can get to know her a bit more."

Easton shook her head, shrugged in defeat. "How the hell should I know? And how do I find out? I have no idea how to do that. Is there a guidebook or something? Rules to follow? I'm so far out of my element here, Shondra."

They laughed then, like junior high girls having a sleepover, but no answers magically appeared.

It was much later that night, as Easton lay in bed trying to sleep, too keyed up from the Diet Coke she'd switched to after the margaritas—*thanks, caffeine!*—when her brain returned to that bit of conversation.

Easton was gay. She'd known for a long time, but had been woefully slow in accepting it. Thus, marriage to her high school boyfriend, a child, a house in the suburbs, her happy parents. She'd done a pretty good job of destroying all those things aside from her child in one fell swoop, that was for sure. Her parents' heads were still spinning.

What if Bella is gay?

That question had stayed with her since Shondra posed it. It had faded a bit into the background as they laughed and teased and discussed other things. In quiet moments, like driving home with a sleeping Emma in the back seat; like now, it stepped into the spotlight and waved to her.

She had no idea how to do this.

Shondra had suggested an online dating site or two. That scared the bejesus out of Easton, though she had trouble verbalizing why. She could go out to a gay bar, she supposed. That idea was less scary and Shondra said she'd happily tag along. But other than those two things, how would she know if a woman "played on her team," as Shondra liked to call it? Easton wasn't an idiot. She could sometimes tell. But not always. What if she thought somebody was and she wasn't? That was an actual fear that lived in the back of her mind. Being new to something when you were in your thirties wasn't the most relaxing thing on the planet.

She inhaled a big breath, filled her lungs to capacity, and held it for a count of five. As she let it out slowly, she willed her body to relax, her muscles to melt down into the mattress. It was an old yoga trick she'd learned for when she had trouble falling asleep. Tomorrow was Sunday, true, but Emma didn't yet understand the meaning of the phrase "sleep in," and would be up by seven, demanding breakfast.

A turn of her head told Easton it was nearly one a.m., so she did the breathing exercise once more, concentrated on relaxing, letting go of the tension. As she did so, a face filled her mind's eye. Bella. Smooth, creamy skin, freckles dotted across the bridge of her nose, a few rogue locks of dark hair escaping her ponytail and framing her face, those hazel eyes, the dark brows accenting them as they seemed to catch everything...

Wow. Had she really looked at Bella that closely? She must have if she had these intricate details, but she didn't remember doing so. At all. How weird was that?

Try as she might, her brain now would not focus on anything but that pretty face. She forced herself not to think about the rest of Bella because then she'd never get any sleep, would probably wake up even more. So she compromised, and instead of fighting it, she let her thoughts settle on her instructor. On her face.

Only her face.

It was more than enough to deliver very, *very* pleasant dreams.

Chapter Six

Framerton High, 2003

"Hey, 1994 called. It wants its pants back."

The new girl kept her head down, but not before Easton saw a flash of pain zip across her face, and in that instant, Easton was sorry she'd laughed with the rest of them, stopped abruptly, and swallowed any sound left.

"Why do you have to be so mean to her?" she asked Tara, voice low. She didn't want the guys to hear, but she didn't understand. Yes, Easton went along with it 99 percent of the time because that's what people her age did, right? Peer pressure and all that crap? But she didn't really understand the joy Tara seemed to get from making somebody else—somebody she didn't even know—feel awful.

"Why not?" Tara shrugged and grinned as she switched out her notebooks and slammed the locker shut. "Besides, she dresses like a fucking homeless person." She made a show of shuddering like her skin was crawling.

Easton let it go and said nothing more. She didn't really like Tara, but she was pretty much the queen bee around Framerton High, and the last thing Easton wanted was to ever end up on her shit list. She'd seen the destruction that came with it. Just look at that poor new girl—what was her name again?—and she hadn't even done anything wrong. All she did was exist, but that seemed to be enough for Tara. If Easton had the audacity to correct Tara, or worse, embarrass her in front of their friends, she couldn't even *imagine* the punishment she'd have to endure. Really, it was just easier to go along. She knew it was cowardly, but she couldn't see any other way.

"Hey, did you do the homework for bio?" Connor interrupted her thoughts to ask the same question he asked her almost every day. He hated bio. Worse, he didn't *get* bio.

Lucky for him, Easton did. She slid a sheet of paper out of her notebook without responding and handed it to him.

"You're the best, babe." He gave her a quick peck on the lips, then spun her around so he could copy her answers onto his own paper using her back as a makeshift desk. Easton didn't really mind. Connor was a good guy, but he struggled in some of his classes, and if he wanted to stay on the football team, he needed to keep his grades up. Easton was happy to help him with that.

As she stood, doing her best impression of a piece of furniture, Easton let her eyes wander over the others in the hall. Bodies moved along as if made of water, flowing together in one direction or the other, moving along to their next classes, the hum of conversation like the buzzing of bees in a hive, steady and constant. Her eye caught the waves of auburn hair coming down the hall before anything else and Easton watched as Kristin Harrington threw her head back and laughed loudly, her throat exposed, at something Josh Danforth said to her. Easton's eyes roamed along the creamy expanse of skin as she wondered if it would feel as soft as it looked, how it would taste...

"Done." Connor's voice jerked her back to reality. Thank freaking God. She swallowed down the lump of...what was it? Shame? Embarrassment? Want?

No. No, not that last one. Not want. Never want. That was silly. Why would she even think that? So what if she looked at Kristin? The girl was pretty. Everybody thought so. It didn't mean anything other than Easton could appreciate an attractive girl. Okay, she had a dream about her the night before. So what? Who cared? Dreams didn't really mean anything, even if there happened to be the tiniest bit of making out in them. Just a tiny, itty-bitty bit of making out. Miniscule amounts of making out. With tongue.

Didn't. Mean. Anything.

"Ready?"

Easton looked up into Connor's blue eyes. He was such a good guy, and she was so lucky to have him. He was handsome and funny and kind. True, he could also be loud and obnoxious, like most guys. And once in a while, he could be a complete douchebag. But who—? Her thoughts were interrupted when she was knocked into, almost to the point of losing her balance.

"Oh, my God, I'm so sorry, Easton."

Kristin Harrington had her hand on Easton's arm, her grip firm. Warm. Helping to steady her. A wave of...something shot through Easton's body like fire, fast and hot, and she opened her mouth to speak, but no sound came out.

"My bad," Kristin said, then continued on her way, Josh Danforth still doing what he could to entertain her.

Easton followed their retreat with her eyes, and that lump was back in her throat. She cleared it away, turned to Connor, reached up, and pulled his face down to hers. She kissed him, made sure it was inarguably an R-rated kiss that left him blinking in shocked wonder.

"Wow," he stammered. "What was that for?"

Sliding her hand down his arm, she linked her fingers with his and tugged him toward their classroom. "Come on. We're gonna be late."

Take that, Kristin Harrington.

❖

"Excellent." Bella was impressed. "Absolutely perfect." Easton had handled the role-playing exercise deftly, listening to her "employee," making her point in a kind way that invited discussion. She didn't get frustrated. She didn't talk down to him. She couldn't have done a better job. Yeah, Bella was impressed and, not for the first time, was clear on the fact that what her boss had been told by the Hart Commodities rep was true—Easton didn't really need to be there. Nor did a couple others...which wasn't to say all of them. There were two or three who were definitely going to benefit from this class.

"All right, that's it for tonight. Don't forget to go to our website and take a look at the videos we have there on dealing with employees whose personalities clash with each other. That's always a fun one." Chuckles went around the room as people gathered their things. "We'll discuss that next week." She watched as her students trickled out one by one.

It had been a busy day. She'd seen several clients, including the young man devastated by his breakup with his girlfriend, the forty-year-old woman who'd had an abortion and was unable to forgive herself, and the twenty-five-year-old CEO whose crazy successful business had given her a major identity crisis. Exhausting enough, those people, but she'd also had a staff meeting, lunch with her boss, and a committee meeting, gone home to give Lucy and Ethel dinner, and then sped back here for class. Normally, Bella would be wiped by now, but she was inexplicably...awake.

"Hey, do you maybe feel like grabbing a cup of coffee?"

Easton's voice surprised her, and when Bella looked up from her things, she realized there were just the two of them left in the room.

Easton scrunched up her nose. "I'm kinda keyed up. Not sure why." With a shrug, she added, "I just don't feel like going home yet. I mean, if it's against any rules or anything, I understand. I just..." She shrugged and repeated herself. "I'm not ready to go home."

God, she's pretty. That was always the first thought that hit Bella's brain whenever she laid eyes on Easton Evans. From the very first day she'd ever seen her. Everything about her was just...pretty. Pleasing to the eye. Her shining hair in at least three varying shades of gold. Her enormously expressive blue eyes, accented with dark lashes and surprisingly dark brows. Her very feminine hands. Her warm, inviting smile. She wore a pantsuit today, gray with a pink top underneath the jacket, black heels, some of her hair pulled back and the rest down, sitting in gentle waves on her shoulders. *God, she's pretty.*

Easton Evans. Part of the dreaded Crap Pack (Bella's own play on Brat Pack) at Framerton High.

Of course, she didn't want to go to coffee with this woman.

That was a terrible idea.

Absolutely not.

"That sounds great," were the words that actually came out of her mouth, and she tried valiantly to hide her own horror at the sound of them.

"Awesome." Easton's face lit up, her smile wide and gorgeous. Okay, so Bella's answer had obviously made her happy, and that made Bella happy...something she tried to ignore and she certainly didn't analyze in any way. "Are you familiar with Perk? Just around the corner?"

"Are you kidding? I practically live there. Why don't you go ahead? I have to drop some things in my office and give my email a quick check. Then I'll meet you. Yeah?"

Easton continued to smile as she nodded. "Perfect. I'll save you a seat. See you in a bit."

On her way down the hall to her office, Bella texted Amy and Heather in their three-way chat.

Mayday! Mayday! I've made a huge mistake! Save me!

Twins texts of *What happened?* were returned in under a minute.

About to have coffee with the Blast from the Past. Am I crazy?

Enough time went by this time to let her toss her stuff in her office and click open her email before a response came. It was Amy.

Is that a real question?

LOL, Amy, from Heather.

You guys. I'm serious. What am I doing?

Amy played the role of Voice of Reason. *You're going to have coffee with a new friend. It's fine. No need to freak out.*

Agreed, from Heather.

Sigh. Fine. H, you're wordy today. She was usually the one with all the advice.

Sorry. Busy. I agree with A. Have the coffee. It's just coffee. This text was followed by three coffee cup emojis, apparently to make up for the lack of words earlier.

Since nobody else seemed concerned about this impending coffee meeting—she refused to refer to it as a date—Bella decided to do her best to just chill. Besides, Perk had an amazing hazelnut French roast and Bella was more than ready for a cup.

The evening weather was typical for May. Cool, but with that feel in the air that inexplicably said spring was here and summer was well on its way. Bella could still detect the smell of late-blooming hyacinths around the office building and there was a new freshness in the air that forced her to breathe in deeply and slowly, as if it wasn't her decision at all.

Perk wasn't terribly busy on a Wednesday night after eight, with just a smattering of customers scattered around the shop. Bella spotted Easton easily—seriously, how do you miss somebody who looks like that?—in the little sitting area, parked comfortably on a soft-looking love seat. She waved to Bella, big orange mug halfway to her lips, and shot her that damn smile. Bella found herself suddenly in a hurry to get her coffee and sit next to Easton. Yeah, what was that about? That urgency? Never mind. She didn't want to know. She was pretty sure of that.

"You made it," Easton said unnecessarily, as Bella took a seat next to her. The love seat made them sit closer together than Bella would have normally, and Easton's scent tickled her nostrils, a subtle perfume of gentle sweetness with just a hint of spice to it.

"I did." Bella tried to settle into the cushions but was unable to fully relax. Something about being this close to Easton tensed her up like a cat on alert.

"Do you come here often?" Both of them seemed to hear the question at the same time, and Easton's cheeks were suddenly a pretty shade of pink. "I didn't mean…" She stuttered a bit and Bella couldn't help but smile. "It's just that your office is really close." Easton closed her eyes. "God." She blushed more deeply.

Bella touched her knee, still smiling. She couldn't help it. Easton in the throes of embarrassment was kind of cute. "Don't worry. It's been ages since anybody asked me that, so I'll take it, even if it was just an innocent question. I should come here often, but I don't. I forget how close I am."

"Well, that's a shame. The coffee is excellent."

They each sipped their coffee, eyes gazing over the rims of their mugs at each other, and Bella had a sudden, inexplicable feeling of contentment, like she was right where she was supposed to be.

Weird. So very, very weird.

"How old is your daughter?" Bella's need to make Easton feel more comfortable was strong, so she grabbed at the topic she thought Easton would be most happy discussing in the hopes of shifting the focus. It worked. Easton's face lit up, her smile widening, her gorgeous eyes crinkling a bit at the corners.

"She's seven going on thirty-five."

Bella laughed. "She was great with my dog."

"She was, wasn't she?" Easton sipped, her gaze in the middle distance. "She's always loved animals and has wanted a dog since she was old enough to know what a dog was."

"Sounds like your ex thinks it's time? I heard him say something about that."

Easton's grin slipped a bit, and her eyes refocused on her coffee. "Yeah. It's fine. It'll make her happy."

"How long have you been separated?" Bella kept her voice soft, knowing she was approaching very personal territory, but somehow needing this information. She didn't understand it.

"Almost two years. We got married right after college and had Emma pretty soon after that." Easton's voice was almost wistful, like she was recalling happier, easier times. Then she seemed to sober as she added, "My divorce was finalized last week."

"Why did you split up? I mean, if it's okay to ask. Feel free to tell me it's none of my business. 'Cause it's not. I know."

Easton's smile returned, a softer, dimmer version of it. Again, she looked off into the shop as if she was searching for the right thing to say. "I wasn't happy."

It was a simple statement. It was also far from the whole story. Bella was trained to recognize these things, and she saw that as clearly as if Easton had said it out loud.

Taking a deep breath and blowing it out, Easton redirected the conversation. "Tell me about your dog. Wait, dogs. You said you had two, didn't you?"

"I did. Good memory." Bella could feel herself relaxing a little at a time, though she didn't want to admit it. "Lucy and Ethel were together at the shelter. I only went to *look*."

Easton let out a snort. "Silly, silly woman."

"Right? Anyway, I saw Lucy first, all curled up in the corner. She lifted her head and just looked at me and she was so deceiving, this intimidating-looking animal with her huge square head. But her eyes were so sweet and soft." Bella swallowed, emotion welling up a bit as she recalled the moment she'd fallen in love with her dogs. "She stood up to come to the front of her kennel to see me, and that's when I saw that there were actually two of them. They'd been curled up so tightly together that they looked like one big dog when there were actually two medium-sized dogs."

She remembered that day like it was yesterday. "My friend Heather was with me. Her job was to make sure I didn't adopt the entire animal population of Junebug Farms. Let me tell you, it was tempting. Seeing so many homeless pets? God, it's heartbreaking. I wanted every last one of them."

"I can imagine." Easton had also seemed to settle back into her seat. The two of them were now arranged like old friends who met for coffee all the time, each with her back against an arm of the love seat, one foot on the floor, a leg bent up onto the cushions so they faced each other. It was alarmingly comfortable.

"Anyway, Lucy sauntered up to the kennel door very slowly, like she was sizing me up as she did so. In the meantime, Ethel finally noticed me, jumped off the bed like she'd been ejected from it, and shoved right past Lucy to get to me first."

"Uh-oh."

"I know, right? I only wanted one dog. One!" Bella held up a finger for emphasis.

"Famous last words." Easton grinned, then sipped, her eyes never leaving Bella's face. Bella could feel them even when she wasn't looking.

"I was in the midst of trying to figure out if I could possibly just take one when the adoption manager came over and told me their story. They were sisters, had always been together since they were born. They were five at that point. They belonged to an older gentleman who lived alone and loved them to bits. When he died suddenly of a heart attack, there was nobody to take them. I'm pretty sure I could actually feel my heart breaking in my chest a little bit. He had no children, only an older sister who's in an assisted living facility that doesn't allow pets. The adoption woman said it broke the sister's heart to have to send them to the shelter, but she didn't have the knowledge to find them a home or a place to keep them while she tried to figure it out. The shelter didn't want to separate them if they could help it."

"And along came you."

"I wasn't even wearing my hat that says I'm A Sucker that day, either."

Easton's laugh was light, feminine, contagious. "So, you took them both home."

"I did. Haven't regretted it for a second. They're great dogs. I can't imagine my life without either one of them."

"How come you only had Ethel at the park?"

Damn, she has a good memory. "I said they were great dogs. I didn't say they were similar dogs. If I didn't know they were siblings, I never would've guessed. They're so very different."

"Really?" Easton wrinkled her nose. "I was going to say that's surprising, but I've known lots of people—myself included—who have siblings they're nothing like. I guess it makes sense that animals might be like that, too."

With a nod, Bella explained her babies' personalities. "Ethel could chase a ball until she dropped. Actually, I'm pretty sure she would if I didn't monitor her and take it away when she starts to slow down. She lives for Tennis Ball. Now, Lucy? She couldn't care less about the ball. Or any toy. Can't be bothered. Food, on the other hand…" She let that dangle in the hopes of getting another peal of laughter from Easton. She did. "Food and sleep. Those are the things Lucy lives for."

"That's so funny."

They were quiet for a moment, their coffees almost drained, and neither seemed in a hurry to go anywhere. Interesting.

"Where is Emma tonight? Babysitter?"

Easton shook her head. "Connor has her Wednesday through Saturday."

At the mention of Connor Douglas, Bella's relaxed demeanor stiffened just slightly. "You guys went to school together?"

"Since eighth grade, yes. Isn't that crazy?"

"I've never met high school sweethearts before."

Easton made that snorting sound again, half scoff, half sarcastic laugh. "Yeah, we were way too young. We waited until after college, so we were both twenty-two, but…" She shrugged. "Yeah, still too young." She set her empty mug down on the table and returned her gaze to Bella. "You married?"

"Me? No."

"Ever been?"

Bella's turn to shake her head. "Nope."

"Do you want to?"

"Are you proposing?" It came shooting right out of her mouth before it even partially registered in her brain, and it took every fiber of energy Bella had to play it off as a joke and not look as horrified as she felt. Thank God, Easton burst out laughing, too.

"Not yet. I'll have to get to know you better first."

And something about *that* response set off a flurry of butterflies in Bella's stomach. She smiled softly at Easton and finished her coffee.

"More?" Easton pointed to the empty mug.

Bella hesitated—actually hesitated! "I should probably get home to my girls."

"Ah, yes. They've been cooped up all day, huh?"

"Pretty much, yeah. They could use a walk." Bella glanced outside. It was dark but clear. She'd stroll around the neighborhood with the dogs a bit.

"If you ever want company on dog walks, I'm your girl." Easton's expression was open and warm as she stood, and Bella got the instant impression that she was looking for new friends. While it wasn't unusual for a person fresh off a divorce to feel she needed new people in her life, it *was* unusual to think of the popular Easton Evans from Framerton High looking for friendship from somebody like Bella. Hell, looking for friendship *at all*. Bella had some trouble wrapping her brain around that, despite her background as a therapist.

"I'll keep that in mind."

"Thanks for indulging me," Easton said as the two of them gathered up their things and strolled toward the door. "I had a good time talking to you."

"Same here," Bella replied, holding the door for her. And she meant it, which was strangely unexpected.

"Maybe we can do it again next week." The brightness of Easton's smile increased.

"Maybe we can." That response? Also strangely unexpected.

They'd parked in opposite directions, so they parted ways and Bella watched as Easton walked away, the way her free arm swung down by her hip, the way her hair gently swished from one side to the other along her shoulders.

Once more, the thought ran through her head. *God, she's pretty.*

Eyebrows raised, lips rolled in, Bella watched for a few more seconds before heading home to lie awake all night thinking about the past sixty minutes.

❖

"Seriously?" Shondra's voice was an octave higher than usual when Easton answered her cell. They'd been texting, but Shondra often got frustrated with that medium. She claimed she talked faster than she typed, which was very true, and would rather just call. "You actually asked the woman to coffee?"

"I did." Easton was absurdly pleased with herself after hearing Shondra's reaction.

"Girl, I am so proud of you right now, I don't even have the words." Easton could hear the fridge open and close, and assumed Shondra was making lunches for the kids. "How was it? Did you have fun? Is she gay? I need details!"

The laughter burst out of Easton. She couldn't help it. Shondra's excitement was contagious. "It was nice. Yes, I had fun. I still don't know if she's gay. It's not like I just blurted out the question."

"Why the hell not?"

"I'm sure that would've gone over well. Hi there, want to get coffee with me? Have a chat? By the way, do you like girls?"

"I don't see what's so hard about that."

Easton shook her head as she picked up one of Emma's toys and walked it to the toy box in the family room where her things lived. "How was your day?"

"Oh, no. Nuh-uh. We're not done talking about your date."

"It wasn't a date, Shon."

"The hell it wasn't. Tell me about her."

Easton plopped onto the gray couch and blew out a breath. Her brain took her back to the coffee shop, to sitting a mere foot away from Bella. She liked being that close to her; she realized that now. She liked being able to make out all the different colors in her eyes. At first glance, they were light brown. But up close, they were more hazel, with little flecks of green and gold sprinkled in them. The most unique eyes Easton had ever seen, no lie. And the way her face lit up when she talked about her dogs? It was beautiful.

"She's beautiful." Easton had said it out loud to Shondra before she even realized it. The surprising part was, she didn't want to take it back. It was the truth. Bella was a very beautiful woman.

"Wow. That's quite an endorsement."

"She is. She's beautiful and she's smart and she's funny. She asked me a lot of questions and I really felt like she *listened* to my answers, you know? Not like she was just being polite. Like she was interested."

"No clues about who she dates, huh?"

Easton scrunched up her nose. "Not really. She's never been married, but that doesn't mean anything. She has two dogs, but that doesn't mean anything either. We actually talked much more about me. Which embarrasses me now that I realize it." It was only in that moment that she remembered Bella was a therapist. Getting people to talk was probably a specialty of hers.

"You people need a secret handshake or something."

Easton feigned a gasp. "'You people?' How dare you?"

Shondra's laugh shot out of her like a bullet. "You know what I mean." She was quiet for a moment, then asked, "What are you doing on Friday night?"

"I feel like you're plotting something. This feels like a trick."

"Just answer the damn question."

Easton squinted as she thought. "Pretty sure I'm free."

"Good. Stay that way. I'll get back to you."

They hung up several minutes later, and Easton reached for the remote to watch something on her DVR. She chose a legal drama and settled in but found her mind drifting back to Perk, to the love seat there, to the company. She had a feeling Bella Hunt was going to be making herself comfortable in Easton's head. Easton both liked that idea and was terrified by it. She hadn't been this distracted by somebody—by a woman—in a long time.

Not since Olivia.

CHAPTER SEVEN

Yeah, I'm gonna need alcohol tonight. The text was from Amy on the three-way convo. *And dancing. Definitely dancing.*

Bella looked at her watch. 3:45 p.m. on Friday. She had one more appointment, then she was free. A night out with her girls didn't sound like a bad idea. Maybe it would help her focus on things other than how many more days there were until Wednesday, when she'd see Easton again. She hated that this was where her brain was, so she hadn't confessed to either Amy nor Heather. No, this was information she was keeping to herself. At least for the time being.

I'd be down for a drink or two, she typed.

DANCING was Heather's one-word, all caps response, followed by a dancing dog emoji that made Bella giggle. Heather was Queen of Emojis.

Are we dancing it out tonight, Amy?

We are. If I don't show up, find bail money and come get me because I'll be in jail for killing one of these fucking little high school pricks! Taking a cue from the Queen of Emojis, she followed her plea with the wide-eyed, shocked face emoji.

It was okay to chuckle at Amy's comments because Bella knew her well. Nobody loved her job—nobody loved her *students*—more than Amy. But let's be honest, they were teenagers, and teenagers could be giant pains in the ass. Once in a great while, Amy had to let loose and call them every name in the book. She only did that with Bella and Heather. It was her outlet. Her release. That and dancing it out, like on *Grey's Anatomy.*

It had been a crazy day, and Bella usually liked that. She liked when she moved seamlessly from one appointment to the next, from one meeting to another. It kept her brain engaged and focused on work. She'd seen Arielle, her patient who really, really needed to leave her sham of a marriage—and Bella was sure she knew it—but was having trouble pulling the trigger. She'd been seeing Bella weekly for nearly a year now. Bella had also seen Jonas, a man in his late twenties whose girlfriend had left him several months ago. It had, quite simply, wrecked him. He just could not understand, couldn't wrap his brain around the why of it. He spent most of his sessions with Bella crying. Or at least tearing up. He was one of her tougher cases because she wanted to shake him and be firm with him about letting go of the ex and moving on, for his own sanity. But that wasn't her job. Her job was to help him get there on his own. Bella vacillated between feeling sympathy for him and being frustrated with him.

Today, though, and yesterday, if she was being honest, she had the weird desire for time. Downtime. Time to sit and think, to daydream. *To fantasize, Isabella, tell the truth.*

Yes, to fantasize a bit, because the fact of the matter was she hadn't been able to get Easton Evans out of her head since coffee on Wednesday night and she wasn't quite sure what to do with that. If anything.

She hadn't had a full-on sex dream about her, not like in high school, but Bella had definitely had flashes. She hadn't been this attracted to a woman in a long time, possibly since Easton fifteen years ago—God, was that even possible?—and the fact that it still seemed to be that way messed with Bella's head a bit. She'd run fast and far away from Framerton High, away from the inappropriate, confusing, devastating crush she'd had on Easton Evans. Finding herself in the exact same boat fifteen years later was not sitting well with her. Not at all. Going out tonight with her girls, having a couple drinks, getting all sweaty on the dance floor sounded great. They might be older than much of the crowd, but Bella didn't care. She needed this. Badly.

I'm in. What time? she typed.

DJ starts at 8, so let's do 7:30 was Amy's response. She'd obviously looked into things, and Bella grinned at the image of her sending one of her "fucking little pricks" out of her office and quickly googling the schedule for their local gay hangout.

Heather's text made Bella's smile widen. *Remember when we didn't go out until 11?*

YES! Amy said. *We wouldn't shower and get dressed until almost 10. Now I'm in bed by then.*

We're officially old at 33, Bella typed and dropped in an emoji with a horrified face.

Speak for yourself! Amy said. *See you bitches tonight.*

❖

Bella felt guilty leaving Lucy and Ethel for the evening again, so she took them for a walk and spent extra time in her small backyard tossing the ball for Ethel while Lucy watched, obvious in her boredom. Then Bella changed into dark skinny jeans, a white tank, and a lightweight jacket in black that was tapered at the waist. She pushed the sleeves up her forearms and added a watch. The cool spring weather did not warrant a tank yet, but Bella knew layers were her friend when it came to a dance floor filled with writhing, sweaty bodies. A touch-up of her eyeliner and a couple spritzes of hair spray and she was good to go.

She pushed through the door and into Teddy's at 7:40, knowing she'd possibly arrived before Heather and absolutely before Amy. Seeing neither of them, she found a spot at the bar and ordered herself a vodka and cranberry, then turned her back so she could lean against the bar and scan the place.

Teddy's had originally been established in the '80s as a gay bar that catered to the bear crowd. It changed hands in the mid-'90s, and the new owners bought the building and expanded the bar up so there was a dance floor and DJ on the first floor, and for people who wanted to actually have a conversation they could hear, a bar and sitting area on the second floor. It changed hands again in 2010, but the basic atmosphere and layout remained the same. The crowd tended to be mostly men, of course, because lesbians are homebodies and don't go out for a night of drinking and dancing like the gay boys do. It was still early, so the dance floor was only sporadically occupied, a handful of men dancing here and there, the bass to the song by Ariana Grande pounding enough for Bella to feel it in the pit of her stomach as if somebody was tapping on her from the inside.

Bella was about to take a stroll up to the second floor when she saw Amy come in the front door, followed closely by Heather. Instantly, the worries in her head dissipated.

"Where my bitches at?" Amy said loudly. Bella closed her eyes and shook her head, then let herself be wrapped in a hug from Heather.

"We're right here," Heather said, as she bumped Amy with a shoulder. "And don't be so vulgar."

"Please," Amy snorted. "Like you don't hear that kind of language every day."

"I do, which is why I don't need to hear it from my friends." Heather was unusually firm, and Bella watched as she and Amy held eye contact until Amy relented.

"Okay. Sorry. What are you drinking?"

Heather peeked over Bella's shoulder. "What do you have?" Bella told her, and Heather nodded and pointed. "One of those."

Amy placed the order with the bartender, got herself a beer, and the three of them stood in a little triangle. Amy held up her bottle. "To Friday."

They all sipped, then Heather lowered her voice. "You guys are gonna protect me, right?"

Bella grinned. It was the exact same line Heather had uttered ever since a woman bought her a drink and asked her to dance more than six months ago. "Yes, Heather, we will protect you from all the big, bad, scary lesbians. Right, Amy?"

An odd look zipped across Amy's face so quickly, Bella barely saw it. "Absolutely. No worries." She smiled widely as the DJ introduced himself and played a Lady Gaga dance mix to get things started. Grabbing each of them by the hand, Amy dragged both her friends onto the dance floor, and so began their Friday.

Two hours later, the crowd had tripled in size, most of them on the dance floor. Bella was down to her tank, sweating and feeling awesome. There was nothing quite like dancing to elevate her mood and it was obvious that her friends felt the same, judging by how they were laughing and falling into each other. Heather was pretty drunk. Amy, not so much. Bella was somewhere in between the two and glad they'd all taken Ubers so they didn't have to worry about driving home.

Back at the bar, they agreed on one more round, Heather's turn to buy.

"I need the ladies' room," Bella shouted in order to be heard. She excused herself, but as she approached the back corner of the bar, she could already see the line. Five women that she could see, and she knew there were most likely another three or four inside waiting. With a groan of annoyance, she headed upstairs to see if that ladies' room had a shorter line. "Not by much," she uttered as she got to the top of the stairs and saw three women waiting. But it was quieter upstairs, and Bella decided to stay, catch her breath, give her ears a break.

With a nod and a smile to the woman at the end of the line— shaved head and more piercings than Bella could count—she leaned against the wall and let her eyes wander the open space that made up the second floor of Teddy's.

The bar started in one corner of the big square area and stretched out from there. It was smaller than the one downstairs, which was in the middle of the room and was accessible from all sides, but not by much. One bartender and one barback were on duty up here, as opposed to three and three on the first floor. A handful of patrons sat at the bar, the buzz of conversation low and comforting. Bella could feel the bass line from the dance music below, but that was all. Having a conversation up here was totally possible. As a woman came out of the ladies' room and they all moved forward one space, the clack of pool balls drew Bella's eye in the direction of the pool table where four women were in the midst of a serious-looking game. To the right of the pool table were several couches and overstuffed chairs arranged in small groupings. Bella scanned the various patrons occupying them.

And then she went still.

It was as if she was suddenly shot with a paralyzing agent of some sort that ceased any and all movement of her body. There were two comfy-looking chairs with matching ottomans. They were tilted slightly toward each other, a small, round table between them. On one chair lounged an attractive African American woman that Bella put around forty. She was talking animatedly to a blond woman in the other chair, using her hands to punctuate her story. Bella squinted as the blond threw her head back and laughed.

Yeah, she'd recognize that laugh anywhere. Light. Feminine. Contagious. Bella was smiling before she realized it.

"You're up."

A gentle tap on her arm brought Bella back to herself as the woman next to her smiled hesitantly and pointed to the open door of the bathroom. Bella hurried in, locked the door, and took a seat.

What the hell is Easton Evans doing in a gay bar?

It was a question with only two answers, really. Either she was gay or she was there with somebody who was gay. Right? What other reason would there be? And it couldn't be the first one, could it? She was recently divorced from a man. Bella immediately scolded herself. *You're a therapist, for God's sake. You know better than to shove people into boxes like that.* She racked her brain to remember what Easton had said about her divorce. "I wasn't happy." That was all she'd said. *Well, that doesn't help.*

Bella dug her hands into her hair, her confusion over why any of this mattered at all threatening to drown her when there was a knock on the door.

"Hey, you almost done in there? There's a line, you know."

Not having accomplished anything, she flushed anyway and grasped the doorknob. *At least she didn't see me* was the only thought in her head as she exited the bathroom and muttered an apology to the next woman in line.

"I thought that was you."

Bella didn't have to look up to know who was talking to her, but she did, right into the big, blue, gorgeous eyes of Easton Evans. She looked beautiful in her jeans and denim jacket. She smelled amazing, that signature spiciness of hers finding its way to Bella's nose. She was warm; Bella could tell by the temperature of the soft hand that grasped hers and tugged her toward the chairs where Bella had seen her last.

God, I've had too much to drink for this.

"Shondra, *this* is Bella Hunt."

The African American woman that Bella had seen earlier sat forward in her chair and held out a hand to Bella, who managed to pull herself together long enough to shake it. "Shondra Carletti. It's nice to meet you," the woman said. "I've heard a lot about you."

Bella felt her own brows rise toward her hairline. "You have?" She hadn't meant to sound surprised, but she was. Easton talked about her?

"Oh, yeah. Easton here *really* enjoys your class."

Did Easton shoot the woman a look? Bella couldn't be sure. She suddenly felt more intoxicated than she had just two minutes ago. What the hell was wrong with her?

"Can I get you a drink?" Easton asked, her smile gorgeous. Magnetic. That was it. The woman was magnetic. And Bella was a big, helpless piece of metal.

Bella squinted at her for a beat before answering. "Oh, no. Thank you, though. My friends are downstairs. And probably wondering where I am. I should—" She jerked a thumb over her shoulder and took a small step backward. She couldn't stay there, but if pressed to verbalize why not, she'd have remained silent, no idea what to say. All she knew was she needed to leave. It was a weird, inexplicable feeling, but she followed it. "It was nice to meet you," she said with a nod to Shondra. "And it's always nice to see you. Easton." Before she could stop herself, she reached out, laid a hand on Easton's upper arm, squeezed. "Always."

Then she fled.

"Well, at least I got my questions answered." Shondra looked far too satisfied as she sipped her no-name white wine and settled back into the comfy chair.

Easton finally sat down after letting her gaze follow Bella's retreating form—her very quickly retreating form—until she descended the stairs and was out of sight. "Yeah? Which questions are those?"

"Question number one: is your instructor as hot as you said she was? The answer to that is, 'Why yes, Shondra, yes she is. She is incredibly hot, just as I told you, and she and I would make stunningly beautiful babies together.' Because, girl? You've been holding out. Wow. Did you see her? Just wow."

Easton laughed. She couldn't help it. Also, Shondra was right. *Oh, I saw her. Believe me, I saw her.* Bella looked…incredible. Her outfit was simple: just jeans and a white tank top—a tank top that showed off all kinds of arms. And skin. Collarbones. Shoulders. Her hair was loose and wavy, kind of tousled. Her cheeks were flushed like she'd been exerting herself a bit. Dancing? Those beautiful eyes were wide, maybe a little glassy. Easton suspected she'd had a bit to drink and that was probably why she'd left so quickly. Embarrassed, maybe?

"And question number two: is she gay? While I can't answer that with a hundred percent certainty, we are in a gay bar and she did seem rather comfortable here, so I'm going to go with, 'Yes, ma'am.'"

Easton shook her head, still grinning. What were the chances? She'd been to other, smaller bars before, but she'd been wanting to come to this one. She'd found it online, had stalked its social media pages for a while, had intended to go for several weekends in a row now, but had always chickened out. Having Shondra offer to be her wing woman was all she needed to bolster her courage. She'd been sitting here in this nice chair, enjoying both the conversation with Shondra and the ability to simply...observe, when who should catch her eye but the one woman she couldn't seem to get out of her head lately? It was all so very strange.

"So?" Shondra's voice brought her back to her present surroundings.

"So...what?" Easton sat back in the comfy chair, finished her drink.

"So...are you going to ask her out?"

Easton scoffed, pretended the thought hadn't crossed her mind. "I wouldn't know how to do that."

Shondra gave her a look that, if it had sound, would've said, "Bitch, please." She kept that look focused on Easton until Easton began to squirm.

"Stop."

"No, *you* stop. Stop being ridiculous. You've already asked her to coffee. Right?"

Easton pursed her lips, nodded grudgingly. "Yeah..." It was true. She had. And the world hadn't crumbled around her. Bella had even said yes. "Yeah, I did."

"See? There you go. Just do it again."

Many questions flew through Easton's mind then. *Does it make me desperate if I ask again? What if she's not interested in me that way? What if she says no? God, what if she says yes?*

"I can see that brain of yours working, bringing up every possible scenario. I can hear the mechanisms whirring from over here." Shondra's half-grin gave the mocking a lightness, made it playful.

Easton blew out a breath that raspberried her lips. "I hate that you know me so well."

"It's a good thing." Shondra squeezed her arm. "Trust me."

Deciding against another round, the two decided to head home. Easton craned her neck on the way down the stairs and on the path toward the door but didn't catch another glimpse of Bella anywhere. She'd either left already or was somewhere Easton couldn't see her. Maybe she was hiding from her.

Oh, well. It was probably better this way, because if Easton was going to ask Bella out, she needed some time to plan. To outline. To rehearse...

Wait.

Am I going to ask her out?

CHAPTER EIGHT

Framerton High, 2003

Izzy had perfected the art of watching while appearing like she wasn't. It came with the territory when you were trying to blend in and be invisible. She stood practically inside her locker—the better to be ignored—and peered through the vent on the door as Easton Evans jammed her tongue down Connor Douglas's throat.

Ewww.

And yet, she couldn't seem to look somewhere else. Couldn't tear her gaze away from the long, exposed column of Easton's neck as she tilted her head up to meet Connor's lips. Couldn't help but let her eyes wander down the curves of Easton's body. Couldn't stop looking at the peek of skin on her side where her shirt rode up, the snugness of her jeans, the perfect shape of her ass. Heat and…something else, something she couldn't name, didn't want to name, raced through her body as she stood there, a voyeur, wishing—

BAM!

The locker next to hers slammed shut and the sound was like a gunshot, shocking enough to snap Izzy out of her little fantasy world as her entire body flinched in place. She blinked rapidly and swallowed hard.

Jesus, really? Pull it together, Iz. You're being a creeper.

This chiding of herself was becoming a regular thing. She couldn't help it. She blamed the dream. Having the same dream more than once was something Izzy had heard about but never experienced. Until this one. She'd had it twice now, but it didn't mean anything. Right? It was just a dream.

With an almost violent shake of her head, she whipped the thought away. Then she grabbed her books, slammed her locker shut, and hurried down the hall toward her lit class. Head down, books held tightly to her chest. The same way she walked everywhere in school. The better to not be seen.

❖

Bella made it until the following Wednesday before she slipped up on the group text.

Amy had typed, *It's Hump Day. You get to see your Blast from the Past tonight, Bells.*

Without thinking, Bella had responded with *Twice in less than a week* and then added an eye roll emoji. The second she hit Send, she realized her mistake and braced for the fallout.

Why didn't text have an Unsend button? Who could she send a letter to about that?

Wait, what? When was the other time? Heather had been fairly quiet, but was suddenly right there with her questions.

"Shit, shit, shit," Bella muttered as she tried to analyze the situation. It wasn't that she had anything to hide. So Easton had been at Teddy's on Friday. So Bella hadn't told her friends. So what? Didn't mean anything. At all. Plus, Easton was there with somebody. Was it a friend? A girlfriend? Would Easton have mentioned a significant other at coffee last week? Bella racked her brains to recall whether there'd been an opportunity but was interrupted by the ping from her phone and Amy's impatience.

Hello?

Bella growled low in her throat as she sat back in her desk chair. There wasn't a way around this and she didn't make it a habit to lie to her best friends, so she clenched her jaw and typed out the truth. *She was at Teddy's on Friday.*

Two emojis arrived within half a second of each other. Both were wide-eyed shocked faces.

WTF? from Amy.

Why didn't you point her out? from Heather.

I'm sorry! I panicked! Again, it was the truth. Bella had spent the past several days first trying not to think about those five minutes at the bar and then reliving them over and over again. Wondering what she could have done differently. Wondering what she should have done differently. Wondering what she should have said differently. She'd come pretty close to driving herself completely mad; it had only been work that had saved her.

EM! I'm calling it. They didn't use the Emergency Meeting, or EM, as Amy had named it, very often. It really was reserved for emergencies. So, when she called this one, Bella balked.

No way. I call overreaction. Everything's fine.

Can we do EHH then? Heather took things down a notch to request an Emergency Happy Hour.

Tomorrow, Bella typed out. *Yes. I can do that.*

They settled on time and place and Bella signed off. She had to get home and spend a little time with Lucy and Ethel, but she also wanted to step away from that conversation. Now she had time to gather her thoughts, organize them in a way that made sense.

Which had proven difficult recently.

As she sat on her kitchen floor between her dogs and stroked their strong backs as they ate dinner, she tried to focus on her feelings. Her current feelings, right then, in that moment. There were several, the first and foremost being her love for her animals. That was a constant and it swelled her heart and warmed her from the inside out every time. She'd often joked that she'd take a bullet for her dogs...except it wasn't a joke. She absolutely would.

The other feelings she wrestled with as she sat on the linoleum were harder to pinpoint, they took more effort to grasp.

Easton Evans represented a lot of things. Bella had to accept that. The biggest thing was her past. Bella had worked hard to first run away from it, but second—and more reasonably—leave it behind. Most people would've run a lot farther, but Bella wanted to at least be in the same state as her parents. She was all they had, and she loved them dearly. Leaving *them* behind wasn't an option—or a desire— so she'd run a good three hundred miles away instead. And that seemed to work. Framerton High wasn't huge and she'd never, in her fifteen years since graduation, run into any of her former classmates.

Until now.

Suddenly, both Easton Evans and Connor Douglas were here, in *her* town, the town she had claimed for herself, and she did *not* like it. At all. It felt like her worlds were colliding and there was not a damn thing she could do about it but stand there and watch, wide-eyed. Feeling like she had no control of her life was something Bella thought she'd left behind as well. Apparently, she was wrong because that's exactly how she felt now. And she blamed Easton for that. Easton and her friendly smile and her gorgeous figure and her showing up at Bella's gay bar. Yes, Bella had decided that everything in her town belonged to her and Easton was trespassing. The therapist in her head tossed her notebook away in exasperation and left the room.

It should be easy to separate. In her line of work, that was an essential skill, one that she'd never had an issue with. But there was one wrench in those gears currently: Bella was attracted to Easton. Was *still* attracted to Easton. Was *still very* attracted to Easton.

"Some things never change," she muttered, and Ethel turned to give her a kiss that smelled like dog food and made Bella chuckle. "And thanks for that." She ruffled Ethel's ears and pushed herself to her feet. Seeing Easton in a gay bar had shifted Bella's perspective and she had to figure out what she was going to do about it, if anything.

Because she was going to see Easton again in less than an hour.

❖

Trouble concentrating.

Hard time focusing.

Distracted.

All those things described Easton in the conflict resolution class that night. Try as she might, she couldn't seem to aim her attention at the *information* in the class because she was too busy letting her eyes roam over the *teacher* of the class.

Ever since Friday night at the bar, Easton hadn't been able to get her mind off Bella. Oh, she could find other things to do to occupy herself, but Bella still danced around in the back of her brain, waving her arms, reminding Easton that she was there, that she hadn't gone anywhere, and hey, don't forget how good-looking she was. Her flushed face, all that tousled hair, her beautiful eyes, her ass in those jeans. It was as if those recollections suddenly grew hands and grabbed on to Easton, gave her a little shake now and then just to make sure she was paying attention, wouldn't let go of her.

As she sat through the class, she tried hard to listen to the actual words being said, but her focus was more on the sound of Bella's voice, the way her facial expressions changed as she spoke. It was so easy to tell when she was passionate about something because her eyes brightened and her posture seemed to straighten, made her small frame just a smidge taller.

Maybe because Easton took part in the role-playing exercise last week, she simply observed this week. Rather than a supervisor/employee issue, this exercise featured two employees with decidedly different work styles who had trouble working together because of it. Mara and Paul played the employees while Kim took the role of the supervisor. She handled it differently than Easton would have, but all managers had different ways of dealing with their staff members.

"What did you guys all think?" Bella asked. "Would you have done anything differently?"

Easton raised her hand, and her heart rate kicked up a notch when those hazel eyes settled on her. "I think Kim handled it just fine, but I might have had Mara and Paul do a bit more talking to each other first."

"In Kim's presence," Bella clarified.

"Absolutely. She'd need to be there, to hear it. But I think allowing your staff to—for lack of a better phrase—air their grievances *to each other* helps cultivate more understanding between individuals. More so than a supervisor telling them this is what I heard and this is how it's going to be."

Bella nodded, and when a smile broke out on her face, aimed Easton's way, weird things happened to Easton's body. Weird, wonderful things. A wave of warmth washed through. Her own smile grew wider. She was pretty sure she blushed—Blushed? God, was she fifteen? It was as if Bella's approval of her answer controlled her mood as well as the physical reactions of her body. Damn, that was some *power*.

The class went on like that and felt infinitely longer than it actually was. Easton found herself literally squirming in her seat once. *Good Lord, what is wrong with me?*

Again, she dragged her feet, taking her time gathering her things once class was over. She pretended to be checking her phone until she was sure everybody was gone from the room except her and Bella. When she finally looked up, Bella was standing still and looking at her.

"Hi," Easton croaked, then cleared her throat and tried again. "Hi."

"Hey," Bella said, and she looked more relaxed than Easton could remember seeing her. "Coffee?"

The slow smile that blossomed across Easton's face was something she could feel. Turned out she didn't have to psych herself up to ask Bella out again. Bella had been on the very same page. "Love some."

They made arrangements to meet at Perk again, Easton heading right over and Bella to follow as soon as she locked up.

The coffee shop was a little bit busier than last week but still had plenty of room. Easton ordered herself a latte and realized with disappointment that she didn't know what Bella had ordered last time or she'd have gotten it for her. Had it ready and waiting. She'd be sure to ask this time.

The same love seat was surprisingly free, and Easton took that as a sign, so she snagged it. Before she even realized what she was doing, she put her purse and her light jacket on her left, between her body and the arm of the love seat, forcing her to sit a bit closer to the center of the cushions and thereby closer to where Bella would sit. "Strategic," she muttered when she saw what she'd done, and a corner of her mouth tugged up as the little bell over the door jingled.

How was it that Easton had seen Bella not fifteen minutes ago, but the sight of her walking through Perk's front door made her heart skip a beat and her stomach flip in her body? She hadn't been so physically affected by a woman—by anybody—in her entire life. Part of her loved it. The other part was terrified. When Bella smiled at her, Easton's entire body broke out in goose bumps. Bella held up a finger and went to the counter to get herself some coffee.

"What did you order?" Easton asked when Bella sat down on the love seat, much closer than last time. Their knees brushed.

"Dark roast, little bit of cream." Bella scrunched up her face cutely. "I've never been able to drink the sweet stuff. I'm jealous of those of you who can."

"Don't be jealous. We're all slowly rotting our teeth and widening our hips."

"Oh, I beg to differ." The second the words were out, Bella's eyes widened as if she'd surprised herself.

Easton smiled and let herself enjoy the compliment, the heat it caused. "So," she said after a moment. "Class was interesting."

It was Bella's turn to smile. "Oh, okay. We're doing that, are we?"

Easton furrowed her brow. "Doing what?"

"Making small talk."

"As opposed to?"

"Discussing what's going on here." Bella moved a finger between the two of them.

"Oh." Just when Easton thought she was through blushing, she felt herself blush some more. "Yeah."

"Okay, let's see." Bella picked up her mug, sat back against the back of the soft love seat, and crossed her legs. Easton's gaze was pulled in that direction as if she had no control over where she looked. "Have you lived here all your life?"

Grateful for the change of subject, Easton relaxed the smallest bit. "No. I'm from a town farther east. I'm sure you've never heard of it. Framerton."

"I know exactly where that is."

"You do?" Easton was shocked. Usually, people just stared blankly at her when she mentioned her hometown. "What are the chances of that? I mean, it's not a tiny town, but most people have never heard of it."

"I think I've driven past it. Or through it. Or I've heard of it. Something." Bella blinked rapidly and turned her attention to her coffee, took a sip. "What brought you here?"

"My job. I'd been working for Hart for a couple years, but my commute was brutal. Ninety minutes each way. Try that in the dead of winter." Bella made a worried face, eyes wide. "Exactly. Anyway, when a position opened up here, I decided to give it a shot." She shrugged. "I got lucky."

"I bet it had a lot less to do with luck."

"You excel at flattery."

Bella's smile held a hint of mischief. "Do you like your job?"

"You also excel at questions."

With a chuckle, Bella said, "Sorry. Occupational hazard."

"I thought, in your occupation, you were just supposed to listen, then ask me how I feel about that."

"And how do you feel about that?"

"About my job? Or about all your questions?"

"Yes." Bella sipped from her big, blue mug to hide her grin, her eyes watching Easton over the rim.

Easton felt a little zing hit low in her body. "I feel fine about my job. I feel…many things about your questions."

"Oh?"

"Mm-hmm." Easton's turn to sip. Several beats went by as they held each other's gaze, the eye contact almost physical in its intensity. *It's now or never.* Easton's brain shrieked it at her. *Now. Or never.* Silently, she took a deep, fortifying breath and stepped over the edge. "I like you."

Bella cocked her head slightly, half-grin on her lips. "I like you, too."

"I'd like to take you on a date."

"Aren't we on a date?" There was a twinkle in Bella's gorgeous eyes that told Easton she was teasing, and it was everything. Its message was loud and clear: *I'm with you here.*

"A *real* date."

"This isn't a real date?"

"Pfft. This is coffee. Coffee isn't a real date. Coffee is where you *decide* if you want a real date."

"And you've decided."

"I have."

"I see." Bella sipped, took her time. Easton loved this game, this back and forth. It was…delicious somehow, and she found it to be a surprising turn-on. Her legs tingled. Her stomach fluttered. "And where would you take me on a real date?"

"Dinner. Maybe a movie. Maybe dancing. I have a lot of ideas."

"Intriguing."

"Yeah?"

"Oh, yeah." Bella waited a beat, then nodded slowly. "Okay."

"Okay, you'll go on a date with me?" God, she felt like a nervous teenager. Did she sound like one? *Please don't let me sound like one.*

"Okay, I will go on a date with you."

And just like that, the nerves were gone. Easton bit down on her bottom lip, trying to keep her grin from being too wide. She needed to keep some semblance of cool here. At least a little. Like, an iota. If that was even possible. Which it probably wasn't. "Excellent." She blew out a breath and sat back, relief flooding her. *Nope. No cool here at all.*

Bella's chuckle was low and throaty. "Did you think I'd say no?"

"Honestly? I was worried there might be some rule I was asking you to break or some line I was about to cross, given your job."

"Well, there would be if you were my client. If I was your therapist. But since you're simply taking my class for your job—and I already know you're going to pass, so it's not like there's any weirdness about you trying to bribe your way into that—I don't see a problem."

"Oh, good." While this had all worked out very well and had gone super smoothly, it hadn't been Easton's plan. Coffee, yes. But asking Bella out? Noooo. All she'd wanted was to spend a little more time with Bella. Get to know her a bit. Maybe flirt a titch. But that "now or never" thing started up in her head and she'd lost all control of her carefully planned evening. Typical.

But now she had a date. Which was awesome. She wanted to high-five herself. She didn't care that it would be corny and weird. She wanted to. Her smile grew wider on her face, she could feel it, and then she gave a quiet little laugh.

Bella's brow furrowed over those beautiful eyes of hers, but she sported a little half-grin. "What's funny?"

"I asked a girl out." Easton said it before she could stop herself, then made a face that made Bella laugh heartily.

"First time?"

With a spark of self-deprecation, Easton rolled her eyes. "Like that's not obvious."

Bella just looked at her, held her gaze, and again, something almost tangible passed between them. "Is that why your marriage ended?" she asked softly.

"I just…I wasn't happy." Easton inhaled slowly, took in the comforting aroma of freshly roasting coffee beans, and turned her gaze toward the front door. Darkness had fallen. The crowd at Perk had thinned a bit without them noticing. "Connor's a great guy. He really is.

I love him." She turned back to Bella, who was watching her intently. "I've been with him since high school."

"Wow."

"Yeah. He was my first love. He was always sweet to me. He's gentle and kind and a great father." She let her voice trail off and raised her eyebrows.

"But it wasn't enough."

"No." Easton's answer was quiet. Almost inaudible. She swallowed hard, then forced a chuckle. "As you can see," she said, waving a hand at herself, "I have issues around that."

Bella's face lit back up and she put a warm, comforting hand on Easton's thigh. "It's okay. We've all got our stuff."

"And I'm totally monopolizing the conversation here."

"Not at all." Bella set her now-empty mug down on the table and said, "I want to know all about you. How about we save it for our date?"

"It is getting late, isn't it?" Easton felt a little internal panic attack. Had she just scared Bella away with her depressing talk of high school sweethearts and failed marriages? God. She'd blown it. She was sure of it.

"Stop."

That one word from Bella, spoken softly and coupled with a squeeze of her leg, halted Easton's crazy train of thought. She swallowed again and met Bella's eyes.

"I can see your brain whirring," Bella said, her voice kind. "Just stop. I'm having a great time with you, but we both have to work tomorrow, I have two dogs at home, and I'd rather we get caught up in sharing our stories when we have lots of time. Okay?"

Bella's tender tone, the warmth of her hand, and those deep, wonderful eyes all worked together to take away any and all of Easton's worry. At least for that moment. "Okay." She put her hand over Bella's and gave it a gentle squeeze. She realized it was the first time her skin had touched Bella's in any way, and the moment imprinted on her brain.

Later that night, Easton lay in bed, lights out, alarm set, eyes wide open. She wasn't sure she'd ever been so awake, her heart beating quickly, butterflies of excitement bouncing around in her stomach. They'd settled on Friday night for their date. She had a few ideas of places she'd like to take Bella, but she hadn't decided on which one, so they agreed that she'd text Bella on Friday afternoon with a location and give her time to go home from work and get ready.

And this time, Easton allowed herself to bask. To savor the day.

She had a date. With Bella.

Corny or not, this time, she *did* high-five herself.

CHAPTER NINE

One of the first things Bella, Amy, and Heather had wondered as they'd all pinpointed that they each wanted to do some sort of therapy or counseling for a living was whether it was hard to focus on your client when you had your own stuff going on in your own life, in your own head. And there were definitely tricks and things they'd learned to deal with that, because it was a very real distraction.

Like today.

I have a date tonight with Easton Evans.

Never in a million years did her sixteen- or seventeen-year-old self ever think she'd get to utter those words, let alone have them be fact. Never in a million years.

Holy shit.

Bella rolled her lips in and bit down on them—hard—to keep the ridiculously goofy smile from erupting across her face while her patient was talking about a very serious problem he was having.

A glance at the clock told her she had ten more minutes with this man, then one more client, then she could run home and change. Easton had texted at lunchtime, told her they had reservations at Brie, which Bella knew to be a very classy French-American restaurant. She couldn't believe she'd be walking in there tonight to meet Easton, to share a meal with Easton as her date for the evening.

The girls were going to meet her at her place to help her find the right outfit. It had sounded like a good idea at the time, but after being bombarded all day with salacious texts from Amy—*"cleavage, baby!"*—and worried lines from Heather—*"it's just a date, don't get sucked in too fast, okay?"*—Bella was beginning to wonder if she should've kept her damn mouth shut and told them after the fact, when they couldn't send her already nervous heart into panicked overdrive.

Giving her head a mental shake, she forced her focus onto her patient and finished out his session. When he left, she made a few notes in his file and gave her phone a quick check.

I'm really looking forward to tonight.

A text from Easton. Simple. Sweet. Turned Bella's insides warm and mushy.

Same, she texted back and added the smiling, blushing emoji. *See you soon.*

She pressed the intercom button and told the admin she was ready for her next appointment.

❖

Two hours later, Bella's front door burst open.

"It's date night!" Amy shouted from the foyer. "Let's make you sexy!" Except she said it like "sex-eh!" Bella rolled her eyes.

"Would you stop?" Heather said, and gave Amy a playful slap. "She's nervous enough. Don't make it worse."

"How do you know I'm nervous?" Bella asked.

Heather tipped her head to the side, an expression of pity on her face. "Oh, honey. You're adorable."

"Shut up and help me," Bella said with a mock glare, and they all trooped upstairs to her bedroom.

"What the fuck happened in here?" Amy asked as her gaze roamed the room. "Hurricane? Tornado? Monsoon?"

Fabric was strewn everywhere. The floor. The bed. Some things were still on hangers and dangling from dresser handles and doorknobs. Some were in piles on the floor. Shoes were all over the room like cargo from a sunken ship floating in the ocean.

"Oh, my God, Bella, you have more clothes than RuPaul." Heather's eyes were wide with astonishment. "How did we not know this about you?"

"Now is not the time to analyze me. Now is the time to dress me. Make me presentable because I am at a loss. Help me, damn it!" Bella's voice was a plea.

"All right, all right," Heather said, pointing a finger around the room. "But we are revisiting this."

"Fine."

Heather dropped her purse and coat, parked her hands on her hips, and surveyed the clothes that were…everywhere. "Where are you going?"

"Brie."

Heather gave a little gasp. "Ooh." Turning to Amy, she said quickly, "You need to take me there."

Amy furrowed her brow, as did Bella.

"I mean, all of us. We all need to go there some time. I hear good things." She waved a hand dismissively, reached down, and picked up a pile of fabric from the floor. "Okay, that means a dress."

"I thought so, too," Bella agreed. "The weather's making it a little tough." It had been a very cool day for May.

"Psshh. No worries. We will find something." Heather moved to the closet and let out a tiny gasp. "How is this closet still full given that half of the Macy's women's section is on your floor? My God, you have a problem, don't you?"

"Focus, Heather. Focus." Bella picked a cream-colored dress off the doorknob and held it up.

"No, it's too early in the season for something that light. Plus, this is dinner. We need dark and elegant. Black. Navy. Burgundy. Something deep." She grabbed a hanger and held it behind her without looking at Bella. "Put this on." Bella took it from her hand and Heather dove back into the closet.

Bella glanced at Amy, who was sitting on the bed, scrolling on her phone. "You're a huge help."

"Hey, my expertise comes in *after* the clothes are on. We work as a team, Bells. Just put the dress on."

Bella grinned. "Yes, ma'am."

As the three of them had shared a suite in college, Bella was not at all self-conscious and whipped her clothes off in the middle of the room. She donned the dress, then backed up to Amy, who zipped it without needing to be asked. Bella turned and stood.

Amy pursed her lips and stretched them to one side in indecision. Heather turned from the closet and immediately said, "No. Try this."

Bella took the hanger from her hand and backed up to Amy again for unzipping.

The next dress was burgundy, with long sleeves and a conservative neckline. Bella put it on, then turned to face her friends.

"Ugh, no," Heather said. "You're going on a date, not to a funeral."

"Gee, thanks. I like this dress."

"Good. Wear it to a funeral." Another hanger was handed over.

This went on for six more dresses. Amy made no comments—she either nodded or squinted. Bella soon learned the squint was a no; the nod left things up to Heather.

Heather's opinions were impressively instantaneous. "No," "Meh," or "My God, what possessed you to buy that?" were her most common responses. Until the black one with the plunging neckline, which caused a very quiet and simple, "Oh."

Honestly, it was a dress Bella had forgotten she had, and when she turned to look in the full-length mirror, she was sad about that. It really was beautiful, made of a soft rayon-cotton combination that felt light against her skin. The waistline hugged her, then the skirt became full, a little playful. The sleeves were three-quarter length, which was great for the cool weather. The neckline...made her pause.

"Do you think it's too much?" she asked Heather in the mirror.

"Do I think what's too much?"

"The cleavage?"

"No such thing," Amy chimed in.

"Yes, there is," Heather said, playfully smacking her. "But not with that dress. It's perfect."

Bella looked down at her chest, doubt coloring her tone. "You're sure? Seems like a lot."

"Sweetie, that's because you have the best angle. Unless this girl is six feet tall, she's not going to be able to see what you do." Heather came up behind Bella and spoke to her reflection. "This dress is elegant and classy and just sexy enough for dinner at a really nice restaurant. It's perfect. I promise."

"You look gorgeous, Bells," Amy said with a smile.

Heather's gentle tone and the honesty in Amy's eyes made Bella relax a bit. "Okay. As long as you guys think so."

"We do. Now, let's find you shoes."

Half an hour later, even Bella was surprised by the woman

standing in the mirror. The dress was perfect, as Heather had promised. Her strappy black heels were just the right combination of classy and sexy and the heel was high enough without being too high. Bella didn't wear a lot of makeup in general, but Heather had helped with some nice touches that made her look elegant—*"You really should play up your gorgeous eyes, you know."* Adding some gentle waves to her hair was the finishing touch, and Bella did a little turn.

"You're a miracle worker," she said to Heather.

"I had a lot to work with."

"Seriously, Bells, you sure do clean up nice." There was nothing at all lecherous in Amy's voice, and that made Bella shoot her a look of affection.

"Thanks, you guys," she said to her friends.

Heather handed her a black clutch. "Use this. It goes nicely. You only need a few things for the evening, so your whole purse isn't necessary."

Bella nodded as she took it.

"Your old high school classmate isn't going to know what hit her." Amy stood from where she'd sat on Bella's bed for nearly an hour. "Hey, was she freaked to find out?"

"We haven't gotten that far yet." Bella turned back to the mirror and pretended to fluff her hair.

"Seriously? How has that not come up yet?" Amy laughed, glanced at Heather. "I'd have led with that."

"I just...I'm not ready. I worked so hard to get away from all of that. I'm not ready to bring it back in. You know what I mean?" She could tell from their expressions as she looked at them in the mirror's reflection that they didn't, but they each smiled and nodded dutifully. It was the first time she'd told the girls she hadn't mentioned to Easton that she went to Framerton High. It wasn't like she wanted to lie to them. She just...wasn't ready to put it all out there yet. After all, she had no idea where this was going, if anywhere. It was just one date. They could be one and done after this. It was just dinner. With one of the most gorgeous women she'd ever seen, of course. With a woman she'd crushed on since she was fifteen, yes. But it was just dinner.

Just dinner.

Yeah. That's all.

No big deal.

CHAPTER TEN

Framerton High, 2003

Easton had had the dream. Again. Well, a variation of it, but the gist was the same: she was having sex with a girl. Not just any girl. Kristin Harrington. Again.

It had scared her the first time. By now, it was a semiregular occurrence, but it still freaked her out a little bit because what was she supposed to think? In the dream, she was always with Kristin, either making out with her or in the process of removing her clothes. Kristin's mouth was always sensuous and pliant under hers. Kristin's skin was always like silk, warm and smooth. And without fail, Easton woke up hot, with her heart racing and her body more turned on than she'd ever been with Connor. There really was only one thing it could possibly mean, but Easton refused to grab on to that. No. Absolutely not. No way in hell. That was not who she was. Not even close.

Kristin was two rows over and one row up and she looked so pretty today. Her auburn hair was up in a ponytail, the color like a late summer sunset. She was wearing her cheerleading uniform, as was Easton, for tonight's game against the Wildcats, and she looked super cute. She was surprisingly tan for somebody with red hair, and Easton let her gaze run the length of Kristin's bare legs. She followed the hint of muscle, the feminine shape, the rounding of her knee that led to a tease of thigh...

"Ms. Evans?"

The voice snapped Easton back to reality, as did the chuckling of her classmates. She felt the heat rush to her face, was sure her cheeks had gone very, very red.

"Did you need me to repeat the question?" Mr. Darnell was their lit teacher, a nice guy who was actually one of the more fun teachers. Most of the kids kind of liked him. He raised his eyebrows in question, probably well aware that Easton hadn't heard him.

She cleared her throat. "Um, yes. Please."

As she listened—and made a show of paying very close attention— she tried not to notice the way Connor squinted suspiciously at her.

❖

Whenever Easton pictured a fancy restaurant in her mind, it was just like this. Just like Brie. Round tables covered in white linen tablecloths. Dim mood lighting and centerpieces with tea lights. Waitstaff dressed in black pants, white shirts, and black ties and carrying large trays of food with what seemed to be minimal effort. The hum of conversation was low and pleasant, and the smells coming from the gourmet kitchen were nothing less than mouthwatering.

"If you'll follow me, Ms. Evans." The hostess could've been a model, all shiny blond hair and long legs, and Easton followed her to a corner table for two. It was perfect: a little bit private and very charming. Okay, it was also pretty romantic, but Easton tried not to think about that just yet. She had two worries she was currently battling, and things being presumptuously romantic was one of them.

She hadn't read Bella wrong on Wednesday. She was sure of it. The differences between the Bella at the bar and the Bella at the coffee shop were certainly interesting—and Easton would bring that up at some point—but for now, she just wanted to spend time with her. Get to know her.

The second worry was simply this: was she being pretentious inviting Bella out to such a fancy, upscale place? Honestly, she loved Brie. Thought it was beautiful, and she knew for a fact the food was divine. And she'd asked Bella out, so she was definitely paying.

Did that matter to Bella? Would things like that be a concern? Was it even Easton's business to wonder?

Gah! My poor brain!

Giving her head a good shake, Easton vowed to not overthink

things anymore this evening, to simply try to enjoy herself and the company she was about to have. She allowed the hostess to seat her and push her chair in for her.

"I'm expecting a date," Easton said, as she took the menu handed to her. "She's about five four, long, dark hair, gorgeous hazel eyes."

"I'll keep an eye out for her," the model/hostess said, with a smile and…was that a wink?

Easton grinned as she walked away. "Well, okay," she said softly.

The restaurant was very busy; it was a Friday night, after all. Mostly couples with a few larger parties sprinkled in. A server came by with water and a wine list for her, which she opened and perused with a knowledgeable eye, stopping on a cabernet and a Montepulciano before realizing she should probably wait and see if Bella even liked wine. She had so much to learn about her…so much she *wanted* to learn.

"Excuse me, is this seat taken?"

Easton looked up into those gorgeous hazel eyes, sparkling down at her in the soft lighting of the restaurant. Bella's brows were raised in question and she was wearing the sexiest black dress Easton had ever seen. The top half sleekly hugged her small frame, the neckline showing enough cleavage to tease but not enough to widen eyes.

Easton stood and held a hand out toward the second chair as several smart-ass quips ran through her head. She chose none of them. "Please." Bella pulled the chair out and took a seat. "You look incredible."

The pink that gently tinted Bella's cheeks was worth the entire evening, and Easton sat back down.

"And you," Bella said, her gaze roaming slowly over what she could see of Easton. Then she shook her head, as if in disbelief. "You're stunning."

"Thank you," Easton said softly. Okay, yeah. This was going well so far. With a clear of her throat, Easton bolstered herself to push past the nervousness and take the reins. "So. Do you like wine? I almost ordered but realized I didn't know if you drank it."

Bella's eyes went wide. "Wait. You mean, there are people who don't?"

"Only sad, sad ones."

"I love wine." That smile again.

"Me too. Do you have a preference?"

Bella tilted her head to one side as she studied Easton, and Easton was sure she could feel it. "I get the impression you know your wine. Surprise me."

As if privy to the conversation, the waiter showed up—a tall, lanky redhead who introduced himself as Tyler—and rattled off the specials for the evening. When he asked if they cared for something from the bar, Easton pointed to the wine she'd chosen.

"Very nice, ma'am," Tyler said.

"Also," Easton said before he could go. "Can we start with the brie appetizer for two?"

"Absolutely." And he went off to retrieve it.

"Okay with you?" Easton asked, shifting her attention to her date. "I thought we might as well commemorate eating at Brie by eating some brie." She did her best to give a playful, lopsided grin.

"The only thing I like more than wine is cheese." The corners of Bella's eyes crinkled when she smiled. Easton added that to the ever-growing list of things she found attractive about Bella.

"So," Easton said, propping her elbow on the table and her chin in her hand.

"So," Bella echoed, then made a show of looking around. "This place is beautiful."

"Have you ever been here?"

"Every time I hear about it or read about it, I tell myself I need to come, but I haven't yet." Bella was completely in her element, her elegance matching that of the atmosphere, the setting around her. "You?"

"Same. I keep meaning to come but just haven't gotten around to it."

"Well, then, I'm glad we're making our inaugural trip together."

Tyler returned with their wine. He went through the ritual of showing Easton the wine bottle, uncorking it, allowing her to taste. At her nod of approval, he poured two glasses and said he'd be back soon to take their dinner order.

Bella held her glass up. "To finally getting a chance to visit this restaurant. Together."

"I'll drink to that."

"Oh, that's lovely," Bella said, swirling the wine. She tucked her nose into the glass and inhaled, then took another sip as Tyler wordlessly delivered their appetizer and left it in the center of the table.

"It's an Amarone. Italian. One of my favorites." Easton was not only thrilled Bella loved the wine, but she was entranced by watching her drink it. The delicate way her hands grasped the stem of the glass. The intensity in her focus, like she was really and truly concentrating on the flavors coating her tongue. When her gaze met Easton's, her eyes darted away, seemingly embarrassed.

"What?" she asked, and her self-consciousness was clear.

"I'm just enjoying you enjoying the wine." Easton said it in a relaxed tone, her chin propped in her hand.

"Oh." Bella's smile appeared slowly, and it seemed to take her a moment to gather herself again.

They sampled the brie together, spreading the warm, creamy cheese onto slices of fresh baguette. Each of them made humming sounds of delight as they chewed.

"Oh, my God, that's delicious," Bella said with wide eyes. "Is it because we're in a French restaurant? I mean, I've had brie a hundred times, but it's never been this good."

"Maybe it's the company," Easton said before she could catch herself. She meant it, though, and Bella's answering smile and blush were totally worth it.

"Maybe it is."

Not long after that, Tyler reappeared and took their dinner orders, then left them to each other once again.

"Tell me about your day," Bella said, and it seemed she was back to her usual confident self.

"Oh, no," Easton said, waving a finger. "No work talk. I want to talk about other things."

"Like?"

"Tell me about your family. Siblings? You get along with your parents?"

Bella took another sip of her wine. "Okay. Let's see." She rested her forearms on the table and spun her wineglass in a slow circle, and Easton's gaze seemed riveted there. On the bare skin of her arms. On her pretty hands, her delicate fingers. "I'm an only child, so no siblings. My parents are still together and we're close. I talk to my mother every day or two and I don't see them as often as I should, but I'm working on that."

"Do they still work or have they retired?"

"My father should retire—he has back problems and his job is fairly labor intensive—but he refuses. I think he's worried he'll be bored if he doesn't have to work, you know? And my mom has waitressed at the same diner for a million years."

"Hard workers," Easton observed. She enjoyed the way Bella's eyes sparkled, how her face changed, was a bit more animated as she spoke about her parents. A tickle of envy scratched at her.

"Very. What about you?" It was Bella's turn to park her chin in her hand and focus those eyes on Easton. What was it about her eyes? The color? The intensity? Easton couldn't name it, but she had the strangest feeling she'd be unable to escape from them if there ever came a time she wanted to. Which, right now? She absolutely did not.

"I come from a family of doctors."

"Oh?" Bella picked up her wine, took a sip.

"All of them. I'm not kidding. Both my parents are surgeons. Both my grandfathers are doctors. My older brother. My younger sister."

"Wow. Lotta doctors in your family." Bella chuckled. "Not you, though."

"No." It was a sore spot. Always had been.

"How come?"

Tyler showed up with their food then, and Easton silently thanked him for giving her extra time to think. It was a subject she didn't discuss often, mostly because of the awful way it made her feel about herself. But Easton was determined not to close it off tonight. Not from Bella. There was something about her...Easton wanted to be as forthcoming as she could without examining the reason why. Which she was pretty sure would scare the crap out of her.

Once their plates were in front of them—filet mignon for Easton and fettuccine Alfredo for Bella—they took a few moments to sample dinner, to smile at one another, to chew and comment on the food. It was obvious when Bella was back in listening mode, chewing thoughtfully as her eyes settled on Easton again.

"I thought I would be a doctor," Easton began. "It was always the plan. I went to college, pre-med and everything seemed as it should be."

"Until?"

"Until I realized I hated it." Easton shot a half-grin across the table, hoping to signal to Bella that it was fine, funny even.

Bella caught it and let a small chuckle go. "Wow. That must have been a wake-up call for you."

"You have no idea. Needless to say, my parents were not thrilled. None of my family was. Disappointment all around. Except for my grandpa."

"Really?" Bella's interest was obvious.

"Yeah, my dad's dad. He and I are really close. He's kind of my life coach." Easton laughed because the statement was frighteningly accurate.

"Your grandpa is? That's so cool."

"He's really smart and really open-minded. Way ahead of his time."

"My grandparents are all gone, so I'm envious. You talk to him about a lot?"

Easton scooped mashed potatoes into her mouth, chewed, then pointed a fork at Bella. "Oh, my God, I talk to my grandpa about everything. He even knew all the details of why I left my marriage."

Bella's eyebrows rose slightly, as if she was surprised, but was trying not to show it.

Easton made a face that was half-grin, half-grimace. "Well. I guess I've opened that door now, huh?"

"I'd say so." Bella kept her tone light and her face open. "You certainly don't have to talk about that if you don't want to, Easton. I understand how personal that is and we don't know each other well..."

Was it Easton's expression that made Bella's voice trail off? Because she wanted nothing more than to spill. To tell Bella every single thing, every little secret she had. "I trust you, Bella." Easton said it very quietly, then had to swallow down the weird lump in her throat. "I don't know why or how, but I do. I feel like I can tell you anything."

"Well, I'm glad. And you can."

"No wonder you're a therapist. You have this quality about you..." Easton studied Bella, held her gaze. Bella didn't waver, and they stayed that way for what felt like a long time, and it was so many things. Comfortable. Exciting. Exhilarating. Delicious. Easton hadn't experienced this in so long. Not since… She cleared her throat quietly and said, her voice low, "I met a girl."

Bella twirled pasta onto her fork, took a bite, and returned her gaze to Easton with a nod.

Another lump. Another swallow. "It was four years ago. At a neighborhood block party. Her name was—is—Olivia and she and her husband and kids lived three houses down the street from us. Our street has a party every summer where we close down the cul-de-sac and everybody brings chairs and grills and food and we cook and the kids play and it's just a lot of fun. I'd never really paid attention to her before, but for some reason, she caught my eye that year." Easton could still remember the very first time she'd seen Olivia. It was the middle of August and it was humid. Olivia was in denim cutoff shorts and a sleeveless white button-down shirt, her dark hair in a ponytail, locks of it framing her face. Flip-flops were on her feet and her toenails were polished a bright purple. Easton could still see them in her mind, that grape color, so eye-catching and fun. She'd been taken in. Instantly. "I couldn't keep my focus off her and the funny thing was, as many times as she caught me looking, I caught her doing the same thing."

"Ah, so it was mutual," Bella said.

"Absolutely. Right away. It's so weird how that happens. We'd never really been on each other's radar before then, but suddenly, she was all I could see."

"Was she the first girl you'd ever found yourself attracted to?" There was something underlying in the question, but Easton wasn't sure what.

"Now that I look back? No. But Olivia was the first one—the only one—I acted on. We had an affair for nearly two years." There. She'd said it. She let a beat go by, then looked up at Bella. "I've only told two people that." A nervous laugh bubbled up out of her, and Easton wondered if it sounded as oddly insane to Bella as it did to her ears. Bella's expression only softened, though, so maybe she was okay. "My friend Shondra knows. And my grandpa. That's it. I haven't even told my ex-husband."

"Really?" Bella was obviously surprised. "Isn't that why you ended your marriage? I mean, I just assumed."

"No, it is. You're right. I didn't specifically tell him about Olivia.

She still lives there. She's still married. They'll see each other on occasion."

"You protected her."

"Yes." Easton took a bite of her filet, chewed slowly as she allowed herself to remember Olivia. She glanced at Bella, gave a self-deprecating smile. "I try not to think about her anymore, but once in a while…"

"Yeah, that's a tough one. The second we tell ourselves not to think about something—or someone—that's all we can think about." Bella studied her for a moment and Easton could almost hear her mind working. "You left your marriage, hoping she'd do the same. But she didn't."

Easton met Bella's gaze, surprised she'd figured it out so easily. She stayed quiet as the familiar pain and emotion rolled through her before giving one nod. "Exactly." The day Olivia told her she'd misunderstood, that she'd never intended to leave her husband to be with Easton was one of the worst days of her life. Easton picked up her wine, sipped, swallowed, sipped again. "We'd sort of touched on the idea, but I ran with it. I shouldn't have. But I couldn't help myself. I could see it. I could see us with a house and our kids and a life together. I was so in love with her." She inhaled slowly, let it out, raised her eyebrows and widened her eyes as she told Bella, "She thought I was *fun*."

"Ouch."

"Yeah."

Tyler stopped by to check on them and refill their wineglasses. Once he'd moved along, Bella asked, "So, what did you tell your ex about why you were leaving?"

It was strange to Easton that she didn't find Bella's questions even the slightest bit intrusive. She felt inexplicably safe with her. So much so that part of her feared she'd spill every last secret she had right there on the table in the midst of their first date. She'd already told her the biggest one. "Connor knew that I wasn't happy. That I hadn't been for a long time. I told him I've liked girls since high school and was just too afraid to do anything about it, that it was time for me to—at the risk of sounding like a cliché—explore that part of me."

Bella smiled, and it seemed genuine to Easton. It felt genuine. She felt utterly unjudged by Bella, and that was a surprise. Even Shondra had given her hell when she'd told the entire story. "Following your true self, being who you are? It's not always easy. I think what you did was brave."

"You do?"

"God, yes." Bella took her white linen napkin from her lap and dabbed her lips with it. She picked up her glass and propped her elbow on the table. "You'd be surprised by the number of clients I've seen over the years who know they're not being true to themselves. Who *know* there's another part of them that they've trapped inside. Yet they stay stuck. They stay in the lives that stifle them because the idea of a drastic change—and it is drastic, don't think I don't understand that—is just too much for them. They'd rather stay where they are, where it's safe and familiar."

"And suffocating," Easton added. She was quiet for a moment, watched Bella as she sipped her wine. She wet her lips and looked down at her plate before she raised her head and said, "You're the first person who's ever told me I was brave."

"You are. I truly believe that, and you should, too."

"Thank you, Bella." Easton had trouble pinpointing the emotions she felt right then. Pride? Relief? Comfort? Attraction? A combination of all of that and more? "Thank you for that."

Bella smiled, and her cheeks tinted just the tiniest bit of pink. "You're very welcome."

A beat went by before Easton gave herself a mental shake and asked, "What about you? When did you realize you liked girls?" She set down her fork, finished with her meal. Wineglass in hand, she sat back in her seat, crossed her legs, and focused on her date. Her gorgeous, unbelievably sexy date. The date she really, *really* wanted to kiss, she realized in that exact moment. Which made Easton's heart rate double and her mouth go dry. She sipped.

Bella followed suit, sitting slightly back in her chair, wineglass in her hand. "Like you, I knew in high school, but it scared the hell out of me and I denied it for a long time."

"Did you crush on any girls in school?" At Bella's slightly surprised look, Easton added, "I sure did."

Bella cleared her throat. "I wasn't really sure what it was at that point."

"So, college then."

Bella tipped her head from one side to the other. "A little bit, yeah. I was kind of a late bloomer."

"Around sex?"

"Around life."

Easton grinned. *God, this woman.* "So…late in college?"

"Yes. It took me a long time to figure out who I am. More accurately, *to be comfortable* with who I am. Long time. So, I dated both boys and girls in college, because as I said: denial. The first girl I slept with is still one of my best friends today. We didn't really have a relationship. Like, we didn't date. We slept together because we were trying to figure ourselves out. I didn't really find somebody I cared deeply about until I was twenty-five."

"A woman."

"Yes."

"How long were you together?" Easton watched the very subtle emotions as they played across Bella's face. The memories. Happiness. Sadness. Wistfulness.

"Six years. She works for a national advertising firm. She's very successful. They offered her the promotion she'd been working toward for years, but with the caveat that she had to move to Atlanta."

"She didn't ask you to go with her?" Easton wanted to reach across the table and smooth out the little divot that had appeared when Bella furrowed her brow.

"Oh, no. She did. But my practice was finally up and running. I had a solid schedule of clients. The wellness center was giving me more responsibility. I didn't want to move farther from my parents than I already was. And frankly, she and I had started to drift quite a bit."

Easton nodded. "Yeah, that's a huge move to make if you're not feeling it."

"I wasn't."

"So, you split up."

With a nod, Bella said, "We did. And you know what? While it was hard and sad, it also didn't crush either of us. Which was a pretty good sign we'd made the right decision. She's doing really well out there. We're still friends. We talk on Facebook here and there. It's good."

Easton let go of a tiny snort. "Olivia and I do *not* talk on Facebook. Or anywhere."

Bella's grimace was laced with sympathy. "Nothing?"

Easton shook her head. "It's better that we don't." She emptied her glass. "At least, that's what she decided." Trying to lighten the mood, she added, "But I'm not bitter."

Bella laughed, and it was as if the sound reached right into Easton and hugged her heart, it was so beautiful. "You can be bitter. Nothing wrong with that. Have you dated since?"

"Not really. I mean, I've got Emma. She takes up a lot of time. And nobody's really caught my interest..." Easton let her voice trail off as red flags flew up all over the place in her head, warning her not to say too much. She ignored them. "Not until you."

What the hell is happening?

How in the world had she ended up sitting in a fancy-schmancy restaurant across from this woman? This woman who was stunningly gorgeous. This woman who was treating her to the best night she'd had in months. In a lot of months. In over a year's worth of months. This woman she'd had such a crush on in high school...the same woman who hadn't even known she'd existed then. How? How was this possible? What was the universe trying to do to her? Was this a test? If so, she was failing miserably because she should've told Easton who she was, and now she couldn't. She'd let the opportunity pass her by and now the window had closed. It would just be weird at this point. No, she was having way too good a time and refused to ruin it. She'd tell her next time. For sure.

Next time.

Would there be a next time? God, she sure hoped so.

Easton could not have been more beautiful. Her dress was also black, but the style was completely different than Bella's, slim-fitting and with an open back that begged for Bella to put her palm there. She hadn't been able to see her legs, as she'd been behind the table when Bella had arrived, but she was looking forward to the view. Easton's blond hair was curlier than usual, bouncy, shiny. Bella wanted to play with it, sift the locks through her fingers, bury her nose in it and inhale deeply.

"Do I have something on my face? Food in my teeth?" Easton's voice yanked Bella back to the present reality.

"Pardon?"

"You're staring at me."

"Yeah." Bella blinked several times and picked up her glass, needing something to occupy her focus. Somehow, while gazing into the deep crimson of the wine, she found a spark of courage. "I'd say I'm sorry, but…I'm not." *Oh, my God, who am I?*

Easton's answering smile was a number of things: a little bit bashful, a little bit glowing, a lot happy, and ridiculously beautiful. After a moment, she raised those beautiful blue eyes and posed a question. "Can I be frank?"

No, but you can be Easton. That's what Amy would've said, and Bella had to force herself not to chuckle at her own thoughts. "Absolutely."

Easton folded her hands in front of her and leaned forward slightly. There was something almost intimate about having such intense focus on her, and Bella felt a flutter low in her body—a feeling she hadn't experienced in a very long time.

"I have never really actually dated," Easton began, her voice quiet, forcing Bella to lean toward her. "I married Connor right out of college. And it's not like Olivia and I had a traditional dating life." She looked at Bella as if wondering if she understood. Bella nodded. "So, this is all very new to me."

She paused, wet her lips, and Bella felt her own thighs clench involuntarily. "That being said, I am…alarmingly attracted to you." She gave what Bella could only classify as an uncertain smile and half shrug. "And I want to be careful to stay at a good pace. Not to rush. I just…" She inhaled, let it out, seeming mildly frustrated. "Am I making any sense at all?"

Charmingly self-deprecating. That was the best way to describe Easton in that moment, and the words filled Bella with a warmth she couldn't—didn't want to—try to explain. "You are."

"You're sure? 'Cause all I'm trying to say is that I'm having a really, *really* good time with you and I'd like to do it again. Soon."

How in the world could Bella say no to that face? To those eyes? Even if she wanted to. Which she most certainly did *not*.

Tyler the waiter arrived before Bella could respond, asking if they wanted dessert.

"I would love some, but I honestly cannot eat another bite," Easton said, and seemed genuinely sad to admit it. Which was awesome because Bella felt the same way.

"Me neither, and I'm not happy about it."

"Next time, we get dessert," Easton promised as Tyler left the little black portfolio containing the check and Easton grabbed it before Bella even realized what it was.

"Next time, I get the check."

Easton tucked her credit card into the pocket. "So, there will be a next time?" And that answered Bella's internal question.

"There will." Bella had no qualms about that one. She wanted to see Easton again. Definitely.

Tyler scooped the check away as Easton said, "I was thinking."

"Uh-oh."

"Ha ha. I don't have to pick Emma up at the park tomorrow like I usually do. Will you be going there with your dog again?"

Bella was relieved by the idea that she wouldn't have to meet up with Easton and her ex again. "We usually go earlier than last week. I had an emergency appointment that morning."

"I'm not scheduled to pick up Emma until four tomorrow. She has a birthday party for a classmate. Connor will bring her by after that. Do you want to, maybe, walk your dogs and then get some brunch or something?" Bella only took a second, but Easton jumped right back in, her sentences running into each other until they were just one long one. "Unless it's too soon, I'd totally understand if it's too soon, I could be moving too fast here, like I said. Am I moving too fast? Because just tell me to slow down and I will. I don't want to make you uncomfortable and I—"

"Stop." Bella said it softly and with a smile as she closed a hand over Easton's forearm.

"Okay." Easton swallowed audibly.

"Now. Take a breath."

Easton did. "Okay."

"You're so incredibly cute right now." Nothing was truer in that moment. Nervous Easton Evans was something Bella had never seen, never expected to see, didn't even think existed. And it warmed her heart, even as Easton scoffed and lowered her eyes toward the table. Bella squeezed gently, and when Easton looked back up, she said, "I would love to meet you in the park tomorrow."

If they weren't the perfect words, they were damn close, judging from the gleeful expression on Easton's face. Tyler brought back the check, Easton signed, and then she and Bella stood wordlessly, gathered their things, and headed for the door.

Bella hadn't had the chance to absorb much about the restaurant upon her arrival because she'd caught sight of Easton and hadn't been able to look away. The situation was much the same on the way out, Easton walking in front of her. Those legs and that tight-fitting black dress snagged Bella's gaze and didn't let go until they'd reached the door and Easton held it open.

The night had cooled, but not unbearably so, and they sauntered together toward the parking lot. They reached Bella's SUV first.

"This is me," she said, indicating the vehicle.

"I'm down there," Easton said, pointing away.

They stood. Lingered. Shifted weight from foot to foot.

"I know I said it already, but I had a great time tonight, Bella." Easton's eyes were less visible in the yellowish glow from the parking lot lights, but Bella could see the sparkle in them.

"Me, too. Thank you for dinner and for a lovely evening." Bella grimaced. "A lovely evening? God, did that sound like I'm seventy-five years old?"

Easton's laugh tinkled out of her. "Not at all. I had a lovely evening, too."

"Oh, good." Bella swallowed, and in her mind, she was trying to come up with the best way to make a move here.

She didn't have to worry.

Easton's mouth pressed to hers before she had time to prepare, and that was probably a good thing. The kiss was tentative. Gentle. Warm. Bella raised her hand, laid her palm against Easton's face, and deepened the kiss just a bit, Easton's words about not rushing anything popping into her head. She didn't want to get carried away—which she knew by the way her instantly heated blood seemed to rush faster through her system and her heart rate kicked up a notch or twelve that she absolutely could. That getting carried away with—by—Easton Evans was suddenly a frighteningly real possibility.

Forcing herself to focus, Bella slowly ended the kiss but stayed close enough that they were breathing the same air. A million things went through her head to say, but instead, she simply stroked her fingers down Easton's cheek and whispered, "Good night."

She turned and got in her car. When she glanced out the window, Easton was walking slowly backward, a sexy smile on her face. She finally turned and disappeared into the shadows.

Bella sucked in a huge breath, then let it out little by little and tried her best to concentrate on driving home rather than the incredible evening she'd just had. The indescribably delicious kiss she'd just experienced. *My God...*

It was a wonder she made it home in one piece.

CHAPTER ELEVEN

Easton pulled her car into an empty spot and glanced at the clock on the dash. She was early. Like, way early, which was her default when she was nervous. Job interviews. Meetings with Emma's teachers. Doctors' appointments. While it was lovely to be known as a person who was never late to anything, the drawback, of course, was that she then had tons of time to sit and get even more nervous as she waited. Tons of time to think, in intricate detail, how she could possibly screw up the very thing she was early for.

Like now.

It was a surprisingly warm morning for May, which tended to start off cool. Easton had put on a pair of tight black workout pants, a white T-shirt, and a lightweight pink jacket, which she suspected would end up tied around her waist at some point. The park was busy with a different crowd than she usually saw when there with Emma on some afternoons. Then it was moms and babysitters and lots of kids in a range of ages. This early, it was dog walkers and joggers and bikers. Fitness folks, who served as reminders to Easton that she hadn't been to the gym in over a month.

Reaching for her phone to punch in a note to try to find time next week, it dinged before she grabbed it. A text from Shondra.

You're already there, aren't you?

Easton grinned. Her BFF knew her so well. *Guilty.*

You're almost half an hour early!

Easton nodded as she typed. *I know. It's a sickness.*

Well, get out and walk around or something. Otherwise, you'll get so nerved up you'll explode. And that's a nice car. Nobody wants to have to clean up your exploded organs.

This time, Easton chuckled out loud. *Eww.*

Exactly.

Getting out now.

Good. Text me later. And breathe!

Easton grimaced. *Trying!*

It had been a bit of a rough night for Easton. Sleep had been elusive, which was unusual on nights when she didn't have Emma. Those were usually her best nights' sleep because she didn't have to listen for or worry about her child waking in the night. Last night, though, her body was on fire. That was the only way to describe it. Bella had set her aflame. Easton tried to remember the last time she'd been kissed like that. Tenderly but sensually. Seemingly with such knowledge of exactly what would turn her on. And she realized the answer was never. Easton had *never* been kissed like that. Even with Olivia, despite a newfound, unfamiliar passion, it had never been like that. When she and Olivia had kissed, it was more…desperate. Hurried. With Bella, it was slow, easy, erotic, like they had all the time in the world. It was intoxicating. Easton had literally felt the tiniest bit drunk as she strolled to her car afterward.

Her mind was a whirlwind of thoughts and images, most of them sexual in nature, but she made it home without issue. The same thought kept rolling through her mind: if her first kiss with Bella—which had been sensually gentle—had completely liquified her insides, what would happen if they went further the next time? What would it be like if they actually had sex? That simple kiss had woken up Easton's entire body. What on earth would *more* do to her?

Looking for things to occupy her mind, she'd done some dishes, cleaned up some toys Emma had left around the living room, and then took a bubble bath before bed, hoping to relax and rid herself of all the nervous energy. Instead, it somehow turned her on more and she ended up taking care of herself right there in the water, biting her bottom lip hard as her orgasm tore through her submerged body with unexpected intensity.

It was a good thing, because she flopped into bed with rubbery limbs and dropped immediately off to sleep…

...where she had a sex dream about Olivia. Olivia, who was still as beautiful as ever. Olivia, who professed her love to Easton in gentle whispers. Olivia, who, as she was moving rhythmically above Easton, sliding her fingers in and out, suddenly morphed into Bella. The shape of her face shifted, her eyes darkened from green to hazel, her expression melted from intense concentration to an easy, sexy smile. Easton didn't have time to be surprised by the change because Bella then picked up speed, brought her mouth down on Easton's, and Easton came barely three seconds later. Orgasmed in her sleep, which had only happened to her a few other times in her life, and which left her body shaking as she woke up to the dark of her room and the emptiness of her bed.

She lay awake for a long time after that.

Now she pushed herself out of her car because Shondra was right. Her nervous energy had returned and was firing on all cylinders, and she felt a bit jumpy. Some fresh air and a brisk walk should help calm her down before she met up with Bella.

The park was massive, one of the largest in the city, with a huge field broken into several areas for playing with dogs, Frisbees, balls of any kind. Space for picnics. A paved trail for jogging or biking that ran all the way around the field. A sign posted at the edge of the parking lot said the loop was 2.7 miles total. Through texts, she and Bella had agreed to meet on the west side of the park, away from the playgrounds and the kids, near an enormous open space so Ethel could run. Easton decided she had enough time to walk the path before their scheduled meet if she kept a brisk enough pace, so she headed on her way. Burning off nervous energy was the name of the game here.

Walking had always been something Easton enjoyed, especially through a park or along some kind of water. Being in nature was best for her head. She could run on the treadmill at the gym or swim in the pool or take a spin class. But nothing allowed her the same type of thinking time, of head-clearing self-discovery, as walking outside. There was something about being among the trees, the birds, the earth. It centered her, did something to her brain so she began to breathe in slow, even breaths like a normal person again. Her muscles slowly relaxed, let go of their tension. Her shoulders dropped a bit. Her back and her jaw softened in a way she could actually feel. And it happened now. She'd started off at a brisk walk, but then her pace had slowed.

She inhaled deeply, let it out, listened to the birdsong in the trees, took in the sights and sounds of other folks in the park that morning, and her body relaxed. Her mind relaxed.

Easton was about two-thirds of the way around the loop when she looked up to see a big, square-headed dog tearing through the grass, eyes on a tennis ball sailing overhead. She recognized the dog instantly and scanned the field until she saw Bella, who waved. A second dog sat at her feet. Easton waved back, fully expecting her body to dump all the recent calm and go right back into nervous and jerky, but she was pleasantly surprised because the exact opposite happened. The calm stayed. Settled in further. She felt warm and there was definite happiness, but she felt…like she was exactly where she was supposed to be.

Easton couldn't recall the last time she'd felt so content.

It was weird. *Not gonna lie, this is a little freaky.*

She stuffed the thought away as she walked toward Bella, who was strolling in her direction. The second dog lumbered along, obviously in no hurry. Ethel had the tennis ball in her mouth and was running in circles around Bella.

"I think she wants you to throw that," Easton said, pointing at Ethel.

"Really? I don't know where you got that silly idea." Bella's smile was even more beautiful in the sunlight than it had been in the restaurant last night. She wore light-colored jeans with a hole in the knee, a soft-looking gray T-shirt with the word Nashville across the front in faded blue letters, and bright blue Nikes on her feet. Her dark hair was pulled back in a messy ponytail and her face was devoid of pretty much all makeup. Easton thought she was just as attractive now as she'd been last night, all dressed up. Maybe even more so.

"Hi," Bella said as she reached Easton, holding out a hand.

Easton grasped it, pulled her into a quick hug. "Hey there."

"I wasn't sure if you were here yet, so thought I'd just get the girls out and ready to go, and then I saw you walking."

"I was a little early." Easton wrinkled her nose. "It's a sickness I have."

Bella's answering giggle was very cute on a Saturday morning, as she picked up the tennis ball and heaved it for Ethel. "I'd much rather be early than late."

"Right?" Easton squatted so she was eye level with the other dog. "So, I assume this is Lucy?"

"It is. Lucy, Queen of All Things, Our Lady of Perpetual Laziness."

Easton feigned a gasp, then whispered to Lucy as she held a hand to her nose. "Don't worry. I'm not listening to your mean mommy. I don't believe a word she says. You're beautiful."

Lucy responded by giving Easton's hand a lick. Easton took that to mean permission to pet had been granted. The dog's fur was short, her coat velvety, light brown with hints of red. She turned her head slightly, as if showing Easton exactly where to scratch.

When Easton glanced up, Bella's gaze was fixed on her, something...deep and hard to identify in her eyes.

Ethel returned, dropped the ball, and waited impatiently, pink tongue lolling to one side, big brown eyes riveted on Bella, tiny whines emanating from her doggie throat.

"She obviously hates this game," Easton commented.

"It's torture for her. I don't know how she stands it." Bella threw the ball again, and Easton found her eyes glued to Bella's body, the stretching of her limbs, the subtle flexing of muscle in her bare arm, demonstrating both strength and femininity at the same time.

"Did you play any sports in school?" Easton asked. Bella could throw a ball, that was for sure.

Bella shook her head, kept her eyes on Ethel as the dog sprinted for the ball. "No. I play a little rec softball here and there."

"You have a team?"

"My friends play. I'll sub on occasion." Ethel trotted back and dropped the ball at Bella's feet. Lucy sighed heavily and walked her front paws out in front of her until she was lying down in the grass. Easton laughed as Bella looked down at them and said, "Her life is hard."

Easton stood. "Why only a sub?"

"I'm not that good," Bella said with a wistful smile and a shake of her head. "Honestly, I'd rather watch." She turned to Easton, those hazel eyes fixed on her. "What about you?"

"Don't laugh," Easton warned, holding up a finger.

Bella crossed her heart.

"I was a cheerleader."

With a nod, Bella turned and threw the ball. "Of course you were."

There was a slight tinge of…something in Bella's tone, and Easton squinted a bit as she felt the subtle sting. Keeping her voice light, she asked, "What does that mean?"

Bella turned to her, and Easton was sure she saw a darkness cloud her eyes for a split second before it evaporated. Then she smiled, shrugged, and said, "Look at you."

Easton scoffed as Ethel returned with the ball. "I'll have you know, cheerleading takes a lot of athletic prowess." She picked up the ball before Bella could. "Which I happen to have." She threw the ball as hard as she could, and it flew much farther than when Bella threw it. "Seriously, have you never watched *Bring it On*?" She raised her eyebrows in lighthearted question.

Looking suitably chagrined, Bella wrinkled her nose. "You're right. I apologize for buying into the stereotype. Nice throw, by the way."

"Thank you." Easton pushed at her playfully, and while it felt better, it had still been an odd exchange. She wasn't really sure what it was, couldn't put her finger on it, so she chalked it up to the same bad rap everybody else gave to the high school cheerleader, especially if she was blond. There was a slight disappointment that Bella would feel the same way, and she decided to maybe revisit it later.

They took turns throwing the ball for Ethel and watched in amusement as she got slower and slower. Finally, she brought it back, dropped it, and flopped down next to it. Then she stretched her back legs out so her pink dog belly was flat on the cool grass.

"That is known as the flying frog," Bella said as she pointed to her dog.

"I see why." Easton had been petting Lucy on and off the whole time, so she now sat between the two dogs, a hand on each head. Both looked blissful, eyes half closed, tongues hanging out, the warmth of the spring sun shining down on them. When she glanced up at Bella, that hazel gaze was aimed down at her with barely disguised desire— preferable to the other odd expression she'd had—and it made Easton's heart pound. "Hi," she said softly.

"Hey." Bella sat down, too, and they looked at each other for a long moment before Bella spoke again. "I see you've won over my dogs with your charm."

"Wasn't hard. The bacon-scented body wash I use helps, too."

They sat in comfortable silence for several moments. Easton could see the playground in the distance, could hear the squealing children playing on the slide, the swings, the merry-go-round, and it made her think of Emma.

As if reading her mind, Bella asked, "Do you miss Emma on days that your ex has her?"

"Every second," Easton said truthfully. "I always tell myself to enjoy the break. Take some time and do some things for me. She goes with Connor on Wednesdays after school, so when I kiss her goodbye on Wednesday morning, I try to think about all the blissful free time spread out in front of me and all the things I could do with it. And then by lunchtime on Wednesday, I get a little sad because I remember that I won't see her again for three more days. By Saturday, I'm usually a little stir-crazy waiting to get her back."

Bella waved her arm to encompass the two of them, the two dogs, and the park itself. "Is this helping a little?" Her voice was soft, like it was something she hesitated to ask, and her dark brows rose up a bit.

Easton gave her the warmest smile she could, which wasn't hard because it was what she felt. "This is helping *a lot*."

Bella didn't hide her relief well, which was super cute. "Well, good. I'm glad. I love the park."

"Yeah?"

Bella leaned back so she reclined in the grass, her focus aimed at the blue sky. Easton followed suit, but on her stomach, propped on her forearms so she could look down on Bella's gorgeous face as she spoke.

"I find it rejuvenating," Bella explained. "The green of the grass. The trees. Especially a day like this when the sun is out and the sky is blue. I could lie here like this in the grass for hours, just quietly with my thoughts."

They lay in silence then, just enjoying the feel of the grass, the sun, the presence of each other, and Easton was kind of amazed at how easy it was to simply exist quietly with Bella. There was more she wanted to know, and she'd get around to asking eventually, but this? Lying in the grass on a lovely Saturday morning in the park? Dogs pooped out next to them, kids laughing in the distance, joggers passing by, the sun warming their bodies? It was undeniably blissful, and Easton couldn't remember the last time she'd been this at ease with somebody. A long time ago with Connor, sure. But many, many years ago. With Olivia?

Never. She was never relaxed with Olivia because she was always waiting for the other shoe to drop. Olivia kept her feeling like she was on a tightrope and could misstep at any moment, bringing everything to a crushing end. Which had happened anyway. No, she'd never been contented with Olivia, not for a second.

But with Bella? It was easy. Terrifyingly easy. Was it too easy? Was that even a thing?

"Hungry?" Bella asked before Easton's thoughts could carry her away to the Land of Confusion, where Easton owned property and could probably be elected mayor without a problem.

"I am. You?"

Bella nodded. "Starving. Ever been to Hedges?"

"I love that place."

"Me too. How about you head there, and I'll take these girls home and meet you?"

"Sounds like a plan."

Twenty minutes later, menu in hand, Easton was sipping excellent coffee at a black metal outdoor table for two she'd been surprised to snag. Hedges was very busy—not unusual for a sunny Saturday morning—but she hadn't even gone inside. When given the choice between inside and out, she chose out without really even thinking about it. The waitress had left a plate of the restaurant's famous shortbread cookies, and Easton nibbled one. She was scanning her breakfast options when Bella touched her lightly on the shoulder.

"Hey," Easton said. "I feel like I just saw you a few minutes ago."

"That's weird," Bella said, and pretended to be puzzled as she took a seat. "It's almost impossible to get a table outside here. How'd you manage?"

"I have skills."

"Yeah? I didn't know that about you."

"There's a lot you don't know about me." Easton looked at Bella from under heavy lids, hoping the words sounded as flirty as they felt.

"I look forward to finding out all your secrets," Bella replied, her voice equally low and sensual.

"You'll have to buy me breakfast first."

"Deal."

They grinned across the small, round table at each other, then Bella glanced around at the other patrons. Easton took her cue, sat up straighter. "Okay." With her eyes, she indicated the couple to her right and lowered her voice. "First date. They met online, I think." She jerked her head back to gesture behind her. "He snored all night long and she is *over it.*" Bella snort-laughed, which made Easton grin widely as she used her eyes again and indicated to her left where three women talked animatedly. "Old college roommates."

"Wow," Bella said as the waitress stopped by and offered her coffee, which she accepted. "That was impressive."

"Thank you. Thank you very much." Easton bowed her head. "It's a talent I have."

"I can't believe you didn't demonstrate it at the restaurant last night."

"I was preoccupied at the restaurant last night." Again, Easton flirted without thinking about it. Bella seemed to have that effect on her.

"With?" Bella's hazel eyes twinkled with mischief as she propped her elbows on the table, coffee cup held in both hands.

"My stunningly gorgeous date."

"Interesting, since I was the one with the stunningly gorgeous date."

"Huh. So odd."

Their gazes held as Bella sipped her coffee, watching her over the rim of her cup. Easton felt that exciting little flutter low in her abdomen that Bella seemed so good at causing. There was something about having those eyes focused on her that…did things to Easton's insides. Wonderful things. Naughty things.

With excellent timing, the waitress returned and asked if they were ready to order. Bella hadn't even opened her menu, but she gave a nod, then gestured for Easton to go.

"I'll have the Belgian waffle with strawberries, please."

"Whipped cream on that?" the waitress asked, jotting in her pad.

Easton started to decline but glanced at Bella, and something made her say, "Yes, please," instead. Bella's face lit up.

"I'll have the spinach and feta omelet with bacon on the side, please," Bella said.

The waitress thanked them, took their menus, and zipped away. Easton could feel Bella's eyes on her. "What?" she asked finally.

Bella shrugged. "Just thinking about you and whipped cream. That combination." She picked up a cookie from the plate in the middle of the table, dunked it into her coffee, and half of it promptly plunked into the cup. "Okay," she said and pursed her lips.

Easton laughed at the look of indignation on Bella's face. "That's what you get."

"For what?"

"For thinking naughty thoughts."

"I can't have naughty thoughts about you?" Bella's tone was playful, but it was clear to Easton that she was now treading lightly, possibly wondering if she'd crossed a line too early in their pairing. All Easton wanted to do was ease her mind and erase the uncertainty that creased her forehead.

She grinned and kept her voice low. "You can have all the naughty thoughts about me that you want."

"Oh, good."

"Just know that the universe might punish you for it."

"If my cookie falling into my coffee is the universe's punishment, I can live with that."

"Then we're good."

Again, gazes held. Again, a zap of electricity shot between them. *Chemistry!* That was the word Easton had been grappling for. She'd never had this kind of chemistry with anybody, ever. Not even Olivia, and she was pretty sure she and Olivia had been off the charts, chemistry-wise. No, the connection with Bella was different somehow. Steadier, and therefore stronger. Much stronger.

And that's when the thought hit her, loud and clear, putting a lump of concern in her throat that she had to swallow down.

I could be in a lot of trouble with this woman.

One sentence. A simple statement.

"What's wrong?" Bella's question pulled Easton out of her own head.

"I'm sorry?" Easton blinked rapidly, cleared her throat.

"Your eyes went really wide for a second there and it seemed like you were somewhere else. You okay?"

Easton reeled her thoughts back in, forced a smile and a nod. "I'm great."

Their breakfasts arrived then, thank God, and Easton was spared from any more scrutiny for the moment. Bella was observant and was already disturbingly good at reading her. It probably came with the territory of being a therapist, but Easton felt at a slight disadvantage and she wanted to change that. The best way, she figured, was to gather more information. Because she really, *really* wanted to know this woman.

She cut a chunk of her Belgian waffle and looked up at Bella. "What made you want to become a therapist?" She put the bite in her mouth and chewed as she watched the beautiful face across the table from her. "Is that the right title? That you go by? Therapist?"

"I'm technically a licensed mental health counselor. But therapist is fine. Counselor is fine. Shrink? Okay." Bella forked some omelet into her mouth, then looked up and to her left, almost as if searching for the right way to answer. "Well." She chewed the bite, swallowed. "I've always been very aware of how your childhood and teenage years can mold who you end up being, down to tiny details. Not just the way you think, but the way you react to things. One event in your childhood can shape who you are as an adult. And it doesn't even have to be something traumatic."

Easton nodded, thinking about her own upbringing. "I get that. I have footsteps of grandparents and parents and siblings that I've always thought I should be following." She grimaced. "I've struggled with that my entire life, and I'm sure there are thoughts or reactions I have that would trace back to that."

Bella pointed a fork at her. "Exactly. Everybody's got something. I was not at all popular in high school. I was mocked. Bullied a little bit. Add to that I was also struggling with my sexuality, and it adds up to this fact: there's not enough money in the world to send me back there." She chuckled at the statement as she ate some more, but Easton saw something dark run across her features.

"I can't imagine you not being popular." It was the truth. Bella was beautiful. Smart. Funny. Kind.

"I'm a completely different person today than I was at fifteen, sixteen, seventeen years old."

"Aren't we all?"

"Oh, come on." Bella's tone was playful, but that shadow was still hanging around. "You were a cheerleader. You're gorgeous. I bet Connor was on the football team. You were the stereotypical popular girl."

"That's the second time you've made an assumption about me

because I was a cheerleader." Easton, too, kept her tone playful and light, but needed to make her point. Bella looked properly chastised—again—and nodded for Easton to continue. "Like you, I was struggling with some aspects of life, too."

"Such as?"

"Oh, you think you get all my secrets already?"

"You mean I don't?" Bella's eyes went comically wide and she pressed a hand to her chest in mock affront.

"Please. It's only our second date. Plenty of time."

"Fair enough."

Serious conversation ended there. Which didn't mean the rest of breakfast wasn't enjoyable, because it absolutely was. Easton loved not only the way Bella seemed to bring the flirtiness out of her but how she played back. Like they were playing catch. Easton would toss a sexy remark. Bella would catch it, then lob one back of her own. It was fun and delicious and made Easton feel slightly inebriated.

When they finished, Bella paid the bill. Easton put up a half-hearted argument, but Bella waved her off. "Please. I'll need to buy five of these breakfasts to be even with last night's dinner." The quick and flirty grin she shot Easton's way when she looked up took away any perceived undercurrent about finances that Easton might've felt.

Once on the sidewalk, they realized they'd parked in opposite directions.

"Thank you for breakfast," Easton said, standing close to Bella, who smelled like coconuts today.

"You're very welcome. Thanks for suggesting this morning." Bella glanced down at her feet, and for the first time that morning, Easton could see her nerves working on her. Which was a huge relief, Easton had to admit, knowing maybe she wasn't the only one in uncharted waters here. After an audible swallow, Bella asked, "Can I see you again?"

"I'd like that," Easton answered, too quickly, she thought. "I'm not sure what I've got as far as Emma goes this week, so can I check and get back to you?"

"Absolutely."

Then came that moment. The awkward. When you stand there at the end of your date and it's the middle of the day and you're in public, so you can't just make out. But you're more than friends now, so a casual wave and a cheery "Bye!" won't cut it. Throwing caution to the wind, Easton reached out and pulled Bella into a hug. It was warm. The nearly full body contact sent warmth running all through her. The hug lasted.

When they finally parted, slowly, Easton lifted a hand to Bella's face, leaned in, and kissed her softly on the cheek. "I'll talk to you soon."

With that, she turned and headed toward where her car was parked, not daring to look back as a storm of emotions swirled through her head.

Oh, yeah. I'm in a lot of trouble with this one.

CHAPTER TWELVE

Sunday brunch was at Bella's that weekend, and while she'd like to say she got up early to prepare, the truth was that Ethel never let her sleep much past six, weekend or no weekend. Lucy, on the other hand, was still in the bedroom, stretched out on Bella's bed and probably snoring, well after nine.

"Your sister is so lazy," she said down to Ethel, who stood at her feet as she mixed up pancake batter, evidently wishing with all her doggie might that some food might randomly fall on her. Bella pulled bacon out of the fridge and got out her frying pan just as a knock sounded on the door. Ethel barked, looking toward the direction of the living room but apparently hesitant to leave the bacon.

"Good morning! It's time for brunch!" Amy's voice rang through the house. Bella heard Lucy's answering bark from the bedroom, then responding laughter as she walked out toward the door.

Amy and Heather were both there together, which almost never happened. "You guys meet in the driveway?"

Heather, dressed impeccably as always in a pretty dress of spring colors, kissed Bella on the cheek as she walked past, carrying a dish. "We decided it made sense to just drive together."

Bella sent a questioning look at Amy, who merely shrugged. Her dark hair was pulled back in a low ponytail and she wore the fedora again.

"I'm liking the hat look," Bella told her.

"Awesome, as I live for your approval." She lifted both eyebrows once in a teasing gesture and held up a bottle of vodka.

"Perfect. You're on Bloody Mary duty." Bella followed Heather into the kitchen.

"I got this." Amy fell in step behind her.

"Kind of chilly today. Aren't your feetsies cold?" Bella gestured to Heather's newly pedicured feet, toes a summery pink.

"I don't care. It's May and I refuse to wear my winter shoes any longer." She wiggled her toes for emphasis as she poked buttons on Bella's oven. "This needs to go in for half an hour, just to warm through."

Lucy decided to lumber in, and at that moment, there were three women and two large dogs all crammed into Bella's adequate but not huge kitchen. Instead of irritating her, though, it warmed her heart. "I'm so glad you guys are here."

"Us too." Heather looked at Amy, who was standing with a goofy, lovable grin on her face. "Hey. Those Bloody Marys aren't going to make themselves."

Amy flinched. "Right. Right. I'm on it."

As Bella made pancakes and set the bacon to frying, she took glances at her best pals. While Amy made her world-famous—to them—Bloody Marys, Heather set the dining room table. For whatever reason, brunch seemed to end up at Bella's house more than the others', and Bella loved that, though it had taken a while, they had learned where almost everything was and that they were comfortable enough to help themselves.

Within thirty minutes, they were seated at the table, each on her second Bloody Mary, enough food laid out before them to feed another three or four people. Sunday brunch was her favorite, and before she realized it, Bella was picturing Easton sitting there with them, in the seat next to Bella's, their feet touching under the table.

As she tore a piece of bacon in half and gave one to each dog, Bella thought she saw a look pass between Amy and Heather. When they looked her way, she raised her brows in question.

"Yeah, so we're gonna need some details about Friday." Amy put an elbow on the table and propped her chin in her hand as she gnawed on a piece of bacon.

Heather scooped a second helping of the surprisingly good apple crisp she'd made into her dish, forked a bite into her mouth, then turned her attention to Bella as she chewed.

Bella could feel her face immediately heat and she couldn't have stopped the smile the broke out across her face even if she wanted to. "It was…" She shook her head as she reached for her cocktail, took a sip. "Wonderful. Amazing. I had a great time. And then we had brunch yesterday morning."

Four eyes widened.

"Two dates in two days?" Amy said, incredulous. "Bells, that's pretty impressive. How'd that come about?"

"No, no, no." Heather waved her hand at Amy. "No, first she has to tell us about dinner Friday night. Because *somebody* didn't answer my texts." She narrowed her eyes at Bella.

"I know, I know." Bella laughed. "I'm sorry. I just wanted to savor it a bit. I knew I'd see you guys today."

"So? Spill."

And spill Bella did. She told them all about dinner. How incredibly beautiful Easton had looked. How terrific the food was and how it didn't even touch how terrific the company was. How Easton had asked if they could see each other the next morning. How they'd kissed in the parking lot afterward. How it was the best kiss Bella had ever had.

Heather let out a dreamy sigh and sank down toward the table a bit in apparent envy. "That is so romantic."

Bella nodded, sipped some more. "It really was. The most romantic evening I can remember."

"Hey, I took you to dinner a few times," Amy teased.

"Taco Bell doesn't count," Heather jabbed, and Bella snort-laughed. Turning back to Bella, she added, "You looked so hot. I'm not surprised she wanted to see you again."

"Thanks to my crack design team. Thank you guys for helping me."

"No need. I had fun. It was like playing with a life-size Barbie. 'This outfit. No, wait. This one. Hang on, try this one.'"

"You guys talk about going to the same high school?" Amy shook her head as she tore a pancake and slipped a bite to Ethel, sitting patiently at her feet. "Seriously, what are the chances?"

"A little bit. But we mostly talked about family and her daughter and her marriage." Okay, so that wasn't really a lie. Just an omission of some of the truth. She didn't like doing it, but she was embarrassed to tell her friends she'd missed her window and needed to wait for the next one. She didn't want the judgment. Mostly because she knew she probably deserved it.

"What happened with the husband?" Heather asked.

Bella told them the story of Olivia, how Easton had started seeing her, how it had ended.

"Oh, man. That sucks. She must've been devastated." Heather's tone was sympathetic.

"I think she was. I want to talk a little more about that with her."

"Seeing her again?" Amy asked. She didn't seem nearly as fanciful and caught up as Heather.

"Yeah, but we haven't set it up yet. She needed to check on her daughter's schedule. Why are you looking at me like that?"

"Like what?" Amy asked, all wide-eyed innocence.

Bella cocked her head. "Please. I know you and I know when you've got something on your mind. Tell me."

Amy looked to Heather, who gave an almost imperceptible nod.

Bella waved a finger between the two of them. "And what's going on here? With the weird looks to each other?" Amy looked to Heather again, and Bella pointed. "That. Right there. What's that about?"

"We're just a tiny bit worried about you," Heather said, holding her thumb and forefinger close together, and scrunched up her face as if waiting for a rebuke of some sort from Bella.

"It's moving kind of fast," Amy added.

Well, that wasn't really something Bella could argue. She could admit that. So, she gave a conciliatory nod. "It is. You're right. I'm very aware, believe me." And she was. She knew by the fact that she wanted to text Easton. Right now. And see her as quickly as possible. Like, in the next five minutes. She also didn't like the stench of desperation that wafted up from that desire, so she pushed it down and tried to ignore it.

"We just want you to be careful," Heather said, reaching out to grasp Bella's hand. "We love you and we don't want you to get hurt. So just…maybe slow down a little bit?"

Bella squeezed Heather's hand. "Promise."

The concern clouding Amy's face seemed to clear, at least mostly, and brunch went on.

❖

Monday was equal parts busy and not busy for Bella. She had four appointments with clients. She also had four free hours to take care of paperwork, answer emails, catch up on a couple of new articles. Unfortunately, not a lot of paperwork was completed, only a couple emails were answered, and the articles remained unread because Bella's mind was preoccupied. Very preoccupied. Very, very preoccupied by soft blond hair and beautiful blue eyes and an absolutely killer figure.

Bella gave her head a rough shake. What was the matter with her? *We love you and don't want you to get hurt.* Bella heard Heather's voice as clearly as if she was standing in the office with her. *Maybe slow down a little bit?*

This was definitely not that. This constant thinking about Easton, the never-ending replays of their parking lot kiss, the way her fingers actually itched to text her more than the handful of times they already had today. None of that constituted slowing down. None of it. And Bella knew it.

Her 4:30 arrived and she was able to shift her focus for the allotted fifty minutes. For that, she was grateful. The last thing she wanted was to shortchange her client because she couldn't keep her own mind out of the gutter. It seemed to like it there, all hunkered down and snuggling with the dirty thoughts and naked bodies. But she pushed through and centered all her concentration on her client. When she finally left her office and stepped out into the wonderfully pleasant late-May air, Bella felt utterly exhausted, weak in her bones, like she'd been holding up a heavy piece of furniture for the better part of an hour.

She left the office by six, stopped to grab a Quarter Pounder with Cheese from McDonald's, which she'd pay for later but didn't care in the moment, because yum. Once home, she felt better. More relaxed, as if she'd been short of breath all day and could now fill her lungs up all the way. It brought unexpected relief.

Thank God for my dogs.

This thought crossed Bella's mind often, on a regular basis. They were like a salve for an aching soul. Whenever she was sad or confused or angry or had simply had a bad day, Lucy and Ethel had a way of making her feel better. Like she mattered. Like she was special. Loved. She'd finished her dinner and had fed them theirs and was sitting on the living room floor with them while they tried to pretend their forty (Ethel) and fifty-five (Lucy) pound frames were perfectly suitable for being in her lap. They played that game for a good twenty minutes before Lucy decided she'd had enough and adjourned to her big fluffy bed in the corner. Ethel, on the other hand, was completely riled up and Bella decided, since the evening was nice, she'd take her out for a little Tennis Ball.

Instead of going to her usual park, Bella had an urge for a different venue. She took Ethel to the nearby elementary school and onto the grounds, which were completely fenced in. There was so much more space for Ethel, and no people who could give her the side-eye about her loose pit bull mix. Technically, she wasn't supposed to be there, but since it was after school hours and she was always very good about cleaning up after her dog, the security guard on duty always cut her some slack. His name was Ralph and he waved to her now from the double doors nearest her.

Ethel was in her glory as she chased her ball, bounding through the spring green of the grass like a puppy. Bella loved watching her run. Also in its glory was the ice cream stand across the street. The first weeks it was open always seemed so busy, and Bella shot several glances in that direction, the lights becoming brighter as the sun sank slowly toward the horizon, the delighted squeals of children getting ice cream carried through the air. Bella found herself smiling more than once and absently entertained the idea of getting herself her first hot fudge sundae of the season as she threw the tennis ball again and again.

Bella had no idea how much time had passed when she heard a voice.

"Hey." It came from nearby and Ethel detoured on her route back to Bella, bypassing her completely to greet the woman and child who'd come through the chain link gate.

"Hi, Ethel," Emma said, running to greet the dog. Ethel, true to her gentle heart, immediately lay down on the grass and rolled over to show her tummy. Emma giggled, fell down onto the grass with her, and dutifully scratched.

Bella smiled at them, then lifted her gaze to take in Easton as she walked toward her. Worn jeans with a worn-white spot on one thigh, black V-neck T-shirt, gray hoodie, unzipped. Her hair was down and slightly tousled. Blue eyes sparkled with a smile as she stopped in front of Bella and held out a hand.

"I wasn't sure what you liked, so I took a chance."

When Bella was able to tear her eyes away from Easton's glowing face to look down, she saw a hot fudge sundae in Easton's hand, the cherry on top adding a bright pop of color to the falling dusk. She glanced back up, confused. "How——?"

Easton's face broke into a smile and she gestured with her head at the ice cream stand. "We were over there getting ice cream and we saw you. Ethel's pretty distinctive." She winked. "I thought maybe you'd like to have some with us." Something passed across her features then, something quick, but it dimmed her smile just a touch. It took a moment for Bella to realize that maybe Easton was feeling uneasy, uncertain about the ice cream gesture, and she hurried to reassure her.

"Oh, my God," Bella said, taking the sundae from Easton's hand. "I was literally standing here thinking it might be time for my first sundae of the season. Like, literally."

"Yeah?" Easton's face relaxed, and with it came relief for Bella. "What kind would you have ordered?"

Bella held up the sundae in her hand before grasping the spoon. "Hot fudge, baby."

Easton gave her a playful squint. "Seriously?"

"Seriously. Cross my heart." Bella did so with the spoon, then held her hand up, Boy Scout style. "Hot fudge, all the way."

"Good." Easton said it softly and shifted her weight on her feet. Bella heard her swallow as she turned to look at the pile of dog and child on the ground. "She's so good with Emma."

"She loves kids. It's in her nature. She's just a sweet, sweet dog."

"I thought you went to the park to play ball. What made you come here?" Easton spooned some ice cream into her mouth, and Bella took a moment to enjoy how her lips closed over the plastic spoon.

Forcing herself to shift her focus, Bella worked her own spoon through her ice cream, making sure to get some hot fudge as well as some whipped cream in the bite. She looked back up at Easton and said honestly, "I'm not really sure." She took the bite, savoring the creaminess as it melted on her tongue. "We come here sometimes, but the park is definitely our default. I just had the sudden urge to come here instead."

"Well, it got you ice cream, so I'd say you win."

"Ice cream and you. A win-win." Bella felt her face heat up after those words, and she hoped Easton couldn't see it in the waning light of the evening. The way Easton's face seemed to glow a bit minimized any embarrassment Bella felt.

"How was your day?" Easton asked. Bella noticed she maintained a fair bit of distance, physically, and wondered if that was because of Emma's presence.

"Not bad." She recounted the bullet points, never mentioning details of her sessions with clients. The words *I thought about you a lot* were on the tip of her tongue, but she kept hearing her friends' voices in the background. Their warning. Their worry. She somehow managed to swallow those words back down, keep them inside. For now. "How about your day?"

Easton groaned and dropped her head back toward her shoulder blades. "I'm at a point where I really, really need my people to accept that their old boss is gone, I'm what they have now, and just grow the hell up. I understood them being upset for a while, but now they just sound like whiny children." She glanced at Bella out of the corner of her eye, sheepish, and said, "I probably shouldn't say things like that to you, since you work for my boss."

Bella reached out and squeezed Easton's upper arm. She couldn't help herself. It was as if she suddenly needed to touch her in some way. In any way at all. "We're friends, too. You're allowed to talk to me any way you want. It stays between us."

"You kind of have to be good at that, don't you?" Easton's relief was obvious.

"At what?"

"At keeping quiet. At keeping secrets."

Bella nodded, ate some more ice cream. "Part of the job, yes." There was a bench nearby, and Bella gestured to it. "Ethel doesn't seem to be interested in Tennis Ball anymore. Your child has enamored her. Want to sit?"

Easton chuckled. "I think it's Ethel that's done the enamoring."

They sat side by side and watched in silence for a moment as Emma and Ethel rolled around in the grass. Emma pretended to ignore Ethel. In response, Ethel would gently paw at her until Emma giggled and lay down, her head on Ethel's pink stomach. They were adorable together.

"Any progress on the dog front?" Bella asked. "Has your ex gotten her one yet?"

Easton shook her head, kept her eyes on the dog and little girl show in front of them. "No, and I think it's sort of faded away. Though after this..." She pointed a finger at her daughter. "Might come screeching back."

Bella held up her hands like a robbery victim, careful not to spill her sundae. "Hey, you came over here of your own free will. I take no responsibility for any desire for a dog that may result from it."

Easton leaned against her, bumped her with a shoulder. "Funny."

Quiet descended again, and the fact that they could simply sit with it, that it didn't feel awkward or at all uncomfortable amazed Bella once again. She couldn't think of anybody else she could exist with in silence and be totally okay. Not stir-crazy. Not nervous. No need to fill the silence with words. It was a nice feeling. She wondered if Easton felt it, too.

After a few moments, Easton sighed and glanced at the watch on her slim wrist. "It's getting late." Dusk was rapidly morphing into darkness and the air had chilled noticeably. Dew dampened the grass. "Come on, Emma. Time to go."

Emma had her arm around Ethel, who sat next to her like they were best friends in kindergarten, and she let out a long "Awwwww" at hearing Easton's request.

"You'll get to play with Ethel again." Easton's head snapped in Bella's direction and she grimaced, teeth showing. "Right?" she whispered.

Bella couldn't help but let a little laugh go. "Any time."

"Oh, good." Easton fake-wiped her brow with a *whew*.

Emma and Ethel approached, Ethel looking for all intents and purposes like she was Emma's dog and not Bella's. "Traitor," Bella muttered.

Easton used her napkin to wipe some residual ice cream off Emma's face, her daughter doing that thing kids do where they turn their head one way and then the other to avoid Mom and her awful need for cleanliness. Finished, Easton looked at Bella, her blue eyes soft, and pointed toward the ice cream place. "We're parked over there."

Bella pointed in the opposite direction. "We're that way."

"I figured." She paused, then said, "I didn't expect to see you tonight. It was a nice surprise."

"It was a *very* nice surprise." Bella clipped Ethel's leash on, then held up her now-empty ice cream bowl. "Thanks for the sundae."

"My pleasure. I'm glad it was the right one."

"It was perfect."

They stood there, and this time it *was* a little awkward. At least Bella thought so. They were like two schoolkids after their first date, hovering on the front porch, trying to decide what they were supposed to do next.

Easton glanced down at Emma, and Bella was sure she heard a soft sigh. "So, I'll see you Wednesday night, right?"

Bella nodded. "You will."

"Okay then. Come on, Emma-bear." She held a hand out to her daughter and they headed for the gate they'd come through, Emma waving over her shoulder at Bella and her dog.

Bella watched for a moment, but then realized how creepy it might seem if she stared the entire time Easton walked away. She clicked her tongue and turned away, tugging Ethel's leash as she went. The dog trotted beside her, looking extra happy, a spring in her canine step. "Looks like we both got to see our girlfriends, huh?" Then she rolled her eyes and groaned loudly. "Oh, perfect, call her your girlfriend, Isabella. That's slowing things down. Totally. Way to go with that. Good job."

Ethel looked up at her as they walked, clearly puzzled.

Bella scoffed. "Yeah, me too, Ethel. Me too."

CHAPTER THIRTEEN

Framerton High, 2003

It was the third week back in school, and Izzy still felt lost and alone. She had friends. She wasn't a complete loser with nobody. But the fact was, she never felt fully comfortable with anybody. Not her friends. Not even her parents. Nobody. She was dealing with some stuff she probably should talk about with somebody, but there wasn't anybody she felt okay talking to about it. A vicious cycle of sorts that left her feeling frighteningly solitary. Thank God she was a senior now. She only had to survive one more year and then she could go. Leave. Run.

The summer had been…weird. Good because she wasn't in school and so was able to find a little peace. Bad because, despite working two jobs, she still had too much time to be in her own head. And that could be a dangerous place sometimes.

The damn dreams.

They'd stopped for a while but started up again toward the end of summer, and though they weren't constant, they happened more than Izzy was comfortable with.

Sex dreams.

She had to call them what they were, and they were most definitely sex dreams.

Izzy was no prude. Sex dreams were fine. Sometimes, they were awesome. She'd had them before. But these latest ones? They alarmed her because the basics were always the same: she was always totally naked, she was always seriously into it, the person she was having sex with was always a woman. Sometimes, she was faceless. Sometimes, she was Kate Beckinsale. Most often, she was Easton Evans.

And *that* freaked Izzy out. Confused her. Messed with her head.

Doesn't mean I'm gay.

That was her mantra. It was the only thing that kept her from completely losing her shit. So, she said it to herself over and over. In her head. In her journal. Again and again.

Doesn't mean I'm gay.

Does it?

She'd seen Easton in study hall earlier in the day and that had triggered her memories of last night's dream, in which Easton was a prominent player. A naked, beautiful, prominent player. Easton had been looking in her direction from across the room in study hall, so they'd made accidental eye contact. Izzy felt her face heat up, like, a thousand degrees, knew she was as red as the candy apple nail polish the girl in front of her was wearing. She yanked her gaze away, opened her notebook, and spent all of study hall writing about it all. Over the summer, she'd found that jotting down her feelings, her fears, helped. She wanted—needed—to get them out of her head so she didn't go totally insane.

Now, for trigonometry, she was once again in the same room as Easton. Izzy walked in, stack of books and spiral notebooks clutched tightly to her chest, glanced to her left and saw the blond ponytail, the sparkling blue eyes, the damn cheerleading outfit because there was a game tonight. Those legs that went on forever.

Izzy had no idea if she'd actually walked into Tara Carlson or if Tara had purposely stepped in her path. Didn't really matter because, either way, they collided and all Izzy's supplies went crashing to the floor, scattering everywhere. Several of the kids nearby laughed, clapped, or both.

"Jesus, watch where you're going, Dizzy the Runt." Tara's voice was as sneery as always. At least Tara hadn't used the other popular version of her name. The much more offensive one. Izzy didn't look up at her as she crouched, made herself small, and tried to grab all her stuff as quickly as possible. She didn't look at anybody, preferring to keep her head down because she knew how red and embarrassed her face appeared. She tried to ignore Tara, who was speaking loudly. She just wanted to get her stuff and find her desk. She was stretching for her calculator, which had skittered under a chair, when her brain suddenly zeroed in on Tara's words, on what she was actually saying. Or more accurately, *reading*.

"'And this time, she wasn't faceless. She was E.E. again. All blond and gorgeous and all I wanted to do was undress her...' E.E.? Easton, that's got to be you. Hey, you're the object of lesbian sex dreams. Congratulations! You've arrived!"

Izzy gasped, felt her stomach churn in horrified panic. She straightened up to her knees, cracking her head loudly on the bottom of a desk as she did so. She reached out a desperate hand toward Tara, who neatly sidestepped it and kept reading in an overly dramatic voice. The entire room had gone quiet.

"'I can still remember the feeling. It was so...urgent. Like I couldn't wait.'"

"Please," Izzy whispered, her eyes pleading.

"'It was awesome and freaky at the same time. What does it mean?'"

Izzy felt her eyes fill with tears. "Please, don't," she begged, but this time it was so quiet, she knew nobody heard.

"'It doesn't have to mean I'm gay. Right? It doesn't mean I'm gay.'"

Izzy hung her head, still on her knees, as the classroom burst into laughter and somebody shouted, "Pretty sure it does!"

"Shall I go on?" Tara asked.

A few cheered, a couple told her that was enough, but Izzy couldn't take any more. In an instant, she felt herself go from horrifyingly hurt and ashamed to incredibly pissed, which came with volcanic levels of heat. She grabbed her things off the floor, stood suddenly, and marched at Tara so quickly, the girl's eyes widened in genuine surprise, and she stepped backward until her back hit the wall and she and Izzy stood mere inches apart. They weren't eye to eye, as Izzy was much shorter than Tara, but Izzy glared with more hatred than she'd ever felt in her life, and it was obvious that Tara felt it. The shadow of fear in her eyes was almost satisfying as Izzy grabbed her notebook and yanked it violently out of Tara's hand.

"You suck as a human being." Izzy said it quietly, on a cracked whisper, then turned to leave. Easton was looking at her from across the room, her expression an odd mix of confusion, surprise, and pity, and Izzy couldn't bear it. She hustled out of the classroom, bumping shoulders with the teacher as she entered. "Nice timing," she muttered as she sped down the hall, the sheer mortification combining with the look on Easton's face to churn her stomach into a sour mess of anxiety.

She made it to the girls' bathroom with three seconds to spare before she threw up everything in her stomach in several long, painful heaves. When she finally finished, when she had not one more drop of anything to expel from her system, she sat on the cold tile floor and let the emotion come.

She cried like a small child, unsure how she could possibly face anybody in that school again.

At the gentle rap on her doorframe, Easton looked up from her computer screen. Brandi White stood there, her face a canvas of forced neutrality.

Easton braced herself. *Here we go.* "Hi, Brandi. What can I do for you?"

Brandi cleared her throat and did a commendable impression of somebody who was a little bit nervous but trying to look like she wasn't. She shifted her weight from one foot to the other and seemed like she didn't want to step all the way into Easton's office. "I just wanted to let you know that I emailed you the sales reports." She glanced at the wood and brass clock on Easton's shelf—whether it was intentional or not, Easton couldn't tell—and Easton noticed that it was 11:45.

"Oh, my God, that's fantastic." Easton didn't want to gush... mostly because this was the first time since she'd begun working in that building that the sales reports had come in when they were actually due. But she could hear Bella's voice in the back of her mind, talking about being sure to praise your staff as often as you criticize, that it made for much more positive morale. "Thank you so much," she said, shooting a smile Brandi's way. "This is going to make people very happy. I really appreciate it, Brandi. Nice work."

Brandi looked almost as surprised as Easton was by the entire exchange. Easton was pretty sure she'd seen a ghost of a smile on Brandi's face. Which was crazy, as she'd decided a few weeks ago that Brandi, for whatever reason, lacked the ability to actually lift the corners of her mouth. At all.

With a quick one-nod of her head, Brandi said, "Thanks," and disappeared back into the area of cubicles that housed the sales force.

Easton continued to stare at the doorway, smile on her face, slight disbelief still hanging out in her head. Dare she call that episode progress? Maybe. She couldn't wait to tell Bella that night.

And there, she paused.

The night before, she'd found herself reflecting back on the whole sordid situation with Olivia. How it had started, how she'd felt when she'd fallen head over heels—which was harder to recall than the paralyzing pain she'd been saddled with once Olivia had decided to stay with the husband she didn't love so that she didn't have to deal with appearances. It was clear to Easton, when she got stuck in a rut of memories, that she hadn't forgiven Olivia yet. She knew she needed to, for herself, not anybody else. But it was a tall order. She'd gone in blindly, trusting Olivia with her heart, and Olivia had simply dropped it on the floor where it shattered into a thousand agonizing pieces. It seemed like Olivia had merely shrugged, adopted an "oh, well" kind of attitude around them, and Easton had realized how misguided she'd been. How she'd let herself fall, convinced herself that this person she'd given her soul to loved her back the same way, with the same surety and intensity. It made her question her own judgment, and Easton didn't need any extra help with that, thank you very much.

The point of all this reflecting was that it seemed to put up caution signs and bright orange traffic cones around her situation with Bella, around the things she was thinking and feeling. Slowing down, way down, was probably the best idea. Except all she wanted to do was kiss Bella again. God.

Easton braced her elbows on her desk, covered her mouth with the fingers of both hands, and let her breath out very slowly.

Okay. This didn't have to be a big thing, right? She could just… take a step back. Not text every day. Maybe every other day instead. *Good plan.* She nodded to herself. *Yeah. Good plan.*

She was going to see Bella tonight, in a mere seven hours. The way her stomach fluttered made her roll her eyes at herself. *God, I'm easy.*

Seven hours. She'd get her Bella fix in seven hours and then be fine for a while. And they should maybe, probably skip the coffee tonight. For distance's sake.

❖

We'll skip the coffee tonight.

That thought had been on Bella's mind all day on Wednesday. She needed to step back. Monday night at the school had been a lovely surprise, had made Bella realize that any time she saw Easton when she wasn't expecting to see Easton was a good thing. A great thing that set her heart to pounding and made her soul feel a little lighter. Things around Easton were confusing and wonderful and scary and she'd gotten texts from both Heather and Amy, each of them trying to be subtle—and failing—about reminding her to pump the brakes. And they were right. If Easton hadn't had Emma with her, Bella might very well have dragged her to a darkened corner near the building and kissed her senseless.

So Bella did her best to hang on to those messages from her friends, to keep them in her head, as she entered the classroom Wednesday night and got ready for the conflict resolution class. Stepping back. Slowing down. Pumping the brakes. All good ideas.

How was it that any resolutions she had around Easton could evaporate so quickly at the mere sight of the woman? Easton was the fourth person to arrive, and she'd obviously come right from work, her sharp-looking black pantsuit giving her a sexy air of authority. Blond hair down and wavy, Easton strolled in, and when her eyes met Bella's, everything about her seemed to…light up somehow. It was a vision of beauty.

"Hi," she said softly, her expression nothing but happy to see Bella.

"Hey there," Bella said back, and had to force her gaze away as Easton took her usual seat.

Class started, and Bella asked how they were doing, if they'd seen or felt anything they needed to talk about. She was surprised when Easton raised her hand.

"I had a staff member turn in a report on time, which I've been asking her to do since I started working there. She's either balked or been snide about it every time. Until today."

"Yeah?" Easton's obvious happiness around this occurrence brought a smile to Bella's lips. "And?"

"And I think I handled it really well." Easton looked around at her coworkers. "I heard Bella's voice in my head, reminding me to be as positive as I could, to not focus on just the negative." She turned back to Bella. "So, that's what I did. Even though what I really wanted to say was 'it's about damn time,' I thanked her instead. I told her the higher-ups were going to be thrilled. And I told her she'd done a good job."

"That's great," Mara Watson said, and reached across to give Easton's arm a squeeze.

"It really was. We both sort of stayed there for a bit, just looking at each other. I think we were both a little surprised."

"And how'd you feel afterward?" Bella asked.

"Relieved. Glad. Hopeful." Easton's expression showed all of those things right there on her gorgeous face.

"I had a similar thing happen," Paul Antonassio offered, then told his story of connecting with an employee he'd struggled with.

Easton's words jump-started an enthusiastic conversation where everybody hopped on board to talk about some of their recent experiences.

Bella offered a word here and there but mostly just listened, nodded, and grinned. There was no feeling quite like the one where you realize all the things you've been trying to teach to your students are not only being put into practice but have worked for them. She'd never really had any desire to be a teacher, but these moments made her understand the draw.

They spent more time sharing stories and talking over a few situations that might have been handled differently, and the hour went so quickly that Bella wondered for a moment if the clock on the wall was wrong. Folks began packing up their things, still smiling and pumped up, and Bella felt accomplished.

"Perk?" Easton asked as she shouldered her bag and walked toward the front of the room.

"Love to," Bella said automatically.

"Great. I'll meet you there." Easton reached out and gave Bella's hand a squeeze before heading out the door.

What just happened?

Bella stood there and blinked. So much for determination. So much for willpower. She shook her head, knowing this hadn't been the plan. Knowing this was not even close to pumping the brakes.

And she didn't care.

The reality was, there was no place in the world she'd rather be that night than sitting on a comfy couch with a good cup of coffee, getting to know Easton even better.

And it wasn't something she was going to apologize for.

Chapter Fourteen

Easton let a low, quiet growl escape from her lips when she saw that their usual love seat at Perk was occupied. The late-May weather was gorgeous that evening and had apparently brought people out of the woodwork. The whole block seemed to bustle with activity, which was unusual for a Wednesday evening.

There was a small, round table for two in a back corner, so she carried two cups of coffee over to it and set herself up so she could see the door, wave to Bella as she arrived. She got herself comfortable, took a sip of her coffee, let it slide down her throat, and felt it warm her insides like fuel. She didn't want to think about how badly she'd failed her "we're going to slow things down" plan, how the coffee invite had just flown out of her mouth before she had time to think. To shut that subject away for the moment, she studied her surroundings instead. The crowd was rather eclectic tonight, a mix of young hipsters and middle-aged yuppies with a smattering of college kids thrown in. The three guys to her right were having a heated debate about hockey while a group of seeming business professionals conversed about the possibility of layoffs coming to their company. Easton was so intent on her eavesdropping that she didn't realize Bella was there until she spoke.

"Hi." Bella pulled out a chair and pointed to the second cup. "Is that for me?"

"It is. Dark roast with a little cream." Easton slid the cup to her, watched her blush prettily.

"You remembered." Bella sat, her eyes sparkling. That pleasant little fluttering that seemed to only happen when Bella was near her started up in Easton's stomach.

"I did." Easton loved when Bella's cheeks got rosy like that, and she reached across and rubbed her thumb across one, which made Bella blush harder.

It was a moment. An intimate one. They both felt it, Easton was certain.

"What did you find out?" Bella asked, voice lowered, and rolled her eyes first left, then right, indicating the other patrons.

Easton quietly filled her in on the conversations she'd heard and the conclusions she'd drawn. Bella smiled with gentle amusement the whole time. Finally, Easton shifted in her seat and propped her chin on her hand. "So, tell me about your day."

Bella seemed to relax a bit, seemed to sink into her chair a bit, like some of the tension had left her body, and Easton loved that this was her reaction when they were together. She wanted to think she had a hand in Bella feeling comfortable. Happy. Bella's face opened as she began to talk, and Easton had a sudden, unbidden vision of this conversation happening each night at the dinner table as they ate. She tried to ignore the image as Bella spoke about two clients she'd seen that day—always respectful of their privacy and never mentioning names.

"That's the woman who wants to leave her husband, right?" Easton asked, to clarify Bella's story.

"Yes." Bella sipped her coffee. "She's been building up to it for the past fourteen or fifteen months and I think it's finally about to happen."

"Is it the right decision for her?"

"In my opinion? Absolutely. I can't tell her that, of course." Bella held her hands up in surrender. "I am the Queen of Neutrality."

Easton chuckled. "Right, right. Your job is to help her figure out her path on her own."

Bella pointed at her. "Exactly."

"And the other guy is the one whose girlfriend left him?"

With a nod, Bella said, "Yeah. About six months ago. He's had such a rough go of it. I was worried about him for a bit there, but I really think he's turned a corner."

"That's got to be a relief."

"It is. It really is."

They sat in silence for a beat, and Easton allowed herself time to study the glow of pride on Bella's face. "You really like your work," she finally said, and the way the smile blossomed onto Bella's face made her glad she did.

"I love it. I really do. I feel like it's what I was meant to do." She sipped. "I mean, maybe not the teaching upper management businesspeople how to deal with their unruly staff, but…"

Easton laughed. "That's got to be so lame."

"You have no idea."

"But the rest of it is good."

"Yes. Very."

Easton took a sip of her coffee, her eyes on Bella as she did. Eye contact with Bella was…intense somehow. A little bit electric. She was suddenly seized with the urge to know everything she possibly could about this woman who drew her so strongly. "Who's your person?" she asked.

"My person?" Bella furrowed her brow.

"Yeah, like, the person you go to for anything and everything. When you're depressed. When you're happy. Who knows all your secrets?"

"Oh, my *person*. I see. I have two."

"Yeah?"

"My suitemates from college. Amy and Heather. We got so amazingly lucky to find each other. We just clicked, and we still do. We tell each other everything." Bella's face lit up when she talked about her friends. She became more animated. Lighter. It was somehow uplifting to see it, and Easton basked. "What about you?"

"I have two as well."

Bella's grin widened at that. "Kindred spirits. Who?"

"My friend Shondra, who you met at Teddy's that night, and like I told you at dinner, my grandpa."

"Right. I remember that. Tell me more about your grandpa again."

Easton felt her heart swell with love, as it did every time she thought about her relationship with him. "He's the best. He just…gets me. My grandma, too, but him the most. They're so far ahead of their time."

Bella sipped her coffee, her eyes staying on Easton over the rim of the mug. "How so?"

Easton inhaled deeply and let it out, looked off into the distance as she thought about her grandparents, conjuring up their faces in her mind's eye. "They're just so…open. My family can be a bit tightly wound. Like I told you, they're all doctors, so precision in many things is necessary. But it can bleed into parts of life that it doesn't have to." She pulled one corner of her mouth to the side in a half-grimace. "I'm kind of the black sheep, and I think my grandparents are the only ones who not only get that but are fine with it. I told you that my grandpa was the first person I told that I didn't want to be a doctor, but I didn't tell you that he came with me when I told my parents. Thank God, because I think it would've gotten way uglier if I'd told them by myself." She took a sip of her coffee, then looked back up at Bella, who was watching her with calm interest. "He's one of the few people who know about Olivia."

"Your *grandpa*?" Bella asked, her surprise clear. "I know you said he knew about why you left your marriage, but I didn't know he knew the *details*."

Easton laughed softly. "He does. All of them, which was the first time I was ever ashamed to tell him something."

"Why were you ashamed?" Bella's voice was tender, her eyes soft and kind.

"Hey, Grandpa, I miss you. Just so you know, I'm leaving my husband. By the way, I've been having an affair with a married woman, too. Yeah, I like girls now. Say hi to Grandma for me."

"Wow. That is…" Bella shook her head as she seemed to search for the right words, a small chuckle bubbling up from deep within her. "Okay, first of all, stop beating yourself up like that. You've liked girls for a while. You've said so. And, unfortunately, it's really hard to control who you fall for. As far as I can tell, you were just finally learning to accept yourself. You were deciding to live honestly, to be who you are. Olivia being married doesn't have a whole lot to do with it. I'm sure your grandfather understood that."

Easton took some time to absorb Bella's words, to let herself feel the comfort of them. "He seemed to."

"He seems like a super, super cool man."

"He is."

"I envy you." Bella's tone was tinted by…something Easton couldn't put a finger on.

Their gazes held, and the level of absolute ease was almost

palpable for Easton; she couldn't remember ever feeling that way before. She let a beat of silence pass. Two. She used the little black stir stick in what remained of her coffee, swirled it around, and watched the little whirlpool it created. The words were there on the tip of her tongue. She wanted to say them but was hesitant. This was all moving so fast, and the way she'd found herself feeling about Bella was alarming. *I shouldn't say anything.* That thought was prominent. And loud. At the same time, she thought about honesty and being forthright and how important that was. Olivia hadn't understood that, but Easton did. "Can I ask you something?" Her voice was quiet, and she took a second before she looked up at Bella.

"Of course."

"Do you think this," she made a gesture between the two of them, "is moving too fast?" The laugh that burst from Bella's lips in that moment was startling. It shot out like a gunshot, and she slapped a hand over her mouth, as if trying to contain it. Easton couldn't help but laugh along with her. Once they'd calmed, she said, "Why is that funny?"

"Because my friends think it's moving too fast, so it's been exactly the thought running through my head all day."

Easton nodded, simultaneously feeling a little thrill at being talked about to Bella's friends and a slice of disappointment that maybe Bella agreed with them. "Mine, too. I was actually going to bail on coffee tonight."

"So was I."

That sat there, grinning widely at each other. "And what do you think?"

Bella seemed to take a moment. Easton watched as her unique hazel eyes scanned the coffee shop but never stayed on one thing. When the gaze came back to Easton, it was soft. Almost tender. Bella tilted her head a little and said, "I mean, what's fast?" She shrugged. "Think about it." She took a sip of her coffee. "We've been on one official date, we've had coffee a few times, you happened to see me at the school Monday, but that wasn't a planned thing."

"We've only kissed once," Easton added, hoping there was a glimmer of mischief in her eyes.

"And that right there is a downright shame," Bella said, arching an eyebrow in an expression that was sexy enough to send flutters of excitement through Easton's body. "We should remedy that."

"I agree."

And that was how they ended up outside in the parking lot, having a heated make-out session in the almost-dark, Bella pinned between Easton's body and her own SUV.

It was different this time. Easton could feel it. She couldn't pinpoint how or why, but she could feel it. When they'd kissed outside Brie, it had been wonderful and hot, but also a bit tentative. They'd been feeling each other out, testing the waters, learning a bit about each other. This time, though...this time was deeper and slower. Easton took her time, letting herself feel every nuance. The warmth of Bella's mouth, the lingering, creamy taste of coffee, the softness of her lips, her velvety tongue as it pressed gently, then more firmly into Easton's mouth and Easton pushed back. Bella's body under Easton's hands was soft but firm, feminine, and Easton could feel the strength, absently wondered if Bella worked out.

When the need for air became vital, they broke the kiss but stayed in each other's arms, breathing the same air, foreheads touching. They stayed that way for several moments.

"Wow," Bella whispered as she lifted her head to look Easton in the eye.

"Even better than I remembered," Easton said, truthfully.

"We certainly do that well together."

"There's no question." Easton hesitated on a second before continuing with, "Is it bad if I say I wonder what else we'd do well together?"

Bella's snort-laugh made Easton grin. "God, no. Why would that be bad?"

Easton lifted one shoulder. "I don't know. The too-fast thing?"

Bella's voice dropped. "We hashed that out, remember?"

"Oh, right."

And they were kissing again.

Oh, my God. I could just stay right here, doing this, forever. For the first time in ages, Easton closed everything else out of her mind and focused solely on one thing and one thing only: Bella.

The next time they wrenched apart, Easton had zero idea how much time had passed. It felt a little darker, but that could've been an illusion. She and Bella stood in each other's arms, breathing ragged, faces flushed. Easton could only speak for herself, but she was so incredibly turned on, she could barely focus her vision.

"Yeah," Bella said, her chest rising and falling rapidly. "We'd be *so* good at other things."

Easton nodded, feeling the heat in her face, hearing the pounding of her own heart in her ears. "I think we should plan on finding out. Soon. I'd say now, but I have an early meeting that I'm not even close to prepared for." She closed her eyes and sighed. "God, I really want to say now." *Shondra would kill me. Dead. In a heartbeat.*

"I know," Bella said, and pressed her hand to Easton's chest, firmly, but without pushing. Attempting to keep distance between them? Easton wondered. "Me too. But…there's no hurry. Right?"

She was right, and Easton smiled and took a deep breath to steady herself, as she felt strangely off balance. "There's no hurry. No."

"You busy this weekend?" Bella asked then, her eyes hopeful. It was an expression Easton decided she loved.

"Emma and I are going to visit my grandparents." The disappointment in her voice was clear, but she did nothing to alter it. She wanted Bella to know that's what she felt in the moment: disappointed.

Bella nodded and looked off into the darkening parking lot for a moment, then turned back. God, those eyes of hers. They could do things to a girl. "Next weekend?"

Their bodies were still very close together, Easton almost leaning on Bella, their faces still close enough that the tips of their noses almost touched. "Next weekend would be good," Easton whispered. Oh, my God, had she ever wanted somebody more? How would she possibly make it through an entire week?

"Great." Bella nodded some more, blinked rapidly a few times, and Easton heard her swallow.

"Are you okay?" Easton narrowed her eyes, a sliver of worry creeping in.

But Bella reassured her with a slow grin as she said, "I'm terrific. Haven't been this good in a long time. But you're gonna need to take a step back from me now if you plan on keeping your clothes on in this parking lot." When she looked up at Easton then, her eyes had gone so dark, a soft gasp escaped Easton's lips, and a wave of arousal washed through her.

"Okay," she said quietly, and with a quick nod, took a step backward, as requested. The crisp night air rushed to fill the space between them, and Easton felt goose bumps break out on her arms.

Bella reached out then. Lifted her hand and stroked Easton's cheek with the backs of her fingers, and it somehow felt incredibly intimate to Easton. The goose bumps multiplied. "Text me?" Bella asked.

"I will."

Bella grasped her chin, gave her a quick peck on the lips, then turned away quickly and got into her car.

Easton gave her a small wave and then headed to her own car. Once safely inside, she blew out a long, slow breath and rested her head against the steering wheel. Her lips still felt kiss-swollen, her blood was still racing. There was a buzzing in her head, and her underwear was uncomfortably damp.

"This is so bad," she whispered into the quiet of the car. "This is really, really bad." Then a grin burst across her face and she chuckled to herself. "In a really, really good way."

❖

Framerton High, 2004

The holidays had come and gone and Easton was actually grateful to be back in school. She was a girl who liked routine, and being on an unknown schedule and having no solid plans made her feel untethered and a little anxious. At least at school, she knew what to expect, where she had to be at any given time, what was due when.

She'd hoped that while school had been out for almost three weeks, the relaxation would help ease her mind. Her dreams. Her confusion. Her uncontrollable urge to stare at another girl. The second Kristin Harrington passed her in the hallway, she knew that hadn't happened. Hadn't come close to happening. In fact, the urge to stare was worse, and it was accompanied by both an equally strong urge to follow her just to be able to smell her perfume and an overwhelming curiosity about what was under Kristin's sweater. Easton found herself looking at her new schedule to see when PE was, wondered if she'd be in the locker room at the same time as Kristin, if she'd maybe be near her when she undressed…

"You okay?" Connor's voice yanked Easton back to reality and she realized with alarm that she'd been kind of obvious in her staring. When she glanced up at Connor, his gaze was on Kristin as well. "That's Christy, right? You know her?"

"Kristin," Easton said quickly as she reached to spin the lock on her locker. "No. I don't know her well at all." The simmering near panic in her gut made her hands shake, and she made a fist before trying her lock again. *Goddamn it.* What was wrong with her? Staring like that? Connor was still looking at her oddly; she could feel it. She spun the lock a third time.

Laughter from down the hall drifted toward her, and when she looked up, the new girl—who wasn't new any longer, but that was still how Easton thought of her because she couldn't remember her name—was hurrying in her direction, books clutched tightly to her chest like a shield, head down so her dark hair obscured her face.

"Hey, Easton!" Tara called from where the laughter had begun. "Here comes your *lesbian admirer*!" She sneered the last two words, loudly, and Easton heard Connor chuckle.

The perfect opportunity had been handed to her on a silver platter, and when the new girl glanced up at her, Easton pursed her lips and blew her a kiss, then waggled her eyebrows.

The girl's eyes went wide—did they fill with tears?—and any color that might have been left in her face drained quickly so she was simply a pale skeleton who picked up her pace and skittered around a corner.

It seemed like the entire hallway had broken into laughter, and though Easton managed to smile, it didn't reach her eyes because she didn't feel it.

What she felt was horrible.

❖

So, nothing had changed.

I don't know why I'm surprised.

Izzy made it safely to the girls' bathroom before the tears came. It was the one restroom in the school that was kind of off in no-man's-land, at the end of a hall that wasn't used a whole lot. Therefore, it was often empty, and for that Izzy was forever grateful. It had become a sanctuary of sorts for her.

She went to the farthest stall, shut herself in, and slid to the ground, letting her books drop from her lap as she sobbed.

Izzy was angry. Not so much at her torturers, but at herself. Over the holidays, she'd read books on sexuality. She'd found a couple of chat rooms for people struggling, and while she didn't participate in any conversations, she followed along. It was interesting. And frightening. And real. She'd spent a lot of time reading about the experiences of others her age, how they'd learned to deal with/ignore/fight back against their tormentors, and she'd taken all of it to heart. She'd practiced in the mirror the things she'd say the next time Tara Carlson opened her fucking mouth.

As expected, it had happened. Instantly.

And instead of hitting Tara with both barrels, Izzy had hurried away in tears, the laughter of her classmates echoing down the hall after her. She'd stood up to Tara once, sort of, but apparently, that was all she was allowed.

Izzy swiped at her nose with her hand, and suddenly, all her anger evaporated like fog on a summer morning. The only thing left was sadness. A deep well of sadness and loneliness and pain that sat way down inside her. She'd been an idiot to think she could banish it so easily, just by reading some chats.

"God, I'm so stupid," she whispered, as the tears continued to roll down her cheeks.

She didn't know how she would survive another five months.

❖

The drive to Framerton took roughly three hours. While it had started out rainy—Easton hated driving in the rain—the weather had gradually cleared the farther east she drove. By the time she'd pulled into her grandparents' driveway, the sky was blue and the sun shone brightly. The house stood, large and welcoming, as it always had. It was the only house her grandparents ever had, the same house where her father and his siblings grew up. Stately was a good word for it, white siding with black shutters and a big red door that opened onto an open front porch that ran the entire length of the house. Easton's grandmother loved flowers, and her tulips were in full bloom along the front, bursts of red and yellow and orange giving the house a welcoming, springlike feel.

Now Emma was running around the enormous backyard with Skippy, her grandparents'—and by "grandparents'" she meant "grandmother's"—Cavalier King Charles spaniel. Her giggles carried through the air to the screened-in back porch where Easton sat in a wicker rocker next to her grandfather.

"I can't believe how big she's getting," Mya Evans said with a smile, as she watched her great-granddaughter through eyes as big and blue as Easton's. Her blond hair was on its way to a rich-looking silver and her figure was trim. Easton had always admired her beauty, hoped to give off such confidence and class when she was seventy-three. Mya set down a tray with three glasses of white wine and a plate of homemade shortbread cookies, Easton's favorite. "Every time I see her, it's like she's grown six inches." She took a wine glass and then sat in the rocker on the other side of her husband.

Stephen and Mya Evans were fascinating to Easton. They always had been. They were an incredibly interesting mix of open-minded modernist and old-school traditionalist. The fact that they were in their seventies made it that much more intriguing. Easton's grandfather had worked insane hours most of their marriage to get his practice up and running and then to keep it so. Mya Evans had a degree in engineering but hadn't ever used it, choosing to stay home, raise the four Evans children, including Easton's father, and run the household.

"Emma!" Easton called out as her daughter watched Skippy squat in the yard. "You know where the shovel and bags are. Clean that up."

"Moooooooom," was Emma's reply in three very long syllables. "It's gross!"

"Yes, it is. Clean it up, please."

Quiet chuckles rumbled through the porch as the three adults watched Emma literally stomp toward the shed on a very loud sigh. "So dramatic," her grandmother said.

"Just like her mother was," said her grandfather.

"Hey!" Easton said in protest, then laughed when they both turned to look at her with raised eyebrows. "All right, fine. That's true."

There was more chuckling at the expression on Emma's face as she scooped up the poop, grimacing and muttering "yuck" under her breath the whole time. Once it was in the bag, she held it up with a questioning look on her face, nose still wrinkled.

"Tie it up and put it in the garbage can next to the garage," Mya directed. "Thank you, sweetie."

"Welcome," was the response. Then a whispered, "So gross, so gross, so gross..." as she tromped off to the garbage.

"How's work?" Stephen asked, then took a sip of his wine. "Oh, this is good, Mya. Did you taste it?"

Mya nodded. "Jeannie recommended it. She had it at her luncheon last week."

"Is that your friend who works at the winery?" Easton asked, following suit and sipping her own wine. It was delicious, not sweet but not dry, with a hint of vanilla and a tang of citrus on the finish. "Oh, wow. That's awesome."

"Yes, and she gets all kinds of inside information on new wines that are hard to get." Wine tasting had been one of the many things Mya had taken up once her children were all gone from the house and she found herself with more time. She had a million hobbies and Easton envied her, wished she could bottle her energy.

"Is this one? Hard to get?"

"Oh, yes."

Stephen snorted. "Do I want to know how much it costs?"

"No, you do not." Mya winked at Easton.

Stephen shook his head, but there was a twinkle in his eye. Easton had come to believe that he not only approved of his wife's many extracurricular activities but enjoyed them. "Back to my question, Easton. Tell me about work. Going okay? And what about this conflict thing?"

Easton watched Emma run around with Skippy in the lush green of her grandparents' huge yard, her giggles bringing a smile to Easton's face as she told her grandfather about her new position. Then she went on to explain the issues with the current staff and why upper management had sent them to Bella's class. "While I know I don't really need a conflict resolution class—I think three of the six of us fall into that category—I've actually learned some good stuff. I'm not even sure I realized it until I put it into practice." She told the story of Brandi White, her initial—and continued—disrespect and obvious annoyance, and Easton's own frustrated reaction to it. "Then, earlier this week, she handed her reports in on time. Came to my office to tell me so."

"Ah, interesting," Stephen said, nodding. "She's starting to come around. And how did you respond?"

"I had to take a moment," Easton admitted. "But I heard Bella's voice—she's the class instructor—and I just stayed completely positive. I thanked Brandi profusely, told her how happy my boss was going to be, and I smiled the whole time."

"And?" Mya asked.

"We sort of stood there blinking at each other. I think we were both a little surprised at such a pleasant exchange. We'd never had one. It was like neither one of us was sure what had just happened or what to do next. It was amusing." She recalled that moment, and it actually made her feel lighter. "I think it's going to be okay."

"That's fantastic," Stephen said, scratching at his face. "Dealing with a new staff can be hard in general. It can't be easy to have them all resent you."

"It's not. But Brandi's been the worst of them, so if she's coming around, maybe that means the rest of my salespeople will, too."

"And how about your love life?" Mya asked, focusing those blue eyes on Easton as she sipped her wine.

"Subtle, Mya," Stephen said with a chuckle that rumbled up from deep in his chest.

"Wow, Grandma. No easing in gently, huh?"

"Sweetheart, when you get to be my age, you don't have time for preamble. You'll see." Her cheerful face sobered a bit. "Your grandfather told me your divorce is final." She kept her voice low, presumably so Emma didn't overhear.

Easton nodded. "Yeah. That was a strange feeling."

"I'm sure it was. But it's been over a year."

"Almost two. And I'm the one who left, so…" Easton let her voice trail off, that same feeling of guilt settling on her shoulders. "I don't really have the right to feel any sadness around it." Repeating that to herself didn't seem to help, though. She was still sad.

Her grandmother scoffed. "Please. That's crap, and you know it."

When Easton glanced her way, she saw the ghost of a smile on her grandfather's face. They were seriously the best couple ever.

"It's time for you to start thinking about love again," Mya said with determination. "You need to find yourself a nice girl."

Easton wasn't sure she'd ever get used to hearing a sentence like that coming from her grandmother, but she was incredibly grateful anyway. "Well, there *is* one that I'm interested in..." Again, she let her voice trail off, as she hadn't planned on telling them, or anybody besides Shondra just yet, about Bella.

But Mya's little joyful gasp was worth it, and Easton laughed. "Tell me all about her! Give me the scoop. What does she do for a living? Where'd you meet her? Is she pretty?"

Easton laughed harder. "There's the gossip-hound grandmother I know and love. Let's see." She ticked each answer off on her fingers. "She's a therapist, I met her in my conflict resolution class because she teaches it, and yes, she's very pretty."

Mya had scooted to the edge of her chair and held her wineglass in both hands as she leaned forward. Stephen sat back, presumably so his wife had a better view of their granddaughter, an amused smile on his face. "Tell me more."

Easton looked off into the yard. Emma was still running around, Skippy hot on her heels, Emma's giggles being carried on the light breeze of a late May afternoon. "Well, there's not a whole lot to tell right now. We're still in the early stages of getting to know each other." She thought about their coffee date Wednesday, the make-out session in the parking lot, how much Easton had wanted to take her home that very night. "We're trying to take things slow."

"But?" Mya prompted.

Easton inhaled, let it out slowly, then turned to her grandmother. "I *really* like her."

"I can see that." Mya finished her wine, then poured herself half a glass more. "So, how far has it gone?"

Easton raised her eyebrows in surprise. Was her grandmother actually asking...?

"Have you slept with her yet?"

She was. She was totally asking.

"Oh, my God, Grandma." Easton covered her eyes with one hand and shook her head as her grandfather laughed.

"What?" Mya asked, all wide-eyed innocence. "Am I not allowed to ask that?"

Easton couldn't help but join her grandfather in his mirth. "You're allowed to ask anything you want. No, I have not slept with her."

"How come?"

Easton realized this was a legitimate question as Mya held her gaze, her expression open and expectant. "Because it's too fast."

"Too fast for what? It's been almost two years, as you just pointed out, since both Connor and the neighbor woman."

"Olivia."

"Olivia. Yes. Her." Mya cocked her head and seemed to think for a moment before lowering her voice. "Is it too fast because you're scared?"

Easton's eyes welled and that annoyed her. She let loose a soft groan, swiped at the one tear that escaped, and nodded.

Stephen laid a large, warm hand on Easton's leg and squeezed gently. He didn't say anything, but his love was clear. As usual, he was a solid, comforting presence who let his wife do the talking.

"I completely understand. And that goddamn Olivia did a number on you. Let's hope I never run into her in a dark alley."

Easton snorted, and her love for her grandmother swelled her heart.

"I can tell you this, though." Mya waited until Easton looked at her, their gazes locked. "You are ready. You are smart, beautiful, wonderful. And you. Are. Ready."

"You think so?" Easton swallowed down the emotion that had decided to camp out as a lump in her throat.

"I know so."

Easton nibbled on the inside of her cheek as the wetness in her eyes dissipated and her grandmother reached across to grasp her hand. The three of them sitting on the back porch, connected by physical touch and their love for each other, was beautiful to Easton, and she allowed herself a moment to simply bask in the love of her grandparents.

"Thank you guys," she said, when she felt like she could speak without her voice cracking. "I mean it."

"You deserve to be happy, Buttercup," her grandfather said as he stroked her cheek with his thumb. "Don't you let anybody—especially *you*—tell you any different. Okay?"

"Okay."

Mya held up a finger. "Just…play a *little* hard to get. Keep her on her toes. It'll be good for her." Then she winked, and life was better.

After that conversation, Easton felt lighter somehow. While it wasn't surprising because she always felt better after talking to her grandparents, it was interesting. She wasn't sure why she needed to have one or both of them tell her she was okay, but that seemed to be her thing. She often came to them when a big change had happened in her life or when she'd made an important decision, because she needed to hear them say she was okay. And they always did. They never failed her. Apparently, she'd needed to hear it about Bella as well. Which wasn't what she'd expected because Bella wasn't a subject she'd planned on bringing up.

Funny how that had gone.

And later, as they sat around the dining room table and finished up dinner, part of Easton wished she and Emma weren't staying overnight, simply because she'd like to see Bella. But it was probably better this way.

Keeping her on her toes and all that…

CHAPTER FIFTEEN

A my's apartment wasn't huge, but it felt like it. The high ceilings made it feel big and the natural light that poured in the windows made it seem bright and airy, even on a rainy Sunday morning.

Bella kicked off her wet shoes and left them on the boot tray in Amy's hall, then handed her jacket over.

"I take it it's still raining?" Amy asked.

"It's kind of misting. That stuff that makes my hair frizz up like one of those dish scrubby things." Bella patted her head self-consciously, but the sound of pots and pans caught her attention, and that's when she smelled the divine scent of bacon. "Oh, my God, I'm starving." She followed her nose into the kitchen and was about to ask if Heather was there yet, but stopped when she saw her.

"Hey there," Heather said and leaned toward Bella for a kiss, her hands occupied by a pot holder and a pair of tongs. She had a flowered apron that was decidedly not Amy's style tied around her waist. Her bouncy hair was perfect, as usual, as was her makeup. Bella kissed her cheek, then snagged a slice of bacon off the paper towel-covered plate next to the stove. "It's hot. Be careful."

It was, but Bella didn't care, because bacon. "You're here early," she said to Heather as she chewed, then turned toward the open dining area and the table where the ingredients for mimosas were set out, in addition to three place settings. Amy held up a flute and raised her eyebrows. Bella nodded.

Amy handed over a mimosa, held her own out, and she and Bella clinked their glasses together. "What's new?" Amy asked.

Bella watched over the little partition that separated the dining area from the kitchen as Heather opened the spice cupboard to grab a bottle. Then she slid a drawer open, grabbed out another pot holder, and closed the drawer with her hip. "What's new is watching Heather be a whiz in your kitchen. Wow." Oven door open, Heather reached in and pulled out a baking dish.

"I may have found my groove," Heather said with a proud grin.

"Where the hell has it been hiding all these years?" Bella asked, then dodged a flying potholder.

"She's become damn good," Amy agreed, and Bella turned to look at her, wondering if she'd imagined the weird edge in her voice. Amy caught her eye, blinked rapidly, then seemed to stand straighter. "But what about you? How are things with the hideously embarrassing high school crush?"

"Sit down, you guys. Breakfast is ready." Heather pulled a spatula from the drawer and handed it to Bella, then sliced up her breakfast casserole as the other two women took their seats at the already set table.

"It's fine," Bella said, making room in the center of the table where two hot plates sat so Heather could put the baking dish there. "It's good."

"'It's fine. It's good'?" Amy scooped some casserole onto Heather's plate, then scooped another piece onto her own. "Could be you be any less descriptive?" She handed the spatula to Bella.

From what Bella could tell, the casserole contained eggs, cheese, something green—spinach?—and bacon, and it smelled heavenly. She served herself a slice as Heather sat down and then two sets of eyes were on her. "What? It *is* fine. It *is* good."

"And you've slowed down a bit?" Heather asked.

"Oh, my God, this is delicious," Amy said quietly, trying to hide her shock, and touched Heather's arm.

Bella squinted at them, then something bright pink on the floor across the room caught her eye. She narrowed her gaze, and after a beat, recognized it. Her eyes went wide with surprise as a picture began to form in her head. She set down her fork, folded her arms across her chest, and stared at her friends, lips pursed.

Heather and Amy exchanged a glance. Then Amy cleared her throat and said quietly, "What?" She was clearly bracing herself.

"What's going on with you two?" Bella looked from one to the other, placed her hands on the table, palms down, then kept her focus on Heather, who she knew was definitely the weak link of the two and by far the worse liar. If anybody was going to crack, it'd be her. Bella leaned toward her a bit, hoping to intimidate her into talking.

With an audible swallow, Heather looked down at her plate, set her fork down, and stayed quiet.

A wave of worry hit Bella. "My God, what is it? Is one of you dying?"

A laugh snorted out of Amy. "No, nobody's dying."

Bella folded her arms again and sat back. "You two have been weird. Like...weird. Shooting looks at each other when you think I'm not looking. Saying strange things." A feeling hit her then, one she hadn't even realized had taken root, one she hadn't felt since she'd left high school, and she swallowed. "Why are you guys leaving me out? What are you leaving me out of?" The smallness of her voice embarrassed her, and she felt the warmth in her cheeks.

Amy and Heather looked at each other, and Amy's big, brown eyes softened as if they'd telepathically communicated something. She cleared her throat and turned her attention to Bella. "We've been...I mean, Heather and I...we're..."

"We're seeing each other," Heather finished.

Bella furrowed her brow. "You're seeing each other." She let the words roll around, and it took her a good twenty seconds before the meaning became clear and her eyes widened. "You're seeing each other as in, you're dating?" The pitch of her voice raised almost comically on the last word.

Heather nodded, and Amy smiled halfway, as if she wasn't sure a full-on grin would be accepted at this point.

"I..." Bella blinked hard. Once, twice. Rubbed her forehead. Sat up. "But...when? How? When? And why didn't you tell me?" She had so many questions. So many emotions.

Amy and Heather looked at each other again and Bella saw it clearly this time: the...love? Was it love already? Heather reached out a hand and grasped Amy's.

"It's been a few months," Amy began, and she held up a placating hand as Bella's mouth dropped open in shock. "I know. We know. But...it just kind of happened and we weren't sure where it would go, if anywhere."

Heather spoke up. "Mostly, we were worried. About what it would do to the three of us if it didn't work. We figured if we didn't tell you and it fizzled, you wouldn't be in the middle. You wouldn't feel like you had to choose a side." She wet her lips, looking nervous and hesitant, and that made Bella feel the tiniest bit better. "Does that make sense?"

Bella looked at her best friends. Looked from one to the other. Amy's brown eyes, Heather's blue ones, focused on her. Worried, a tad frightened, but also…happy. There was definite happiness there. In the way Heather leaned slightly toward Amy. In the way Amy held tightly to Heather's hand. They were happy. And that really was the only thing that mattered to Bella.

"And…it hasn't fizzled?"

"No," Amy said, and it seemed like she wanted to smile, but she held herself in check. "It hasn't."

"Well." Bella reached for the champagne, filled her glass. "Fuck the orange juice. I need straight-up alcohol for this." She took a long sip, then another, then set it down. "That explains why Heather's overnight bag is over there in the corner. And why she suddenly knows where everything is in your kitchen." The girls looked slightly chagrined but said nothing, seemed to wait Bella out. She inhaled slowly, let it out, and nibbled on her lower lip for a moment. Then she folded her hands on the table and looked from Amy to Heather and back to Amy. "Yeah, I'm gonna need all the deets. Spill."

❖

By the time Bella got home and let the dogs out into the backyard, she was exhausted. Funny how emotional discussions—good or bad—could do that to you. Her friends were happy. That was the bottom line. Yes, Bella would've liked to be in on things from the beginning, but part of her did understand why they'd chosen the path they had. She didn't like it—being excluded brought up painful memories from her past—but she understood it.

As she stood at her sliding glass door and watched Ethel run around the yard like a puppy while Lucy did her business under a tree, occasionally blinking up at the raining sky with obvious annoyance, the corners of her mouth tugged up a bit. She'd never seen Amy so happy. So smitten. Yeah, that was the word, corny as it sounded: Amy was totally smitten. Like, gooey looks and over-attention. The whole nine yards now that Bella knew and they didn't have to be secretive or even discreet any longer. And once the cat was out of the bag, Amy hadn't been able to keep her hands off Heather.

"That's been the hardest part," Amy had admitted to Bella under her breath when Heather was out of earshot. She'd even looked a bit sheepish, and Amy was *not* somebody who looked sheepish very often. "I just...want to be touching her all the time. You know?"

There was a prickle of jealousy, if Bella was being honest with herself. Just a small one. She was thrilled for her friends. Over the moon. Their happiness was palpable, and Bella couldn't help but smile at them once she got past the surprise of it all. But there was a teeny, tiny sliver that felt envious, that wanted what they had and was irritated they'd found it so close to home.

She slid the door open for Lucy, who stepped inside and immediately shook her entire body, sending a mist of water everywhere. Bella used the towel she kept handy for just such occasions and wiped her dog down, dried her paws, gave her a kiss on top of her big, square head. Lucy marched away with a snuffle, straight to her bed in the corner, where she curled up and plopped down with a long-suffering sigh.

"I know. It's hard to be you, huh, Luce?"

Ethel was next, and she was more than wet from her running around. She was muddy, and it took a lot more effort to get her clean. By the time Bella finished, she was sitting on the floor and dirtier than her dogs had been.

On her way up the stairs to change into cleaner clothes, a ping came from her back pocket. A text from Easton.

How was your weekend?

They'd texted a bit since Wednesday but only sporadically, as if each of them had their conversation about moving too fast in the backs of their heads. She texted back.

Not bad. Yours? How was your visit with your grandparents? She set the phone on her dresser and stripped off her now-muddy shirt.

Really great. It always is. You'd like them. And then a smiling emoji.

Bella vaguely recalled Easton's grandparents. At least her grandfather. He was a well-known and beloved local doctor. Lots of kids at school were patients of his, something that made Easton even more popular than she already was. *I'm sure*, she texted back.

You saw that this week's class is canceled, yes?

That text surprised Bella. Until she looked at her email and saw the note from her boss telling her so. *I did, yes.* She was glad Easton couldn't hear her sigh.

We have a company-wide picnic that evening and my bosses want all the managers there. This time, the emoji was rolling its eyes.

Bella grinned. *Well, that's a bummer.*

Right? A beat went by. Two. Then the next text came. *I was thinking...*

Uh-oh... Bella texted back immediately, her grin widening.

Ha ha. Very funny. There was another pause between texts, and Bella wondered if Easton was thinking, rethinking, gearing up, hesitating...Finally, the phone dinged again. *Are you free Friday night?*

A wave of excitement flooded Bella's system at the thought of spending time with Easton. *I believe so.* She tried to picture Easton's face as a few more beats went by before her next text came.

Would you be interested in coming to my place? I'd like to cook you dinner.

"Ooohhhh..." Bella said quietly into the silence of her bedroom, as a gentle throbbing began low in her body. *I would be very interested in that.* Then she sent her own smiling emoji.

Fantastic. I'll touch base with you as it gets closer.

They signed off, Easton needing to help Emma with some homework. Bella had some work to catch up on, so she finished changing into sweats and headed downstairs to the living room. The light rain had gotten heavier, and a check of the weather showed it wasn't stopping any time before dark. Bella gathered her laptop and work stuff and settled onto the couch with the Food Network on the TV.

It only took a moment or two for her to realize that concentrating on work was going to take some effort because her head was filled with a gorgeous blond with expressive blue eyes and legs that went on for days. She knew what Friday would be, where it would lead. They both did, she was sure of that. They would be alone, not in public, not making out in a parking lot—which seemed to be their thing and made Bella chuckle softly—it would be the two of them. Just the two of them. In a house. A house with, presumably, a bed. And instead of thinking about how they'd talked about speed, moving too fast, slowing things down and all that, Bella thought about Amy and Heather. The way they looked at each other now. How they'd felt something and taken a chance. Bella wanted to feel that courage. She wanted Easton to look at her the way Amy and Heather looked at each other.

Bella needed to tell her. It was time. It was beyond time. If she wanted this to go anywhere deeper, she needed to tell Easton that they'd gone to school together, that she knew exactly where Framerton was because her parents were still there. She needed to come clean about who she was before it was too late to do so. It was already late, she knew. She was dangerously close to it being weird. She'd have to explain to Easton why she'd lied. Well, she hadn't exactly lied. She just hadn't told the whole truth.

"Come on, Isabella," she said aloud as she shook her head at her own ridiculous rationalization. "A lie of omission is still a lie."

Lucy lifted her head from her bed in the corner and stared.

"Don't judge me, Luce." Bella pointed at her. As if trying to make her feel better, Ethel hopped up on the couch and laid her head on what would have been Bella's thigh but instead was the keyboard of her laptop. Bella grinned. "Thanks, Ethel," she said, resting her palm on Ethel's big head.

It would be quite some time before she was able to concentrate on work.

How in the world am I going to make it until Friday?

CHAPTER SIXTEEN

The waitress set the chicken salads down on the table and asked if there was anything else she could get them.

Shondra pointed to her glass. "I just decided iced tea isn't strong enough. I'm going to need some alcohol. Pinot Grigio, please." She looked at Easton, eyebrows raised in question.

Easton sighed. "Fine. But only one. I don't have the day off like some people at this table. I have to go back to work."

Shondra made a *psshhh* sound and waved a dismissive hand. "One glass won't kill you. Might make your hateful staff think you're fun." She winked, then stabbed her fork into some chicken.

"Hey, my staff is coming around," Easton countered, pointing her fork. "In fact, I am reasonably sure they no longer want to beat me to death in the ladies' room."

"I'd still check under the stalls every time."

They both laughed, but it was slightly forced, and the quiet settled over them as the waitress delivered their wine.

Shondra kept her eyes on her food as she said, "Just be careful, okay? That's all I'm asking."

"Why are you so worried?" Easton did her best to keep her tone light, airy, carefree. "It's not the 1950s. Or even the 80s. I'm a grown woman who wants to have sex with somebody she's wildly attracted to. Trust me, this body needs a good workout." She smiled widely, stayed playful. But Serious Shondra was a tough crowd.

"It's not your body I'm worried about, honey. It's that open, tender heart of yours."

Easton was touched. There was no way around that. She felt her best friend's love and it brought tears to her eyes. "I know," she said very softly. "I know."

"And I realize that I'm being a little ridiculous." Shondra made a show of lightening up, sitting straighter, eyes wider. "And such a downer. My God, what's my problem?" She laughed, a sharp bark of a sound. "You are absolutely right. You're a grown-ass woman who can do what she wants to do and who the hell am I to tell you any differently?"

The whiplash-inducing turnaround wasn't unexpected; it was what Shondra did when she was worried. Easton had seen it several times. Shondra expressed her concern, worried that she'd overstepped or was being too bossy, then completely changed her tune. Easton understood, knew her friend well, and she reached across the table to cover Shondra's hand, thereby getting her attention.

"Stop," Easton said calmly but with a gentle, open expression she hoped conveyed her own love. "I get it." She pulled her hand back and sipped her wine. "You saw me after Olivia, at my very lowest, with my heart in a million pieces."

"I don't want to see that again," Shondra whispered, with a shake of her head.

"I know."

"Not ever."

"I know."

"Okay."

And that was that. End of conversation. It always amused Easton that they handled things that way. One of them just needed her concerns to be clear to the other. Once that was the case, they moved on. It was something Easton loved about their friendship: the shorthand.

"That color is fabulous on you, by the way," Easton said as she gestured to Shondra's sunshine orange dress.

"Isn't it? I've been waiting for the weather to be warm enough."

The early-June day was beautiful, sunny and warm, a clear sign the summer was pretty much here. A square of sunlight fell across the white tablecloth and Easton laid one hand out flat in it, feeling the instant warmth on her skin.

"No class last night, huh?" Shondra asked, then finished off her wine.

Easton shook her head.

"So, you haven't seen her since…?"

"Last Wednesday."

"Over a week. Wow. You text?"

"A little bit, yeah." Easton was amused by how she and Bella went in spurts with their communication. "We can talk for quite a stretch and then we'll go for a while with nothing. It's…different."

Shondra lifted one shoulder. "Maybe she's doing the same thing you are. Stepping carefully. Staying in control. Maybe she's been hurt, too."

"Maybe." It was something Easton didn't know about Bella. In fact, she knew a lot less about Bella than Bella knew about her.

She'd have to remedy that on Friday.

❖

"Are you nervous?" Heather didn't look at Bella when she asked. Just kept sifting through the closet, stopping at a top, sliding the hanger along, giving a dress a second look, sliding the hanger along. She looked all springy today in her white slacks and printed top in blue and pink. Her blond hair was in a messy bun and Bella, as usual, envied her easy style.

"Yes and no." It was the truth and it surprised Bella as she sat on her bed and watched Heather that Thursday evening. She thought of herself as terrified, but that wasn't really the case if she took a hard look at the situation. "I mean, I'm nervous. Of course I am. The chances of us sleeping together are pretty high, and it only makes sense to be nervous when you've never been with somebody."

"I sense a 'but.'"

"But I'm completely comfortable with her. I don't really understand it. I just am. It was instant." She crossed her ankles and leaned back on her elbows. She inhaled and let it out very slowly before adding, "Plus, she's ridiculously hot."

Heather turned and shot her a grin. "That helps."

"Right?"

Arms full of hangers, Heather walked to the bed and set the clothes down. "Okay. I think we need to go kind of elegant but casual. Super sexy, but not too available. It's a fine line we're walking here."

"I love all this 'we' stuff," Bella said with a chuckle, as she sat up.

"We're a team, Bella," Heather said, feigning insult. "Do you want to get laid or not?"

Bella didn't think of being with Easton in such raw, derogatory terms, but she knew Heather didn't either, that she was playing with her. "Yes, please."

"All right then."

They spent the next forty-five minutes chatting and trying on outfits, mixing and matching tops, pants, dresses, jackets, shoes. Bella loved it. She loved clothes but didn't necessarily trust her own judgment when it came to putting things together. She was the person who bought the entire outfit right off the mannequin; it was the only way to be positive everything worked. She'd whined more than once about how she needed a stylist to help her match things up. Luckily, Heather was a master. Her style was effortless.

"Tell me about you and Amy." Bella watched Heather flush a pretty pink. "Is it going well?"

Heather held a shirt out in front of her with both hands, inspected it, then dropped her arms to her body. "Oh, Bells." She released a long breath that made Bella laugh.

"Wow. If that wasn't the dreamiest of sighs…"

Heather covered her eyes with a hand. "I know, right? I've become a giant mush ball."

"I hate to break it to you, sweetie, but of the three of us? You've always been the mush ball."

Their gazes held, and they shared a moment of joyful friendship without using any words. Bella finally spoke. "You look so happy. It's nice to see. I'm really glad." She lowered her voice and leaned forward slightly. "And if she ever pisses you off, you call me. I'll knock her around a little bit."

"If anyone can take her, it's you." Heather handed over a top. "Here. Put this on."

Bella took the pale green silk shirt off the hanger. "What happened to make you guys take a chance? I mean, you've known each other forever. Why now?"

Heather cocked her head and looked toward the ceiling as she thought. "You know, I don't know that I can pinpoint a moment. I texted her one night because I'd moved a picture in my house and ended up with a hole in my wall that was bigger than I'd expected. Amy's good with drywall and stuff, so I texted to see if she could help me. She came right over. You know how she is, how much she likes to get her butch on."

"I do," Bella said, with an affectionate smile. "She needs us to think she's tough."

"Exactly. Anyway, we got talking about our days and she'd had a date with that flight attendant the night before that didn't go well, I guess."

Bella nodded, familiar with the woman.

Heather took a pair of black pants off a hanger and handed them to Bella, mid-sentence. "I was trying to offer a little advice and she jokingly said, 'You know, I should just take you out on a date instead.' And we laughed about that for a few minutes, but then…somehow… we both stopped laughing and…it became a good idea and we decided to do it." She shrugged as if it was the most common thing in the world for two friends who've known each other for more than a decade to suddenly decide to go on a date, and the soft smile that bloomed on her face was simple, honest, and gorgeous. Contented and gorgeous. "And it was the best date I've ever had."

Bella stared at her for several beats before dropping her hands to her sides with a huff. "Well, hell. How am I supposed to top *that* story?"

Heather burst into what Bella recognized as some slightly embarrassed laughter. "What, you can't get cornier than that?"

"Hey." Bella grasped her arm as Heather went to turn back to the closet. When she had Heather's attention, she moved her hand up and laid her palm against Heather's cheek. "I didn't think that was corny at all. I thought it was beautiful. I envy you."

As they stood there, Heather's eyes welled up and she whispered, "I'm afraid it's too good to last."

Bella shook her head rapidly, kept her tone as playful as she could because she wasn't sure what to say if she had to be serious. "No. No, no. You're our optimist. You're the one who always sees the bright side of things. There's no being afraid allowed here. Not from you."

Heather looked down, her expression soft.

Bella grabbed her hand, waited until Heather raised her face. "I'm kidding, sweetie. I am so kidding. I get it." And she did. Though she wasn't into things as far as Amy and Heather were, she really wanted it to work out with Easton and she was terrified of jinxing it. She was already on thin ice by leaving out a very important piece of information, and this conversation with Heather only solidified her resolve to spill it to Easton at dinner the next night.

"Yeah?"

"Absolutely." Bella sat on the edge of the bed, still holding on to Heather's hand, and pulled her down to sit next to her. "Here's the thing: we have no guarantees in life." At Heather's grimace, she squeezed. "But you obviously want this to work, and it's crystal clear to me that you guys are good together. I mean, I haven't known for long, but Sunday? Once you told me, it was so obvious that you're into each other. That there's…more there than just fun." That was true. With all the cards on the table, it was as if the picture of Heather and Amy together had been slightly foggy and it suddenly came into sharp focus so Bella could see their faces, their eyes, the softness there, the fondness. And while she didn't want to get too mushy or overly positive with Heather, something inside Bella knew—just *knew*—that her friends were going to make it. It was a feeling that lifted her, warmed her heart, made her indescribably happy for them. And for herself because she'd get to watch it happen, watch them grow together. What an honor that was going to be. "And that there's a possible future."

"You can see that?"

"Who knows you guys better than me?"

Heather gave a slow nod as her eyebrows rose with realization. "That's true."

"I say do your best not to worry, not to try to see too far into the future. Just be here now, with Amy, and the rest will fall into place."

"That's good advice." She nodded some more, this time with a bit more confidence, as if thinking about it had her feeling stronger. She turned her gaze to Bella, her face a portrait of gratitude. "It's great advice. Thanks, Bells."

There was a beat before Bella broke the emotion with, "Excuse me, aren't *you* supposed to be giving *me* advice, though?"

Heather stood up from the bed, straightened her posture. "Why, yes. Yes, I am. And I have some. Are you ready?"

Bella shifted her position on the bed, made a show of bracing herself. "Ready. Hit me."

"Shave."

"Excuse me?"

"Look, I know it's been a long time since you've gotten down and dirty and that can make us become a little…lax in the grooming department. Shave it." She waved a finger up and down to encompass Bella's entire figure. "All of it."

Bella burst into laughter, and just like that, the mood was light again, happy and fun, all the serious talk tucked away until it needed to be brought out again and discussed.

"All right," Heather said, and she was back in Fashion Consultant Mode. "Let's find you something that's going to have the beautiful and sexy Miss Easton drooling all over herself."

CHAPTER SEVENTEEN

4:30. That's what the clock on the nightstand told Easton the time was.

4:30.

"Okay. Plenty of time." She'd been standing in front of her closet in her bra and underwear for a good fifteen minutes, doing nothing but staring. Accomplishing zero. Making no progress at all. Which was annoying.

She'd taken a half day at work. She wanted to make sure the house was clean, that she had everything she needed to make dinner—a simple chicken dish with baby new potatoes, mixed vegetables, and chocolate mousse for dessert—and that the sheets on the bed were fresh, thereby possibly jinxing herself, but it was a risk she was willing to take.

All of that was done. The predicted rain had graciously held off while she ran around town and only now started to tap gently on the windows. Easton could accept that, as she was in for the evening now, she hoped. The only thing left was to get dressed. She hadn't expected that to be the hardest task of all, but it was. She wanted stylish but comfortable. Pretty but touchable. Sexy but not slutty. Another five minutes went by before she literally shook herself into movement and plucked a pair of dark jeans off a hanger and stepped into them. She moved to the dresser, took out a silky black tank top with spaghetti straps, and put it on. In front of the full-length mirror, she studied her reflection. She was having a good hair day, thank God, her blond locks wavy, partially pulled back off her face and clipped in the back while the rest hung down around her shoulders. The jeans were snug and the tank was one that could be casual or dressed up with some added jewelry. She chose a simple hammered silver pendant her sister had given her for Christmas, then added silver hoops and the silver Pandora bracelet with the Mommy charm, a Mother's Day gift from Emma last year.

Another glance at the reflection was positive. She looked good, if she did say so herself. The idea of cute black sandals crossed her mind but she much preferred to go barefoot in the house, so she left the bedroom without them and headed downstairs to get dinner started.

Bella was due to arrive at 6:30.

The nerves kicked up a notch.

Easton stood at the bottom of the stairs for a moment and scanned her home. The first floor was open concept, so from her spot, she could see just about everything. The housekeeper came by on Wednesdays—not a coincidence Easton hired her to clean on the day Emma left for a stretch—and the dark hardwood floor gleamed in the sunlight. The chocolate brown sofa had been vacuumed and its many throw pillows arranged neatly at the corners. End tables and the coffee table were dust-free. The windows were so clean, the glass seemed nonexistent, though the rain was taking care of that. The kitchen sparkled—part of Easton was bummed she was about to mess that up—and she knew the downstairs powder room, her own master bath, and Emma's bathroom all shined and smelled a little bit like lemons and Lysol.

On the coffee table sat a squat candle in a glass jar. It had the warm, inviting scent of cinnamon and Easton loved it so much, she'd bought three of them. The other two were packed in a cabinet somewhere in the dining room. She lit the candle, then turned on her Bose speaker and selected a nice jazz mix from the music selection on her phone. Piano filled the air, the speaker on a shelf in a nice central location so the music could be heard in every room.

"Time to start dinner." Easton said it aloud, something she found herself doing often when Emma was at Connor's. While she enjoyed their arrangement and having time to do things for herself without having to worry about her daughter, Easton also missed her terribly, even missed the constant noise created by having a seven-year-old. When the house was quiet, Easton had taken to turning on music or the television, even if she wasn't watching, or talking to herself, like just now. She'd had no idea when Emma was born just how enormously her life and feelings would change. Oh, everybody warned her. "Everything will be different," they said. "You'll be stunned by how deeply you love your child," they said. "You have no idea how much your life is going to change," they said. Easton took all of it with a grain of salt—and lots of nods and smiles. She and Connor read dozens of books. They scoured the internet. Read blogs. Joined chat boards. Went to classes. They were ready, and they knew it.

Easton felt herself smile as she pulled the chicken from the refrigerator. Yeah, they'd had no idea. Zero. They were so arrogant in their assumptions of what it would be like. They weren't even close to being ready for what it meant to be parents. Physically. Emotionally. Financially. Not even close.

It didn't matter, though. From that day on, nothing mattered but Emma. She came first in everything. Easton's own needs took a back seat. So did Connor's, something he had not been prepared for. The sun rose and set around Emma. Still did, if Easton was being honest with herself. She just had a better handle on it now.

Expectant parents were presumptuous in (what they thought was) their knowledge of parenting.

New parents were wide-eyed and shocked.

Little cartoon drawings of herself and Connor in those two time periods often appeared in Easton's head. In the first one, the two of them are hanging out casually, feet up on the coffee table, chatting happily, thinking they've got it all figured out and they're ready. Once Emma was born, the cartoon versions of them just stand there, blinking, eyes huge, heads turning this way and that as if wondering which way to go, where to look, what to do now, how had they gotten here... She and Connor had done exactly that: they were obnoxiously sure of themselves, then flabbergasted at how intense it all was once Emma arrived. Connor's hair had gone from neat and fashion-forward to perpetual disarray, sticking straight up from his head, as he ran his fingers through it constantly while struggling with the right course of action when it came to his newborn daughter. And then he'd lost it within the course of two years, as if it couldn't take the pressure of fatherhood any longer and simply...left. They still joked about it. For Easton's part, she had lived in yoga pants and ratty T-shirts stained with spit-up, formula, baby food, or all three, makeup-less and utterly sleep-deprived, for the better part of a year, shuffling through the house like a zombie, rarely aware of which day of the week it was. They were laughably disheveled. Well…she could laugh *now*.

Ah, parenthood.

Easton grinned and allowed herself a moment to miss her baby terribly before she tucked that back down a bit so she could focus on the chicken, which she finished cleaning and seasoning and had ready to go into the oven. The rain had picked up, the gentle rapping on the windows changing to a steadier drumbeat. The sky had gone dark enough to make it feel later than it was. Easton was just drying her hands on a dish towel when her doorbell rang. Her brow furrowed as she glanced at the clock. 5:05. Only two possibilities: she and Bella had gotten their wires crossed about time or somebody wanted to sell her something she didn't want or need.

She geared up for a quick dismissal as she crossed the floor to the front door, but when she opened it, she blinked in surprise.

It *was* Bella.

But not the Bella she was used to. Not the Bella she was expecting. Not the calm, quietly sexy Bella she couldn't wait to talk to, feed, get her hands on. No, this Bella was a mess, standing on the front stoop in the rain, looking like a lost puppy. Her hair was wrecked, black streaks of mascara running down her flushed cheeks, her eyes red and puffy. She must have come right from work, as she wore nice pants and a sharp bright blue top that probably made up a smart outfit before it was drenched by rain. Easton let out a small gasp of surprised concern.

"Oh, my God, Bella." Easton reached out a hand to grasp Bella's arm. "What happened? Are you all right? Get in here." She had to tug a bit to get Bella moving. She seemed slightly dazed. Easton looked out into the rain, saw Bella's car in the driveway. "Did you drive like this? Are you okay?"

Bella stood still on the throw rug just inside the front door. Her beautiful hazel eyes seemed huge, and not in a good way. In a clichéd, deer-in-the-headlights kind of way. In an I-don't-know-where-I-am-or-what's-happening kind of way. In a somebody-please-hug-me-before-I-completely-fall-apart kind of way.

And Easton did.

There was no question. She reached out and wrapped her arms around Bella, pulled her in tightly and just held her. Bella was stiff for several seconds, but then her entire body relaxed and began to tremble. Easton held her. Waited. And when a small sob broke free and Bella's shoulders began to shake, Easton tightened her arms, pressed a kiss to her head, and felt her own eyes well up in sympathy and her heart squeeze in her chest as Bella cried in her arms.

A rumble of thunder rolled through the air and the pelting of rain against the window panes became even louder. Easton led Bella to the couch, sat her down.

"Don't move," she said quietly, then went into the kitchen for a glass of water and snagged the box of tissues from the powder room. When she returned, Bella hadn't shifted an inch, not even to sit back or get more comfortable. She didn't look any less dazed. Easton held out the box of tissues. When Bella didn't move, she pulled one from the box, set it down, then sat next to Bella. With gentle hands, she cupped Bella's chin and wiped away her tears, the smeared makeup.

Finally, Bella showed signs of life and reached for another tissue. She blew her nose, then sat back as if she'd finally let go of a huge breath. "I don't know how I missed it," she said quietly.

Easton sat back with her, close to her, so their thighs were touching. She braced her elbow on the back of the couch and toyed with Bella's hair as she watched her face carefully. "What did you miss, sweetie? Talk to me. Tell me what happened."

Bella reached for the water glass, took a couple of swallows, then sat back again. Whether conscious or not, Easton wasn't sure, but she scootched a bit closer to Easton, and Easton shifted so she was facing her. No lights had been turned on in the living room yet and the darkness from the storm made it feel like twilight. Bella inhaled very slowly, then held it for a moment before letting it out in a long exhale, as if she was gradually deflating.

"My client," she said quietly. "I told you about him. The one whose girlfriend left him. Remember that?"

Easton nodded, recalling the story. "You said it had devastated him, but he was making a lot of progress, finally."

"Right."

Easton felt a pit of dread form and settle in her stomach. "Tell me." She kept her hand in Bella's hair, hoping the contact would help, would give her strength.

"I thought he was doing great. I saw him yesterday. He was happier than usual. Almost upbeat. He had plans for the weekend. He was really doing well."

Easton swallowed and let Bella set the pace. Part of her didn't want to hear the rest of the story.

"I got a call about an hour ago. Jonas—" She turned pained eyes to Easton. "His name was Jonas. He found out his ex got engaged, and he decided the best way to handle that was to hang himself in his apartment."

"Oh, God, Bella."

"I don't know how I missed it." Bella's eyes filled with tears again.

"Baby, I'm so sorry." Easton pulled her closer and Bella let her.

"How did I miss it, Easton? How? He came to me for help. It's my job to see that kind of thing." Bella's voice was so strained, so filled with pain and confusion and self-loathing, Easton wanted nothing more than to wrap her up and keep her safe from the world.

"Maybe he didn't want you to see it," Easton offered quietly. "Or maybe it hit him all at once, so hard he just couldn't deal."

"Why didn't he call me?" Bella's voice was barely audible, less than a whisper, but so achingly sad, it broke Easton's heart a little bit to hear it. "I could have helped him. Why didn't he just call me?"

"I don't know." It was the only thing Easton could say. How did you comfort somebody in this situation? How could she possibly make this any better for Bella? She already knew the answer. The answer was that she couldn't. That there wasn't a way. That nothing would make it better for Bella. Time? Maybe. Her forgiving herself? Probably. But for right now? All Easton could do was hold her, so that's what she did.

They sat on the couch in silence, aside from Bella's occasional sniffles, for a long time. Easton lost track, but the sky continued to fade, going from a light gray to the color of iron to nearly black. It was the only way she could mark the passage of time. And yet, she held Bella and Bella let her, until Bella finally spoke.

"Do you have any wine in this place?" Her voice was hoarse, scratchy, and she cleared her throat.

"I do. Would you like some?"

"Please."

Part of Easton was reluctant to let go of Bella; it was as if she'd already gotten used to holding her and just wanted to continue to do that. Forever. But she forced herself up and into the kitchen. Once there, she took in the chicken breasts, still seasoned on the pan and ready to be cooked, and the small potatoes in the strainer in the sink, waiting to be quartered. "Are you hungry?" she called. "I could fix you something." She poured two glasses of the Sangiovese she'd picked out that afternoon and carried them into the living room.

Bella hadn't moved. "I'm sorry. I don't have much of an appetite right now." Her expression was sheepish as Easton handed her a glass.

"No worries. You let me know if you change your mind, okay?" She sat back down on the couch and Bella leaned against her.

"Thank you," she said quietly.

"For what?"

"For being here. For not being freaked out. For just...holding me." Again, her voice was quiet, gravelly.

"Confession time: I didn't know what else to do." Easton grimaced at her and actually saw the tiny ghost of a smile cross Bella face.

"It was perfect. Exactly what I needed." She looked up at Easton then, her hazel eyes filled with so much emotion, Easton couldn't identify it all. "I may need that again," she whispered.

"I'm right here."

They sipped their wine and sat in surprisingly companionable silence for a long while. Easton didn't feel awkward. She didn't feel at a loss for words or desperate for conversation. She felt...warm. Content. Like she was exactly where she was supposed to be in that moment. When Bella shifted a bit, Easton turned to look at her, and Bella's face had changed...her eyes were clearer, brighter than they'd been all evening. She seemed open, wanting, certain as she sat up straighter, took their wineglasses, and set them on the coffee table. Several moments passed as she simply sat and regarded Easton with something that looked very close to...desire.

"Easton," Bella whispered, then reached up a hand and stroked Easton's face. Softly. Tenderly. Ran her thumb across Easton's bottom lip.

Easton swallowed, as her heart rate picked up. She looked at Bella, studied her face, knew her gaze dropped to Bella's mouth, tried to pull it away. Failed.

Bella's fingers slipped around to the back of Easton's head and pulled her in close, stopped with her mouth scant millimeters from

Easton's. The eye contact in that moment…Easton didn't know how to describe it. Intense was the best word, the only word she could come up with, but it wasn't enough. It was more than intense, like Bella was looking directly into her soul.

"Easton," she whispered again before pressing their lips together. Gently at first. Short little kisses, one, then another, then another, their mouths soft, warm, wet.

It felt amazing. Easton had known the very first time they'd kissed that they were brilliant at it. But now? There was a slight trepidation, and Easton battled it even as Bella's kisses became firmer. Longer.

"Bella, wait," she said quietly and touched her fingers to Bella's chin. When those hazel eyes were focused on her, Easton asked gently, "Are you sure about this?"

Bella's nod came without hesitation. "Please, Easton. I need to feel…" She swallowed what Easton guessed was a ball of emotion, but her eyes pleaded. "Life. I need to feel *life.*"

It made sense. It absolutely did, and Easton felt it. In response, she pulled Bella in and then they were kissing again and this time, Easton didn't stop it. As if Bella could read her thoughts, read that it was okay, she increased the pressure, the sensation, deepened the kiss until it was open-mouthed and hotter than any kiss Easton had experienced in her life. Ever. Bella pushed her tongue into Easton's mouth at the same time she pushed Easton onto her back on the couch, and Easton had no control over the guttural moan that escaped her. The feel of this? Bella's weight on her, Bella's hand in her hair, Bella's mouth doing amazing things to hers? There were no words. The pleasure was immeasurable. Easton's entire body was on fire and despite the circumstances that had put them here, she reveled in it.

She tried to focus on the different sensations that were assaulting her body in the most wonderful of ways. Bella's kissing never stopped, but Easton could feel her hands. Her fingers that slipped up under the tank, scraping erotically across the skin of her stomach, up, up to cup a breast through the fabric of Easton's bra. A gentle squeeze, and then a stroking that zeroed in on Easton's nipple with alarming precision, even through the fabric. Easton swore she could feel her skin tightening under the attention, and when she shifted so her legs parted and Bella settled between them, pushed against her center, Easton felt that, too. Good Lord, did she feel it.

Bella moved her mouth from Easton's and used her tongue to trail along the side of Easton's neck, down to the spot where her neck and shoulder met, spending a little time there before pushing Easton's shirt up over her breasts. Bella looked up then, caught Easton's eye, and again, the intensity of her gaze was almost too much for Easton. She made a sound that could only be described as a growl when Bella freed her breasts and took one into her mouth, sucking hungrily. Easton dropped her head back against the pillows and dug her fingers into Bella's hair. She might have muttered, "Oh, my God," several times, but she couldn't be sure because that was when the sensations blurred. Combined. Melded. From that point on, Easton couldn't pick out any one thing, couldn't pinpoint which parts of Bella were touching which parts of her. Before she even realized it, she was topless on her own couch and Bella was tugging at the ankles of her jeans, sliding them off and tossing them to the floor with a flourish, her underwear not far behind. Bella fell forward and caught herself with one hand, her face close to Easton's as she slipped the fingers of her other hand through the slick wetness she'd caused between Easton's legs.

Easton gasped at the same time Bella moaned with pleasure, her hazel eyes drifting closed as she whispered, "My God, I've dreamed of doing this for so long..." And then fingers pushed into her and everything went white for Easton, hazy. Sensations built quickly as Bella picked up a rhythm, dropped her mouth onto Easton's and kissed her so deeply, Easton couldn't tell which way was up. All she could do was feel. And in that moment, she did something she'd never done before. Not with Connor. Not even with Olivia.

Easton let go.

It wasn't conscious, and she'd analyze it later, but in that moment, she turned herself over to Bella fully. Trusted her with her body, with her soul, with her heart. And the second she did that, her orgasm came screaming out of nowhere to rip through her like a hurricane, tearing sounds from her she'd never made before, arching her body as tightly as a bowstring, the pulsing contractions the only thing in the world she could feel as she wrapped both arms around Bella's upper body and held on for dear life.

Easton had no idea how long it lasted. Could've been a few seconds. Could've been a few days. All she knew was that when she finally opened her eyes, everything seemed sharper, more focused.

Bella's weight was still on her, and when she tried to shift, Easton tightened her grip, wouldn't let her move, felt her gentle chuckle. Her center throbbed still, her breathing a bit ragged, her throat dry. Bella's head was on her chest, her fingers still tucked warmly inside Easton's body, and it shocked her to realize that she was pretty sure she could stay just like that for the rest of her days and be perfectly happy. Which was totally and romantically dreamy and unrealistic, but still...

They stayed that way for a long while, Easton toying with Bella's hair, until finally Bella mumbled, "I can't feel my arm."

Easton grinned and opened her arms. "Fine. Fly. Be free."

Bella pushed herself up but stopped halfway and just looked at Easton. It was the first time in Easton's life that she finally understood what it meant to *feel* somebody's eyes on you. It was as if Bella was touching her all over again—without actually touching her at all.

Easton sat up, reached for Bella as she whispered, "Come here," and kissed her. Bella kissed her back but gently turned her head away slightly.

"It's okay," she said, as Easton furrowed her brow. "Really. Can you just hold me?" Her voice was so small, so uncertain, that Easton felt herself melt a little bit.

"Of course I can." She opened her arms and Bella crawled into them, tucked her head under Easton's chin with a sigh of what seemed to be contentment.

"I'm sorry," she said against Easton's still-bare chest. "I just..." Her voice trailed off and she looked up, her hazel eyes clear and bright. "I'm not...it's not that I don't want you to touch me. Believe me, I do. Just..."

"Not right now," Easton finished, surprised to realize that she completely understood. "I get it. It's absolutely okay. Just know that..." She lowered her voice as she pressed her lips to Bella's hair. "I *will* be touching you. Very soon." She could feel Bella smile against her skin.

"I'm counting on it." They were quiet for a beat or two. "I needed to feel you. I needed to feel your warm skin and your heartbeat and..."

"My orgasm?" Easton supplied when Bella faltered.

"Yes." Bella's shoulders moved with quiet laughter. "That, too. That most of all." Then she added, "I needed to feel alive, and touching you really helped me with that."

"Glad to be of service," Easton said, doing her best to keep things as light as she could, given the circumstances. They certainly weren't the ones she'd expected would surround them their first time together. She felt Bella give her a little squeeze, but they remained quiet and the silence fell over them like a soft blanket. It wasn't long before Bella's body jerked slightly, and Easton knew she'd fallen asleep.

The room lit up then as a flash of lightning crackled through the sky. Easton hadn't turned on any lights, so there was only the lightning and the soft glow of the cinnamon candle to see by. Easton was getting goose bumps on various parts of her still-naked body, so she slowly reached for the fleece blanket folded on the back of the couch, not wanting to wake Bella, and covered them both with it.

Easton was comfortable.

No. She was much more than that. She was…content. Relaxed.

Happy.

Easton was happy.

It was a new feeling. A very new feeling. And she wanted to hold on to it for as long as she could.

Lightning cut through the room once more, this time followed by an ominous rumble of thunder and the pattering of rain on the windows continued steadily.

The question was, how long would that be?

CHAPTER EIGHTEEN

It was nearly 11:00 when Bella slid her key into the lock on her side door. The rain had eased up slightly, now not much more than a drizzle. The thunder and lightning had moved east, the rumbles still audible, though much quieter and less threatening.

Ethel was standing in the doorway to the kitchen, her tail wagging back and forth, always so happy to see Bella. Seriously, was there anything better than coming home to a creature who was utterly thrilled by the mere sight of you? She rubbed Ethel's ears between her fingers and kissed her on her big, square head. "Hi, baby. Sorry I'm so late." Lucy came wandering over then, moseying slowly, as if making it clear that Bella's presence really didn't affect her one way or the other. She was the queen of indifference, but Bella gave her the same treatment: an ear rub and a kiss on the head. She led them to the back door and let them out.

They were going to be her excuse to not stay overnight at Easton's. It would've been easy to get Amy or Heather to stay at her place and dog-sit, but she wasn't ready for that and she knew it. Sex with somebody new was one thing. Sleeping wrapped up in each other and waking up together the next morning was quite another. No matter how appealing the idea was...

A small scoff pushed from her lips as she admitted she'd pretty much done it anyway, falling asleep in Easton's arms the way she had. That had been unplanned, but so had Jonas's suicide.

The lump that formed in her throat was instant and her eyes welled up as Lucy sauntered to the door and waited to be let in. Bella focused on wiping her feet, drying her large back with the towel. God, how had she missed it? How had she not seen any of the signs? They must have been there, right? She'd always thought of herself as very good at her job, but this…this gave her major pause. Had her wondering. Second-guessing. Replaying every conversation she'd had with him in the past couple of months. What had she missed? What was there to be seen that she hadn't?

Bella blew out a breath, a breath born of frustration and confusion and sadness. She would call her supervisor tomorrow, talk it through with her. She needed to. For her own sanity.

Easton had been…amazing. Every second with her. Every minute. She'd been there. She'd given Bella exactly what she'd needed in the moment, without question, without reservation. That meant something. It meant something huge. Bella was torn between thinking about it and pushing it out of her head. But she was tired, and her coping skills were in the toilet, so she didn't have anything left to push with.

As if trying to help with the reminiscing, her brain replayed the image of Easton's naked body beneath her. The unreal softness of her skin…all that gorgeous, creamy skin. Yeah, Bella wanted more of that. Her mouth…for a woman who'd admittedly only been with two people, Easton excelled at kissing. *My God.* Bella swallowed hard, thinking about Easton's lips, her tongue, how she gave back everything Bella put out there. Her breasts. *Oh, my God, how many times did I fantasize about them?* Bella recalled the handful of times she'd been in the locker room at Framerton High at the same time as Easton. How stealthy she'd been about sneaking peeks at Easton undressed, always terrified of getting caught. She was happy to report that Easton's breasts certainly lived up to the hype Bella'd showered them with. They were smallish but full, and fit perfectly in Bella's hands. They were responsive, which was such a turn-on. The second Bella had closed her mouth over a nipple, Easton had sucked in her breath and pushed her hips up into Bella's.

Bella swallowed again, her arousal surging through her at the simple memory of Easton, and she had to shake her head free of the images, open and close her fists as she did her best to regain control of her own body, because the memory of Easton coming for her? Nothing compared. Not a thing in the world.

No woman had ever had such an effect on her. Not like this. Her phone pinged in her back pocket. A text from Easton. *You make it home okay?*

Bella smiled tenderly at the idea that somebody was worried about her. *I did,* she typed back. *Thank you for tonight. For all of it.* It seemed lame, but she had no other way to word it.

It was MY pleasure. Believe me. A winking emoji followed, making Bella's smile grow.

Not just yours. I promise you.

Easton sent back a blushing emoji and the conversation ended there, which Bella was grateful for. She wanted to see Easton again. Absolutely and without a doubt. But she needed to deal with her grief and confusion over Jonas first and Easton seemed to get that. Yet another reason to keep her around.

Ethel finally decided she'd had enough of running around in the rain and stood at the door, her huge face smiling at Bella, and not for the first time, Bella wondered what she'd ever done before she had dogs. How had she survived?

She let Ethel in and dried her off, wiped her feet. Ethel normally hated this, did her best dodging and weaving to avoid the horrible and dreaded towel. But not tonight. Tonight, she seemed to sense Bella's emotions, her grief, and she stood still so Bella could do what she needed to do. Bella finished up, scrubbing the towel gently over the top of Ethel's head. "You're a good girl," she said quietly, and when she looked into the big brown eyes of her dog, she could swear she saw a glimpse of something…human. The tears crawled up from her throat to pool in her eyes, and she wrapped her arms around Ethel's barrel-chested body, hugging her as she cried quietly.

Ethel let her.

The house always felt a little bit…weird when Emma was gone to Connor's, so Saturday afternoon brought back a sense of normality for Easton. Connor had given her a couple of boxes from their attic that she'd apparently left behind when she'd moved, and they were now stacked in the corner of the living room. Emma had her My Little Pony stuff spread all over the floor—it looked like slow-moving lava that was gradually taking over the room—and she was playing and talking quietly with her friend Darcy from school. They were using the boxes as cliffs for the ponies to climb. Easton had to admire the imagination.

Normally, Easton didn't like Emma to have a play date as soon as she got home from her dad's. She wanted mommy-daughter time so they could chat, talk about what she'd done at Daddy's, go over school from the end of the week. It was time that Easton looked forward to, even if Emma was too young to get that yet.

Today was different, though. Today Easton needed some time. She hadn't allowed it this morning. She didn't feel ready somehow, strangely, to give herself a chance to think about last night. Bella had not been in good shape when she'd arrived, and today Easton wondered if having sex on the couch was the smartest thing for them to do, especially since it was their very first time together. Yes, Bella seemed to need it. Her explanation made perfect sense. But it certainly wasn't the way Easton predicted it would go.

Maybe that's what was bothering her this morning.

Which wasn't to say it wasn't good. Because it was. It was beyond good. It had been spectacular. Best sex Easton had ever had, circumstances aside. But she wanted to give back, to return the favor, to reciprocate, and Bella just hadn't been in a place to allow that.

She'd sent Bella a text in the morning, saying hello, asking if she was doing okay. Bella's response had been personal enough but short, and Easton had to remind herself that Bella was dealing with some major emotions right now, that they were probably worse today now that things had had a chance to sink in and solidify. Easton wanted to text again. Several times. But she'd stopped herself each time, not wanting to be that girl, the girl that is constantly poking at you with her never-ending need for attention. Olivia had made her feel like that girl, and Easton had vowed never to fall into that pattern of desperation again.

At the kitchen table with her laptop open and every intention of getting some work done, Easton sat still instead, elbow on the table, chin in her hand, staring off into space. Replaying bits and pieces from last night. Replaying certain ones even more.

"Hey!" Darcy's voice came from the living room. Then both girls dissolved into little-girl giggles and Easton smiled at the sound, forcing herself back to the present. With a sigh, she put her fingers on her keyboard. Her eyes, however, she shifted toward her very quiet phone.

She hoped Bella was doing okay.

❖

"What did Anne say?" Heather asked as she sat next to Bella on her couch. It was Sunday brunch, but not really. Amy and Heather had texted numerous times on Saturday to get the scoop on how things went at Easton's house but instead had been met with utter silence for far longer than they were okay with. By the time Bella had finally texted back and told them about Jonas, it was Saturday night and she was beyond exhausted. They wanted to come right over. She told them no, to come in the morning.

Neither of her friends were happy about it, but they did as she asked.

Sunday morning at 8:00, there was no knocking. No preamble. Amy used her key and they found Bella sitting on her couch, cup of coffee in hand, gazing off at...nothing. She was dressed but didn't look at all fresh, and Heather guessed correctly that Bella hadn't gone to bed. The dogs were both lying down in the same room, Lucy at Bella's feet, Ethel next to her. They hadn't left her side all night.

The two friends had whipped into action, and despite her sadness and fatigue, Bella couldn't help but smile as they moved efficiently around her house. Amy had switched out Bella's coffee for some "more relaxing" tea, then let the dogs out and back in. Heather had scrambled her some eggs and added a slice of toast. The plate now sat in her lap, hardly touched.

"Eat," Amy ordered, poking at the plate. "Come on."

Bella sighed, then dutifully took a bite. Surprised by how good they were—and how instantly her hunger blossomed—she took another.

"Anne," Heather reminded her. "What did she say?"

Anne Haggerty was Bella's boss at the wellness center and often acted as therapist to the therapists. Bella had known her for years and respected her greatly.

She finished chewing, swallowed, and cleared her throat, recalling Anne's words yesterday. "She said she went through my notes, remembered everything I'd said about Jonas, and that I'd done everything right. That I didn't miss anything. That he just couldn't handle the news and fell down a rabbit hole before anybody could get to him."

"See?" Amy said. "Not your fault. Told you."

And she had. Several times. Because Bella wanted—no, she *needed*—somebody to blame. Somebody to take responsibility for the sudden disappearance of a good, kindhearted man whose only mistake was to love the wrong woman too much. The logical place to lay that blame was right at her own feet. After all, Jonas was seeing her for help. Her job was, quite literally, to help him. To guide him, to assist him in seeing his own worth.

She'd failed him.

Heather's warm hand was suddenly on her back, rubbing in comforting circles. As if she could read Bella's mind, she said, very quietly, "It wasn't your fault, Isabella."

For the first time since Friday, Bella heard the words and didn't instantly tear up. Because, logically, she knew them to be true. Emotionally, it was a different story. She gave a quick nod and forked more eggs into her mouth as Ethel lifted her head to watch.

The three of them sat silently for several moments, one or all of them sipping or eating at any given moment. Bella finished her eggs, every speck of them, then set her plate in front of her on the coffee table.

"So," Amy ventured. "This happened on Friday?"

"Thursday night," Bella corrected her. "But I didn't find out until Friday afternoon."

"You didn't go to Easton's then, huh?"

Bella turned her gaze toward Amy. "Oh, no, I went." She caught her bottom lip in her teeth and nibbled, knowing it was an obvious sign of nervousness and her friends knew it well.

"You did?" Heather couldn't hide her surprise.

"Actually, I went there right away. Not long after I heard."

Heather squinted at her as Amy said, "Wait. So, you did have your date with her?"

Bella cleared her throat, picked up the paper napkin from her plate, and fiddled with it. "I mean, we didn't have a *date*, really…" Her voice trailed off. When she finally braved a glance up at Amy, she was arching an eyebrow.

"Bells. Spill. Now."

"I slept with her." Mentally, Bella ducked, expecting instant fallout. Which she got.

"You what?" Amy's tone was incredulous. "After the news you got? You had sex with her?"

Heather seemed to maybe have a better understanding of it. Or at least some. When Bella leaned forward and covered her face with her hands, she felt Heather reach behind her back, probably to calm Amy. "Easy. Just relax for a second. Bella." Heather waited until Bella sat back up. "Tell us what happened."

Amy wasn't looking at her, but Bella swallowed hard and told her story. "I was a mess. I was in…a bad place. A really bad place. And it was the strangest thing, but all I wanted to do was talk to Easton. I know that seems weird because we haven't known each other that long—"

"Only fifteen years," Amy muttered, but Heather shot her a look and she apologized. "Sorry. Go on."

"I knocked on her door. I was way early for our date. She let me in, knew something was wrong immediately. And she just wrapped me in her arms and held me, no questions asked, and I just bawled. I cried so hard and she just held me." Bella recalled now how she'd felt in Easton's arms. How comforted. How safe. "She led me to the couch, got me some water. I asked for wine."

Heather smiled at that.

"And I told her what had happened. What Jonas did. How I felt. All my worries and concerns and confusion. And she listened and touched me somehow the whole time, her hand on my leg or in my hair or on my shoulder. At one point, I looked up at her and she was just so beautiful, so open, and I was"—she looked around the room, as if the word she was looking for was hiding on the ceiling or behind some furniture—"*seized* is the only word I can think of to describe how I felt then. I was seized with this urge, this *need*, to feel her. Her body. Her heartbeat. Her life. I know that sounds crazy, but I couldn't help it. I needed to feel that she was alive. That *I* was alive. I had to touch her. Like that."

When Bella finally dared a glimpse at her friends, she knew they understood. Heather nodded, and Amy looked grudgingly okay with it. They were all in the same field and they all knew that a sudden death could often make a person crave life. Whether it was to do something crazy like skydive or bungee jump or something closer to home, like have sex with a woman you'd only dated once or twice, it wasn't an uncommon reaction.

"So?" Amy asked. "Was it good?"

Heather shot her a look and she shrugged.

"What? It's a legit question."

Bella allowed a small smile to appear. "It was. It was much more than good. She's…" She inhaled, then let it out very slowly as she remembered what it was like to peel the clothes off Easton's body, to have her warmth beneath her. She recalled the perfection of her breasts, how Easton had reacted to her touch. She'd never forget the feeling of sliding her fingers inside, into the warm, wet heat, and if she closed her eyes, she could still hear the gentle, breathy sounds Easton made when she had an orgasm, the whimpered cry. "She was everything I hoped she'd be. I don't remember ever touching anybody and feeling like that."

"Wow," Heather said, eyes slightly widened. "This is a big deal, Bells."

"And when she returned the favor?" Amy asked. "Just as good?"

"Actually, I didn't let her." Bella wrinkled her nose. "That wasn't what I needed. I needed to touch *her*, to feel *her*."

"She was okay with that?" Heather's voice held a hint of skepticism.

Bella relaxed, felt her face slacken in contentedness as she remembered Easton's words, the softness in her eyes when she opened her arms and took Bella into them. "She was. She completely understood. I asked her if she could just hold me and she did. No questions asked. It was exactly what I needed."

The three of them sat quietly for a moment. When Heather spoke, her voice was soft, as if she didn't want to ruin the silence. "Are you okay, Bella?"

Bella took a beat or two to think about it before she gave a subtle nod. "Yeah. I will be." She sat back on the couch so she could see both Heather and Amy without having to swivel her head back and forth. Her voice was low, factual. "I wish there'd been signs, because I'd have seen them. I wish he hadn't felt so awful and alone. I wish he'd called me. I wish a lot of things. But wishing isn't going to change any of it."

"I keep saying this, but you do know it wasn't your fault, right?" Amy's expression was sympathetic and serious as she laid her hand on Bella's thigh.

With a sigh, Bella agreed. "I do. In my head, I do." She looked at Heather, at her sweet face and kind eyes. "I think it's going to take my heart a while to get there."

"It will, for sure," Heather agreed. "So, for today, since it's raining and it's Sunday and we're your best friends, we have a girls' day, and we watch movies. Sound good?"

Thank God for these two. Bella could think of nothing else in the moment but how lucky she was to have these friends of hers. As she glanced down at her dogs, who hadn't left her alone in a room since yesterday, she added them to her list of things to be immensely thankful for. "Sounds perfect."

Which was almost true.

There was one more person she'd love to add to the mix, and then it would be.

The next time, definitely.

CHAPTER NINETEEN

"Emma Elizabeth, I am not going to say it again!" Easton could feel her blood pressure increasing each time she asked Emma to pick up the boots, raincoat, and school bag she'd unceremoniously dropped on the floor near the side door before running off into the living room. In an enormous, and inexplicable, hurry to resume whatever adventure her My Little Ponies were on, she couldn't be bothered to listen to her mother. Just like any typical seven-year-old.

Standing in the kitchen, dish towel in hand, Easton forced herself to count to ten. Then she picked up a wet dish, dried it, and put it away. Shondra laughed at her when she pulled out her dish soap and towels. *"Girl, you've got a state of the art dishwasher, right there under the counter. What are you doing, washing and drying those by hand?"* Easton could hear her humorous disbelief, smiling as she picked up another dish. Truth was, washing and drying dishes helped her to relax, to calm herself. Maybe it was the mindlessness of it. Maybe it was the repetition. Easton wasn't sure. All she knew was that after she finished, she was much less tense and entertained far fewer fantasies of shipping her daughter off to boarding school.

It had been raining since Friday night, on and off. It was now Tuesday, and while the rain had eased up, it was still wet and muddy and gross outside. As evidenced by the raincoat and boots that still sat in a pile near the door. Emma was on a roll lately. Still. The teacher who ran the after-school program had asked to speak to Easton today. Again. Apparently, Emma was being mouthy to the teachers and snarky to her fellow program attendees. When Easton sighed in dismayed frustration, the teacher had gently asked if maybe it had to do with the divorce and said lots of kids acted out around a big change like that.

"But it's been almost two years," Easton had told her, mystified.

The teacher, a heavyset blond of about thirty, had tipped her head to one side, then the other and said simply and gently, "Sometimes it takes a while for this type of thing to appear. Sometimes it's been bottled up for some time and finally needs a release." She suggested maybe some counseling might help Emma cope with her frustrations better.

Easton wondered if Bella could help with ideas around that.

She blew out a breath as she folded and hung the towel on the handle of the oven. She wanted to see Bella. Badly. But she was super cognizant of pushing. Bella had gone through something awful. She needed time to deal with it. Easton knew that.

But they'd had sex.

Right there, her brain reminded her as she looked toward the living room and saw the couch. And then her stomach fluttered as her body remembered. Bella's mouth on hers. Bella's hands on her. Inside her. The sensations that shot through her body, somehow both familiar and unfamiliar at the same time. Her explosive climax. God, it had been explosive. Sex with Olivia had been good, really good, but Easton had never come that hard with her. Not once. There was something… perfect…about being with Bella, even that very first time.

And then there was the way they'd fit so perfectly together as they'd cuddled. The sorrow Easton had felt as Bella cried in her arms was new as well. Olivia wasn't a terribly emotional person, so she'd never really fallen apart around Easton, never made Easton feel needed. And Connor was a guy. So, aside from Emma, Easton had never been somebody's soft place to land.

It felt nice to be Bella's.

Yeah, Easton needed to see her again. Soon.

She picked up her phone from the kitchen table, typed out a quick text. *How are you? Doing okay?*

They'd texted a bit since Friday night. Not a lot on Saturday, as Bella told her she was seeing her boss—who served as her own therapist when needed—to talk about her client's suicide. She'd gone quiet after that, and Easton had been worried, but hadn't pressed. She sent a good-night text and went to bed. She didn't hear from Bella again until Sunday afternoon. She said she was with her BFFs and they were helping her.

She'd left it alone and was proud of herself for that. Monday had been services for Bella's client, so Easton had sent a text or two but largely gave Bella her privacy. That course of action paid off, because this morning, she'd gotten a text from Bella saying good morning and that she was doing better.

Thank you for Friday night. You took care of me and I really appreciated that. She followed it with an emoji that was blowing a kiss.

"I think *you* took care of *me*," Easton had mumbled with a grin as she texted back, *I'm glad I could be there for you.* It was the truth.

Your texts have been wonderful. I'm sorry I've been less than responsive. Rough couple of days.

Easton grimaced. *No explanation needed.* She thought about it for a grand total of three seconds before adding, *Can I see you tomorrow? Coffee after class?*

A beat went by before Bella's response came. *I was thinking maybe a little making out, but I can do coffee instead. Sure.* A winking emoji came next and Easton chuckled.

I like your idea better.

Me too.

The weird sense of relief that washed over Easton surprised her. It occurred to her in that moment that maybe she'd been a little bit worried that Bella regretted what they'd done on Friday, but she hadn't actually given it any attention. Interesting. Well, at least it seemed now like she didn't have to worry. A glance at the side door made her wrinkle her nose.

I have dealings with a 7-year-old, she typed. *Talk later.* She added an eye-rolling emoji, tucked her phone into her pocket, and—Irritated Mom Face firmly in place—marched into the living room.

Emma wasn't playing with her My Little Ponies. Instead, she was sitting cross-legged on the floor in the corner, one of the boxes Connor had sent home with Easton opened up, several of Easton's past belongings spread out in front of her.

Emma looked up at her. "What's this stuff, Mama?" she asked with innocent curiosity. It was interesting in that moment: Easton saw much of Connor in Emma but didn't often see herself. She supposed that was normal, made sense, but right then, the sight of Emma's big, inquisitive blue eyes was like looking in the mirror. Easton felt pride well up within her.

Easton squatted down and sat, making herself comfortable next to her daughter. "Well, let's see." She rummaged through the box. "Looks like this is stuff from my bedroom when I lived with Grandma and Grandpa."

"When you were little like me?"

Easton pulled out a couple of yearbooks, a ratty old teddy bear, two cheerleading trophies. "I was a bit bigger than you. In high school."

"Who's this?" Emma asked with a giggle, picking up the bear. He was threadbare in some places, his brown fur completely rubbed away. One of his plastic eyes hung a bit loose, and his red bow was droopy. But Easton remembered him fondly, couldn't count the number of times she'd gone to bed with him wrapped in her arms. He'd even made the trip to college with her.

"That's Gus. He got me through lots of sad times."

Emma's smile slid off her face. "You were sad?"

"Oh, sure," Easton said. "When I had to go to bed and didn't want to. When Grandpa said I had to take a bath. When Grandma told me to eat my broccoli." She said the last line as if narrating a horror movie and added some tickles to it.

Emma giggled. "Ew! Broccoli!" When the tickle party ended, she asked, "Can Gus sleep with me tonight?"

"I think he'd like that."

"Well, my bed is definitely better than a stinky old box."

"You are very logical, my child."

"What are these?" Emma grabbed one of the yearbooks strewn across the floor. Three of them. Easton looked at the years and wondered why the one from her freshman year was missing, couldn't remember if she'd even bought one.

"That's called a yearbook. You get them when you're in high school and they are full of pictures of you and your friends."

Emma started in the middle, turned the pages slowly on the book from Easton's senior year. When she got to the sports section, Easton pointed to a photo of the football team.

"Do you know who that is?"

Emma squinted, held the book closer. "Is that…is that Daddy?"

"It is."

"Wow. He looks so different!"

"He's eighteen in that shot."

"And he has hair!" Emma said it with such wonder that it made Easton laugh.

"He does."

"Was he good? At football?" Emma looked up at her with those eyes again, but this time, she saw Connor in the expectant expression.

"He was very good." Easton moved her finger to the cheerleading squad, posing in a pyramid. "See anybody here you might know?"

Emma repeated the same moves. She squinted, held the book closer to her nose, then dropped her finger on the blond girl hanging off the right side. "You?"

Easton nodded with a smile. "Me."

"You were really pretty." Emma smoothed her hand over the photo.

"Thank you, baby." Easton kissed the top of her head.

"Are there more pictures of you and Daddy?"

"I'm sure there are."

They spent the next fifteen or twenty minutes flipping pages, Easton pointing to different pictures from different clubs. She found her younger sister in the freshman photos and Emma laughed hysterically at her aunt's half-shaved head. There was a shot of Connor and Easton with their arms around each other, looking off at something Easton couldn't remember now. It was labeled Cutest Couple. Easton smiled, feeling equal parts nostalgic and sad. They came to the senior pictures.

"Are you and Daddy here?"

With a nod, Easton said, "They're in alphabetical order. See if you can find us."

Emma's face went serious, her little brow furrowed as she searched, whispering, "D. D. D," under her breath. Then, "There! Connor Eugene Douglas." She looked up at Easton with wide eyes. "Daddy's middle name is *Eugene*?"

Easton laughed at the shocked horror on her daughter's face. "It was Daddy's grandpa's name."

"Still." They flipped more pages until they got to the Es, and again, Emma slapped her finger down on Easton's senior picture. "Mama!"

God, was I ever that young? Easton looked at the photo and, for the first time, could see the faraway look, the hint of sadness in the blue eyes. Most people wouldn't notice it. For all intents and purposes, Easton was a happy, lucky young woman. She was popular, her family was well-known and had money, she was the head cheerleader dating the quarterback. Basically, in her senior year, Easton Evans was a walking stereotype of the All-American Girl. Nobody knew what she'd been dreaming of back then, who she'd been dreaming of, or how solidly she'd tamp those dreams down, lock them away for the next twelve years, until they exploded out on their own, taking her tidy little life with them. Looking at the photo now, Easton was sad for that girl.

Emma turned the page, looking for "more weird hair." Easton grinned and scanned the book, and all of a sudden, there she was. Kristin Harrington. Object of her very first sex dreams and the beginning of a very long journey for Easton. She tipped her head to one side, noting now that Kristin was actually kind of plain. Pretty but not stunning. Wholesome, with kind eyes and a gentle smile. Easton was filled with a fondness for this girl who had no idea—then or now—how much she'd been thought about. She gave herself a mental shake as Emma started to turn the page when another picture caught her eye and she put her hand on Emma's, stopping her.

What the...?

Easton squinted at the photo. It wasn't one of the nicer senior photos. There were no trees or lush green grass in the background. It was obviously an inexpensive shot, like a portrait you'd get done at Sears or Target. The girl was sort of huddled, her shoulders up slightly as if consistently bracing for a blow. She looked to be wearing a simple cotton top, not terribly dressy. Her dark hair was kind of limp, and if Easton thought her own eyes looked sad in her photo, she had nothing on this girl. Her eyes were filled with so much. Sorrow. Despair. Helplessness. Confusion. It was so weird to be able to see all of that from one photo, but it was the eyes that had snagged her attention. They were eyes Easton knew well. Uniquely hazel. Easton's heart began to pound as she brought a hand to her mouth and muttered, "Oh, my God."

Emma ran her small finger along the name under the photo, then looked up at her, obviously puzzled by her mother's reaction.

"Who's Isabella Marie Hunt, Mama?"

CHAPTER TWENTY

Framerton High, 2004

Izzy liked her job at Swirl most of the time. Seriously, what's not to like about working in an ice cream shop? She hadn't been there long, but she was getting the hang of it. She got to see lots of adorable little kids. She got to make really cool sundaes—her boss, Stacy, was very creative and there was always a new one to learn. And she was making her own money.

Swirl was a cute little place, tucked in the middle of a strip mall between a karate studio and a fabric store. More than one night a week, they'd get flooded with kids in their gis, a word Izzy had only learned because a young boy had gently corrected her when she called it his "karate uniform." Those were the best nights. Nobody appreciated ice cream the way kids did.

It wasn't super busy in the early spring. People were still working themselves out of winter, which often felt like it lasted nine months in the northeast, and ice cream wasn't always the first thing on their minds. It would pick up by a lot once the weather really broke, Stacy had warned her, so Izzy took advantage of the quiet to catch up on her homework, and that was what she was doing when *they* walked in.

Tara the Tormentor. That was her name, as far as Izzy was concerned. That was who she was in Izzy's journals—which she continued to write in because if she didn't, she'd go insane, but she hid them much better than in the past. Tara was accompanied by her crew, of course, because bullies never went anywhere without an audience. Tara's boyfriend, Noah. Kayla and Blake. Easton and Connor. All six of them entered through the doors of Swirl, laughing and happy, the guys fake-punching each other, as high school football players seemed to do constantly for no apparent reason. The second Tara met Izzy's eyes across the shop, her entire face lit up.

Fuck. Izzy let out a long breath and resigned herself to the impending awfulness, hoping it wouldn't last too long.

"Well, well, well. If it isn't Dizzy the Runt." Tara approached the counter, her face sporting its usual, evil expression of torment, the others followed slowly. Tara hurried Easton and Connor with, "Hey, E. Your *lesbian admirer* is ready to take your order." As was always the case, she spoke the words "lesbian admirer" much louder and with more emphasis than necessary, and of the few customers that were already in the shop, a couple heads turned to look.

Izzy felt her face heat up, damn it, and vowed not to even look at Easton Evans. Instead, she kept her eyes downcast and muttered, "What do you want?"

"I want ice cream, of course," Tara said, again, louder than necessary. "I would like a small blackberry cone. Noah wants a large chocolate almond cone. Please." As if adding that last word would take away her horribleness.

Blake ordered a hot fudge sundae to split with Kayla, and was nice enough about it. Connor ordered a sundae as well. "And Easton wants a small vanilla cone with sprinkles."

"Make sure they're the *rainbow* ones," Tara added with a wink. "The sprinkles of your people, right?"

Izzy did her best to ignore them, got to work on the cones first. She handed Tara hers, wishing there was a way to do so without touching her.

"Now, there aren't any, like, gay cooties on this, right?" Tara asked, feigning hesitation over taking a bite. When Izzy didn't answer, she leaned closer and prompted, "Are there?" Her eyes held a nasty spark.

"No," Izzy said quietly and turned away to make Noah his cone. He took it, held it up, and raised his eyebrows in expectation as Tara snorted a laugh. "No," Izzy said again.

"No gay cooties on my ice cream, guys," he said to the others. "But you should probably double-check when you get yours."

Stacy appeared at that moment. She was young to own the shop.

Barely thirty. Hip. Trendy. Her hair was in a ponytail, a streak of hot pink decorating the center of it. She had a diamond stud in her nose, an eyebrow piercing, and the edges of a tattoo visible at the collar of her shirt. She was super nice and funny, and Izzy liked her a lot. "Need a hand?" she asked Izzy, who, despite her fondness for Stacy, wished she'd just go in the back to her office so Izzy didn't have to be further embarrassed. Without waiting for an answer, Stacy glanced at the computer screen and started on the two hot fudge sundaes. "I'll make these together. You do the vanilla cone."

With a nod, Izzy did as she was told, taking her time on Easton's cone, rolling it in the sprinkles. She crossed the floor and held it out to Easton.

"Look at that," Tara said. "Gay sprinkles on your lesbian ice cream cone from your *lesbian admirer*. Easton, you are *so lucky!*" She drew out the last two words with over-the-top exuberance.

Easton took the cone, and Izzy was pretty sure she winked at her. Izzy's stomach rolled over and she cast her eyes down, tried to swallow the shame that came every time she was in the same room with Easton.

Stacy set the sundaes down on the counter, rang up the total, and stared at Tara as she paid. When the transaction was complete, she kept her voice low as she said, "You know, we're all-inclusive here. Everybody is welcome. Everybody is treated with kindness and respect. Our customers expect it of us and we expect it of our customers. If you can't manage to keep your obnoxious comments to yourself, maybe you don't need to come back."

Izzy was torn between acute embarrassment and indescribable gratitude as her six classmates shifted uncomfortably from foot to foot and muttered half-hearted apologies. All except Tara, whose expression was a cross between anger and humiliation.

"My father has a lot of power in this town," she said to Stacy, though the crack in her voice took away a lot of the venom. "I'll have him talk to the owner. He could shut this place right down, just like that." She snapped her fingers for effect.

Stacy, God bless her, rolled her eyes dramatically. "Well, you send him right over, okay? I'll be sure to let him know what a good job his daughter's doing keeping up the family's good name by making homophobic comments in a place of business." She pulled a business card out of her pocket and set it on the counter with a snap. "My name is Stacy Bruner. Have him ask for me. I own this place." She and Tara held gazes for what felt like a lifetime to Izzy before Tara finally backed down.

"Come on, you guys," she said in a huff, and stormed out the door. Noah was right behind her, but the other four sort of shuffled their feet, taking their time.

"Sorry," Kayla said, her nose wrinkled, then pushed her way out.

The other three followed, Easton taking a last glance behind her, making eye contact with Izzy that Izzy couldn't read for sure. Didn't matter. She wished she never had to see any of them again.

"You okay?" Stacy asked once the door had closed and the six were gone. Her voice tugged Izzy back to the present.

"Yeah. I'm fine."

"You don't have to take that, you know. You just call me up front. I'll handle it."

"Okay." Izzy grabbed a wet cloth, wiped down the counter where a few stray sprinkles were hanging out. She needed something to do.

"Hey, Iz?" Stacy's voice was soft. Kind. When Izzy looked at her, she said, "You're fine just the way you are. You know that, right?"

Izzy shrugged, then went around the counter to the area with the tables, needing to get away from Stacy and any talk of anything about her. There were less than three months left in the school year. It couldn't come fast enough for Izzy. She was going to grab her diploma, leave this awful town, and never look back.

And hopefully, she'd erase Tara Carlson and Connor Douglas and, most of all, Easton Evans from her life. Completely. She didn't want to see her ever, ever again.

Not ever.

❖

Doing okay today?

The text had apparently become Heather's standard daily check-in. Sometimes it came more than once a day. First thing in the morning, always. Then sometimes not until noon. Sometimes toward the end of the workday. And sometimes, all three. Monday, Tuesday, and now today, Bella had been checked on by text, by phone call, by email. And while she rolled her eyes and pretended to be annoyed by the poking, deep down, she was incredibly grateful for her friends. She texted back that yes, she was doing better.

Bella *was* doing better. Jonas's services on Monday had been hard. Emotional. His ex-girlfriend, the one who was now engaged to somebody else, was there, much to the dismay of Jonas's mother, if facial expressions were any indication. But the ex looked heartbroken, and Bella felt for her. While she wasn't the cause of Jonas's suicide—it was nobody's fault—she most likely felt that she was and would carry that with her for a long, long time. Bella didn't go to the actual funeral, only the wake, and she stayed in the back, not going through the reception line or up to the casket. Frankly, she wasn't sure how Jonas's mom would feel about her being there either, so she stood along the back wall and silently paid her respects to the client she'd known but couldn't reach. After half an hour, she headed to her office and threw herself into paperwork in the hopes of focusing on something else.

Gradually, things would get back to normal. She knew that in her head. It was going to take her heart a while to catch up.

But today was Wednesday. And Wednesday had a bright spot. A very, very bright spot. Today she would see Easton for the first time since Friday night. For the first time since they'd slept together. Bella was both excited and nervous. They'd done some texting since then, but Bella had sort of kept a bit of a distance. She didn't want to mix Easton in further with the sorrow she felt over Jonas, and she was pretty sure Easton had understood that. She'd kept in touch but hadn't pushed, and when she asked about tonight, Bella's heart soared. Seeing that gorgeous face was just what she needed right now.

It was a little after six and much of the building had cleared out for the evening, as usual. Bella was back after feeding Lucy and Ethel, and waved to the receptionist who worked until seven on Wednesdays so she could point people in evening classes and sessions toward where they needed to go. Before heading to the classroom, Bella had a few things to drop in her office, so she headed there, the proverbial spring in her step as she walked. Yeah, okay, she was really excited to see Easton. She was also a bit jittery, as she knew they needed to talk. Things had gone kind of sideways on Friday and nothing had gone as Bella had planned. It was time to fix that, to lay everything out on the table. It was well past time, and Bella was acutely aware of that, needed to prepare herself for the possibility that Easton might be upset when she found out what Bella had kept from her. But they'd talk and work through it, she was sure.

She'd just sat down at her desk and pulled a drawer open when she heard the very rapid click, click, click of heels coming down the hallway. Somebody walking very quickly. When she glanced up, she was surprised to see Easton walk right into her office and stop next to her desk. Bella had no time to be happy about her presence, though, because this wasn't the Easton she was expecting. This Easton was different. Still dressed in work clothes, still gorgeous, but different. Tense. Serious. Angry? Bella had never seen her angry, but it was pretty obvious by the way her dark brows formed a V above her nose and by the flashing of those blue eyes, usually the color of the ocean, but somehow seeming cooler, icy now.

"Easton. Hi." Bella felt her own brow furrow. "Are you okay?"

Easton looked at her for a moment, tilted her head slightly to one side, squinted a bit.

Bella's stomach churned. "What is it?" she asked quietly. "Tell me."

"Maybe you should tell me," Easton said, her voice equally quiet, but intense. Sharp.

It was Bella's turn to cock her head. "Tell you what?"

Easton reached into the messenger bag that dangled from her shoulder and pulled out something that made Bella's blood run cold. A lump formed in Bella's throat, and try as she might, she couldn't swallow it down. Easton opened a yearbook and set it on the desk in front of Bella. Her finger tapped a photograph, one Bella knew well because it was framed and hanging in her parents' house.

"Is that you?" Easton asked, her voice barely a whisper.

Bella suddenly understood what it felt like when somebody said the floor dropped out from under them. That was how she felt. She sucked in air very slowly, swallowed again, and scratched at her eyebrow. Without looking up, she nodded in slow motion and said, "Yeah," drawing the word out.

At Easton's small whimper, Bella did look up. Easton took a step back. "All this time?" she asked, and now it wasn't just anger, it was pain on her face. "All this time I talked about my hometown and my high school and, God, the things I thought about then. My secrets. And all this time, you knew you'd been right there in the same school? In the same classes? You knew me, and you never said anything? You never said *anything*." She enunciated the last line, accenting each word.

Bella's head was a mess. So many things. So many thoughts and feelings. All at once. All flying around like leaves on a windy fall day. She felt awful. She felt guilty. She should've said something sooner. She knew that. God, everybody knew that. She could picture Amy's *I told you so* expression in her head. "I meant to tell you," she began, her voice embarrassingly feeble. "I was going to on Friday—"

"On Friday?" Easton's eyes went wide. "We'd been talking, going for coffee, for weeks before that. *Weeks.*"

"I know." Bella swallowed, clasped her hands together to keep them from shaking, wondered how she hadn't predicted it might be this bad.

"Why did you wait so long, Bella? Or should I call you Isabella?" Easton didn't quite sneer her full name, but she didn't say it with any kindness, and the sarcasm that colored the word wormed under Bella's skin, lit a spark there that grew to a flame alarmingly fast and ignited the pain and anger from old wounds she thought she'd rid herself of for good.

"No, you know what? Why don't you call me Dizzy the Runt? Or better yet, Izzy the Cunt? That's the name you guys were most fond of. Or don't you remember?"

Easton's face went white with shock. With what looked like realization.

And in that moment, it hit Bella. "You *don't* remember, do you?"

"Oh, my God." Easton brought a trembling hand to her lips. "Oh, my God..." She shook her head slowly back and forth. "Bella."

"You and your friends made my life a living hell, Easton. How is it possible you don't even remember? The names you guys called me. The horrible bullying over my sexuality—which I wasn't even sure of at that point. I was so confused." Bella's voice dropped to a whisper. "The teasing you did, winking at me, blowing kisses, mocking me. How can you not remember?" Bella should be angry. She knew she should. But it vanished just as quickly as it had appeared. And just like that, she wasn't angry anymore. She was sad. Deflated. And for the first time in more than ten years, she felt every bit like that poor, confused high school version of herself. She propped her elbows on her desk and dropped her head, digging her fingers into her hair. "It figures," she muttered. When she looked up, Easton was gazing off into the empty office.

"Was this, like...revenge for you?" She brought her focus back to Bella, but her eyes didn't flash anymore. They were just...defeated and wet, her voice barely a whisper. "Getting to know me? Having dinner with me?" She paused, and Bella heard her swallow. "Sleeping with me?"

"What?" Bella looked at her in shocked disbelief, insulted. "No! God, no. You kind of need somebody to know all the facts in order for revenge to work. Yes, I knew who you were immediately, but it became pretty clear that you didn't recognize me, so I was happy to leave it that way."

"Why?"

"I—" Bella started to answer. She wanted to answer. But the truth was, she didn't really have an answer. It was true that, at first, she'd have been perfectly fine to never reveal their common background to Easton. She'd have been totally happy for them never to connect on any level other than a professional one. But then... "I don't know," she finally said, her own irritation obvious in her tone. "I liked you."

"Oh."

"Yeah, oh. In my defense, I didn't want to. And I didn't expect to. And I would rather not have."

"I see."

It stung. Bella could tell by the quick flash of pain that zapped across Easton's face as she looked around the office, cleared her throat.

"I didn't recognize you. Like, at all."

Bella snorted as she waved a hand over Easton's form. "Yeah, well, not all of us are born looking like you. Some of us take a while to get comfortable in our own skin. I've changed a lot, physically. I did a lot of hiding in high school, trying not to be seen by your crew. Took me years to realize I didn't have to do that."

"And you changed your name."

"Sort of, yeah. I didn't want to be Izzy ever again. I grew to hate her. She was weak and pathetic. Bella is a different person entirely. I knew you had no idea who I was."

"And you thought never telling me was the best idea?" Easton held her arms out from her sides.

"I wasn't sure how, Easton. I didn't plan any of this. It just sort of…happened this way. What would you suggest I say? 'Hi, remember me? I was the poorly dressed chick in high school with a major crush on you that you and your friends bullied and teased relentlessly until I was able to graduate and run as far and as fast as I could from you. Nice to see you again!' Would that have been the best way to approach it?"

Again, she'd stung Easton. She could see it on her face. Her mouth opened, as if she was about to say something, then she closed it again and cast her eyes downward. She said nothing, words seeming to have left her.

Bella glanced at her watch, grimaced. "Damn it," she muttered. To Easton, she said, "Listen, it's almost seven." She was in no mood to teach tonight. Not even close. But she had no choice. "I have to get ready."

"Sure." Easton gave a nod, turned, and slowly left Bella's office.

The yearbook was still open on Bella's desk and she almost called to Easton to come back and get it, but honestly, she needed a minute alone to collect herself. To catch her breath. To figure out how not to burst into tears. There was an ache in her chest now and she didn't know how to deal with it. She and Easton had something. *Had* had something. But she'd let it slip through her fingers because she was too afraid of facing her past.

She closed the yearbook quietly, not wanting to look at poor Dizzy the Runt any longer. She'd been banished, and Bella had no desire to bring her back. She'd worked too hard and too long tucking her away in a tiny box and putting her on a high, high shelf in her brain. The cruel twist of fate—that even after seeing her face in the yearbook, Easton still hadn't remembered Izzy—seemed fitting. Izzy was going to stay in her box. Bella had no intention of ever bringing her out again.

Except that maybe she needed to.

CHAPTER TWENTY-ONE

"Hi, sweetie, how was school today?" Easton was curled on the couch, her feet tucked under a blanket, looking much more like a person weathering an icy winter than somebody in her house on a warm June evening, the daylight still hanging on even as it was after 8:00.

For the next twenty minutes, phone pressed to her ear, she listened as Emma told her every intricate detail of her day, few of which had anything to do with learning. Easton couldn't help but smile at her daughter's exuberance, as well as the impressive speed of her words as she went on and on. The list of important things in life was so enormously different to a child than to an adult, and Emma was no exception. Things that warranted a lot of her seven-year-old attention included the odd texture of cafeteria pizza, Archie the class turtle who went home with a different kid each weekend, and her friend Jessie's super-curly hair. "How can I get mine like that, Mama?" She didn't really wait for any answers before moving on to the next topic, which was her upcoming sleepover Saturday night. Her first.

"Okay," Easton said, finally about to get a word in. "Time for you to get washed up and ready for bed. Let me talk to Daddy and then I'll come back and say good night."

"Wow," Connor said, when he was able to get on the line at last. "Are your ears bleeding?"

"My God, our child can *talk*," Easton said, with a chuckle.

"She's ridiculously excited about the sleepover. Can't stop talking about it. I'm gonna let her sleep in on Sunday, since I doubt five seven-year-old girls will get much sleep when they're all together. So, I'll let you know when she's ready for you to pick her up." There was a short pause as he grunted in exhalation and Easton assumed he'd sat down. "So, hi. What's new?"

His voice was a relief in her ear, and Easton still marveled at how they'd managed to keep their friendship intact, despite their split. Connor knew her better than anybody else, and when she was feeling uncertain or confused or frightened, and her grandfather wasn't available, he made a great sounding board and gave pretty reasonable advice. This subject, of course, wasn't something her grandfather could help with.

"Remember Tara Carlson from high school?"

"Of course. She dated Noah for a while senior year, right? I still talk to him on Facebook once in a while and I see her on his page here and there. Why?"

Easton scratched at her forehead, trying to figure out how to explain the new information she had and not sure where to start. Deciding to just dive in, she said, "Do you remember that girl that Tara was so awful to? The quiet one? She was new junior year, came in from that school that closed."

She could picture Connor sifting through his memories, sandy brow furrowed, probably running a hand over his bald head. "Tiny thing? Dark hair? Carried her notebooks against her chest like a shield?"

"Yes. Her."

"What the hell was her name...?" He drew the words out, indicating he was thinking, thinking...

"Izzy Hunt."

"Yes! Dizzy the Runt, Tara called her."

"Among worse things."

"Yeah." The regret in Connor's voice was apparent now. "We were not nice to that poor girl. Tara was brutal. And us guys weren't much better."

"We all went along with whatever Tara said. God, we were such followers." Easton shook her head now, because on her drive home from Bella's office—she'd bailed on the conflict resolution class—she'd started having sudden recollections of things that were done and said to "Izzy" back in school. By Tara. By her. It was as if finding out Bella's real identity had opened a floodgate of long-forgotten memories that now came washing through Easton's brain like water through a broken dam. None of them made her proud.

"We were kids," Connor said. "Kids are assholes to each other."

"True. But we were bad. Remember when Tara made her drop all her books and then snatched up her journal and started reading it out loud to the class?" That had been a particularly horrifying memory when Easton's mind conjured it up. She'd been in her car at a red light when she remembered Tara gleefully reciting all Izzy's confusion about her sexuality. The horrified expression on Izzy's face as she tried to grab the notebook back.

"Oh, God. Yeah, I do. Ugh." Connor sounded as mortified by their behavior as Easton felt, and she was grateful he didn't just brush it off as the poor decisions of teenagers. "That poor girl. If I remember correctly, she'd had a dream about you, right? A sex dream?"

Oh, my God. Easton had forgotten that part.

"And Tara never let anybody forget it. She brought it up all the time and you'd wink at her or blow her a kiss."

Easton closed her eyes against the guilt that washed over her. "Oh, God," she said quietly. "I did, didn't I?"

"I mean, you weren't Tara..." Connor let his voice trail off, the unspoken *but you were kind of awful* hanging between them.

Bella's voice replayed in Easton's head then, something she'd said earlier. *I was the poorly dressed chick in high school with a major crush on you that you and your friends bullied and teased relentlessly...* "She had a crush on me," Easton said quietly, not sure if she was talking to Connor or herself.

"Tara sure thought so."

"No, she did. She told me."

"Wait." Connor's confusion was apparent. "Who told you?"

"Bella." Easton shook her head. "Izzy."

There was a beat before he said, "I'm so lost."

Easton sighed. "Bella. Remember her? At the park with the dog?"

"The pit bull that scared the shit out of us but ended up in love with Emma? And vice versa?"

"Yeah. Her. That's Izzy." She could almost hear the gears turning in Connor's head as he tried to understand what she was saying. "Bella Hunt is teaching my conflict resolution class. Her full name is Isabella Hunt. In high school, she went by Izzy."

"Holy shit. Really?"

"Really."

"You've kind of…been seeing her. Haven't you?"

Easton inhaled, let it out slowly. "I have."

"But you didn't know she went to high school with us? You didn't recognize her?"

"Did you?" Easton tried not to snap the two words.

"No," Connor admitted. "She looks completely different, but…I honestly didn't really pay a lot of attention to her in school, so it's not surprising I didn't recognize her."

"Yeah, neither did I."

A second or two of silence went by. "You mean she didn't tell you?"

"No. My yearbooks were in one of those boxes you sent home last weekend, and Emma got them out. We were looking through them last night, finding pictures of you and me, when we got to the senior pictures. And there she was."

"Wow."

"Yeah."

"And you talked to her about it?" Connor's voice was soft now. Gentle. As if he knew how hard this was on Easton, though he couldn't possibly.

"I stomped right into her office today, all full of righteous indignation, and I let her have it."

"What did she say?"

Easton felt her entire body deflate like a pool toy being put away for the winter as she recalled Bella's reaction, her face, her pain. "She told me how awful high school had been for her, how hard we all made it on her, how she'd never expected to ever see me again, and when she did, and it was obvious I didn't recognize her, how she didn't plan to tell me who she was at all. But then we got close…and then closer, and she meant to tell me last Friday…" She went on to tell Connor about Bella's client's suicide and how she'd shown up to Easton's house, utterly distraught. Her voice got quieter and quieter as she told him how they'd just curled up on the couch, how Bella said she needed to feel alive.

"Did you sleep with her?" His tone held the tiniest sliver of accusation—because how could it not; he was her ex and he still loved her—but Easton could tell he was trying to be gentle, to be there for her.

"Yes," she answered on a whisper.

"And then you found out she's actually known you for, what? Fifteen years? That she's from the same town? That she waited on you when you went out for ice cream?"

"Oh, my God, I forgot about that." The full weight of it all hit Easton then. The realization that she'd paid so little attention to the small girl called Izzy back then. That she was barely a blip on eighteen-year-old Easton's radar in school, but that Bella remembered every detail of every interaction they'd had.

I was the poorly dressed chick in high school with a major crush on you that you and your friends bullied and teased relentlessly...

"It must have been so awful for her, Connor." Regret and guilt and sadness all rolled together to sit in Easton's throat, and her eyes welled up.

Connor must have sensed her emotion. "E, listen. Kids are rotten to each other. It sucks, but it's true. And most of us grow up to be decent people. We can't change high school. We can't change how we treated others. But *we were kids*." He stressed the last words gently.

It was like a vault in her memory banks suddenly flew open and added to the flood from earlier. In the blink of an eye, Easton could see all the different images of Izzy Hunt back then. The pain in her eyes—how had Easton never seen their unique color?—the shame on her face. The way she always walked: very quickly, head bent down, probably hoping to pass by without being noticed. Not that Tara ever let that happen.

"You can't beat yourself up." Again, Connor's voice was gentle, but it didn't make the visuals of young Izzy fade away.

You can't beat yourself up.

No? Couldn't she?

Shouldn't she?

❖

"Wow."

Heather had said the word three times now, and they sat quietly as the waitress cleared their dinner plates and asked Bella if she'd like a box for her barely touched burger and fries. She nodded in defeat.

"I don't know, Bells." It was the first time Amy had spoken since Bella launched into the story. She hadn't wanted to tell her friends what had happened with Easton over a text, so she'd called an emergency meeting and waited until the three of them were together, face-to-face, having dinner at a local sports bar. Then she'd spilled it all. Every detail. How indignant Easton had been. How angry that had made Bella. The things they'd said. How Easton had walked out slowly, like an extra hundred pounds had been added to her shoulders. How she'd skipped the conflict resolution class—which, in all honesty, was probably best for both of them at the time.

And how very badly she wanted to talk to Easton now.

"I don't know," Amy said again, shaking her head slowly from side to side, toying with the cocktail straw in her vodka tonic.

"What don't you know?" Bella asked, though she was pretty sure she knew the answer.

"I think you should just let this go. It's caused you both a lot of pain, you know? Let it all go."

"Like, don't call her, don't text her, the end?" Bella asked. "We have one more class, but I don't know if she'll come." If Easton didn't show, Bella would credit her for the class anyway. She hadn't really needed it, and they both knew it.

"Yeah. Just move on. I think, just chalk it up to one of those weird things life throws your way. And hey, you got laid, at least. Ow!" Amy flinched as Heather slapped her arm. "What?"

Heather just closed her eyes and shook her head as if she was at a complete loss over how to deal with somebody like Amy. The *what the hell is the matter with you?* went unspoken but hung in the air in the center of the table.

Bella shifted her gaze to Heather. "What are your thoughts?"

Heather picked up her glass, sipped her Cosmo, her face pensive. After a moment, she sighed, long and slow. "I wish you guys could have a do-over. Like, see each other for the first time again and do things differently."

"Yeah, like *tell her you went to school together*," Amy said, one eyebrow arched as she emphasized her main point. "I told you not to wait, and you kept waiting."

"I know, I know," Bella said, then took a slug of her rum and Coke.

"Leave her alone about that," Heather said to Amy. "She heard you."

Amy's frustration was obvious. "Yeah, but, this could've been something awesome. It really could have."

"And I blew it. Believe me, I'm aware." Bella wanted to be annoyed with Amy. With her insistence on reminding Bella that she should've spoken up, should've come clean. "But, you know, this hasn't been easy on me. Seeing Easton again conjured up a lot of memories for me. A lot of really bad, really painful ones. I wasn't popular in school like you guys. My parents had no money. A lot of my clothes were from Goodwill and sometimes, it was obvious. I got bullied before bullying was a thing."

"We know," Heather said quietly, and closed her hand over Bella's. "We do. I'm sorry you had such a rough time in high school."

"When I got the Facebook invite to our ten-year reunion? I laughed. Out loud. Like, cracked the hell up. Why the fuck would I ever go back there? There isn't enough money in the world. I never wanted to see that place or those people ever again. In my life."

"We know," Heather said again. And they did. None of this was news. Bella had come out with all of it the first month of sophomore year in college when the three of them had gotten drunk together in their suite and all the secrets came out, solidifying their friendship forever. But Heather didn't prod her. Didn't hurry her along or stop her mid-sentence. She just let her go on.

"And then, out of the blue, there she is. In my fucking class. Looking all gorgeous and friendly and the best/worst part is, she doesn't even recognize me. When this all came out on Wednesday, it was pretty clear that Easton Evans had barely noticed me in school, while simultaneously making me miserable. Isn't that ridiculous?"

Okay, she might have been a tiny bit tipsy at this point—it was her second drink, and she hadn't eaten more than two bites of her dinner— and she was getting a bit maudlin, not to mention she was dropping way more F-bombs than usual for her. She pushed the cocktail aside and grabbed her water glass instead. "Sorry," she muttered.

"Don't be," Heather said. "Don't you dare be sorry with us. We love you." She glanced at Amy, who nodded and shot Bella one of her cocky half-grins that was a combination of "I love you" and "I'm sorry for being an asshole."

Bella returned it with a small smile of her own. She had her friends, and for that, she'd be forever grateful. Nobody got her through life's crap like Amy and Heather. Bella turned her hand over, grasped Heather's, and squeezed. "Can we talk about something else now?"

❖

Easton didn't think she'd ever get used to having Friday nights to herself. Sometimes she went out to a movie. Sometimes she'd meet up with Shondra or, more likely, go to her place. She and Connor had made this schedule intentionally, so that each of them would have one night of the weekend free to go out, to date, to…whatever might come up.

Last week at this time, I was naked. Right here on this couch. With a beautiful woman touching me, doing things to my body that I haven't felt in…ever.

She lay there, eyes closed, and let herself remember what it was like to have Bella above her. That gorgeous face, those expressive eyes, her alarmingly knowledgeable hands. The heat. The desire. The sounds. God…

Easton's eyes snapped open and she shook herself. No. She couldn't go there again. She'd spent way too much time there over the past couple of nights, reliving what was one of the most intimate experiences of her life. But now she was sad, a little battered, and couldn't go there again.

The television was on for company, its volume low. Easton wasn't really watching it. An old episode of *The Simpsons* was on, but she didn't pay attention, instead focusing on the laptop propped on a throw pillow on her thighs. She had a few reports to look through that she hadn't gotten to that day because she'd spent way too much time gazing out the window, unable to concentrate, visions of Bella filling her head.

Obviously, the same thing was happening now, as she tried to recall anything on the report she'd just read and failed spectacularly. With an irritated scoff, she clicked out of her work app and opened Facebook. Before she could stop herself, she typed Tara Carlson's name into the search bar and hit Enter.

She wasn't hard to find. Still in Framerton. Her relationship status said she was married and that her two-year anniversary was coming up. So, not married very long because…this was hubby number two?

Easton went scanning through Tara's photos, noticing with a glee that made her feel the tiniest bit ashamed that Tara wasn't aging well. She looked a good ten years older than thirty-three, her dark, leathery skin telling Easton she either spent too much time in the sun or in a tanning bed. Easton would bet on the latter. Letting her memory take her back to high school, Easton recalled how short Tara was with people she deemed not worthy of her attention. She was pretty sure Tara only kept her around because her family had money and it looked good to pal around with the child of surgeons, but Tara had never been warm to her. Or to anybody, really. After scrolling past several very conservative political posts, she wondered why Tara had been—and evidently still was—so angry at the world. She also wondered why she'd never asked her. Maybe she'd needed a friend. Then she remembered how Tara took such immense pleasure in reading Bella's most intimate thoughts out loud to an entire classroom. That coupled with an anti-LGBTQ post was enough for Easton to shake her head and click off the page.

She didn't allow herself to think about it before she typed in Kristin Harrington's name. It was a common name and a long list of possible matches came up, but Easton found her within a minute. Interesting, that.

"I guess high school crushes never really go away," Easton said to herself as she clicked on Kristin's little icon.

There she was. Her profile photo was her with two little redheaded kids. A boy and a girl, smiling widely. Just like that, Easton was transported back, because she could see Kristin's features in both children. According to her profile, she was a fifth-grade teacher in a small town just outside of Albany. Easton studied a couple of her photos. She was still pretty, really hadn't changed much. Red hair, kind green eyes, welcoming smile. Easton tried to think back, to remember what exactly it was that drew her so solidly toward Kristin, even though Kristin had no clue at all. It had to be the kindness. Any memories Easton could conjure up, Kristin was smiling in them. She always said hello, was nice to everybody. And she had that wholesome peaches-and-cream aura that pulled people in.

Maybe my taste in women isn't all bad.

The guy in the photos that Easton deduced was Kristin's husband looked a bit familiar, and she wondered if she'd find him in the yearbooks still in the box in the corner. Easton hadn't gotten them out again since she'd seen Bella. Hadn't wanted to revisit.

A huge sigh hissed out of her as she thought about how awful life must've been for Bella. For the first time, she concentrated, really thought about what it must have been like. It was true that Easton remembered very little about Bella—she still wasn't sure if that was a good thing or a bad thing—but as she sat there looking at her former high school crush—she could admit that now—she pictured Kristin doing to her the things that she and Tara had done to Bella. What if Kristin had known Easton had a thing for her? What if she'd used that to make Easton's life a living hell? Teased her, blew sarcastic kisses across a hallway for all to see. Winked at her just to see how long it would take before she either turned red or burst into tears. Took every opportunity she had to out Easton? Make her feel small. Worthless. Unwanted.

It wasn't something Easton had ever thought about. It never occurred to her back then that somebody would do something like that to her, even as she unwittingly did exactly that to tiny Izzy Hunt, who she hadn't even really known then and had barely remembered now. What kind of person did that to another human being?

Easton didn't realize she'd been crying until a tear spilled down her cheek and she swiped at it. No wonder Bella didn't tell her about their shared past. Why would she want to relive that? Easton had no business being angry about that anymore. Not now. Not after memories had begun to seep back in, reminding her that just because she wasn't as horrible a person as Tara was, she was no better because she did nothing to stop her. Did nothing to help Izzy Hunt. Didn't punch any of the guys when they called her Dizzy the Cunt, not even her own boyfriend, who knew—then and now—how Easton felt about that word. Fifteen years later, she flinched at the awful moniker. How could she have just let that slide?

"We were kids. Kids are assholes to each other."

She heard Connor's voice, knew he was right. But she also didn't think that was a good enough excuse. Easton was a mother now, and the thought of somebody making Emma so sad that she couldn't wait to get the hell out of town made her heart squeeze in her chest and her mama bear instincts begin to simmer in her gut. How must Bella's parents have felt? Did they even know?

So many questions. So many regrets. So many memories. Easton sat there and stared off into the middle distance of her living room as her brain went around and around and around. It was a giant, discombobulated jumble, but there was one clear thought. Just one.

I want to start over.

Chapter Twenty-two

The advantage of not showing up at the park mid-morning on a Saturday, Bella found, was that there seemed to be fewer people rather than more. This surprised her as she unloaded Ethel and Lucy from the car and walked them around the paved path to an emptier part of the field.

"Do you think daddies bring their kids earlier so mommies can sleep in?" she asked her dogs, neither of which seemed to have an answer, though Lucy looked as though she was thinking about it. "Or maybe people come here in the morning so they can do other stuff the rest of the day?" Whatever the reason, Bella was glad for the sparse crowd. Fewer people to worry about giving her a look because her (big teddy bear) dogs were scary looking.

She'd had trouble getting out of bed this morning. Then she'd had trouble getting herself moving. Motivated. Finding any ambition at all to go forward. Her fight—and subsequent breakup—with Easton had been three days ago, but she still felt as battered as if it had happened in the past twenty minutes.

"Can you break up with somebody if you're not even sure you're dating them?" she asked aloud. Again, Lucy glanced up at her, wise brown eyes seemingly absorbing her words. "Sure feels like it."

She'd dragged herself through the morning, managing two cups of coffee but nothing to eat. She'd made it from her bed upstairs to her couch downstairs, and she'd killed another two hours lying there, staring at the television. She couldn't recall what she'd watched. At all. No idea.

Both Amy and Heather had texted her, probably from the same

place, she'd thought with more than a hint of envy, but she hadn't felt like talking. Again. She was wallowing, it was true, and she wanted to wallow in peace. For as long as she felt like it. With nobody to tell her she shouldn't.

The far end of the enormous open field was pretty much deserted, so Bella took a tennis ball from her pocket and hurled it as far as she could for Ethel, who went bounding after it with uncontained excitement. Lucy settled down onto the grass with a sigh and watched.

The day was overcast, and for that, Bella was oddly grateful. Cheerful sunshine and inviting blue skies would've just made her feel worse. At least the dull grayish-white clouds matched how she was feeling. No rain. No thunder or lightning. She wasn't angry. She didn't want to lash out. She was simply...sad.

Ethel could play ball all day long, and that was just fine with Bella. And Lucy, apparently, who'd fallen over on her side like she'd given up on life. Bella sat down on the grass next to her and placed a hand on her warm belly as Ethel trotted back toward her with the ball for the nine-hundredth time. Bella threw it and watched Ethel run. A little slower at this point but still magnificent, the power in her lean, muscular body obvious. She got the ball on the bounce, then turned to trot back to Bella.

Except she trotted right past her.

"Hey," Bella said firmly as she turned around to see what had caught Ethel's eye. Her voice stuck in her throat then as she saw Easton, all blond and beautiful, striding toward her as if she owned the park. She stopped to pet Ethel, who seemed thrilled to see her, the traitor. When the tennis ball was dropped at her feet, Easton picked it up and threw it for a surprising distance, sending Ethel off to chase it once more.

"Hey." When she reached Bella, she held out a hand like a traffic cop. "No, don't get up. Just...hear me out. Please." And just like that, she went from quietly confident to glaringly nervous. Her hands trembled, Bella noticed, and she put them together in front of her stomach, fiddling with her nails as if trying to keep her hands busy. She looked out in the distance, at the trees, at the sky, down at Lucy, who'd sat back up and was studying her with interest. Anywhere but at Bella. A shaky chuckle escaped her lips. "You know, I don't have Emma tonight, so I have an entire day to get things done. Instead, I've been sitting in that parking lot for nearly four hours, just hoping you'd show up so I could talk to you. I had plenty of time to rehearse, and now that I'm on…" Her voice trailed off as she shrugged. "Everything I wanted to say just sounds…" She blew out a breath. "So lame."

Bella pulled her gaze away, watched as Ethel strolled slowly back to them.

"I'm sorry, Bella." Easton's voice was small, filled with so many emotions, Bella couldn't keep up. "I'm sorry for now, but mostly, I'm sorry for then."

She looked…defeated. That was the only word Bella could come up with to describe the sadness, the resignation on Easton's gorgeous face. Her dark brows were turned down slightly over her nose, as if she'd been thinking hard about something for a long while now. Her full lips were pressed together in a thin line. Bella didn't like seeing her this way, but her words from Wednesday were still fresh. *"Was this, like…revenge for you? Getting to know me? Having dinner with me? Sleeping with me?"* She understood what might have made Easton feel them. Say them. But they still sliced through her like a razor blade, despite Bella's harboring a pretty significant secret. The fact that Easton thought she could do something so diabolical as to plot a sexual revenge fantasy and then carry it out…she had trouble swallowing that one.

And then she heard Amy's voice. *"I think you should just let this go. It's caused you both a lot of pain, you know? Let it all go. Move on."*

Easton looked up at the sky, scratched the back of her head, and gave a rueful smile. "Yeah, this isn't coming out like I imagined it would, so just let me say it again: I'm really sorry, Bella. I never meant to hurt you. Then or now."

"I'm sorry, too," Bella said. "I should've been up front from the beginning. It was unfair of me."

Easton held her gaze for what felt like a long time, and Bella felt like she was searching for something. Then she gave one nod. "It's okay."

There was so much more to say and nothing more to say. Bella had never felt both things so acutely at the same time before, so she continued to simply look at Easton, her mouth staying shut, her voice box keeping silent. Her swallow was audible.

Easton cleared her throat. "Thanks for listening," she said, barely a whisper. She laid her hand on Ethel's head, then turned and strode across the field back toward the parking lot. Bella watched her the entire time. She didn't want to, but she couldn't manage to pull her eyes away. Something tugged at her heart. Something important and she clenched her jaw as Easton got into her car and drove out of the parking lot. Bella had the strangest feeling that Easton had just driven off with a small part of her.

And she needed to get it back.

❖

Why did she feel like this?

Easton had to stop crying. This was ridiculous. She hadn't known Bella that long. A few dates. One night on the couch. This couch. Where she lay now, used tissues strewn across the coffee table, the Food Network on the television as it was the only channel she could count on to not have anything remotely resembling a love story.

She'd screwed it up in the park. Somehow. She'd rehearsed it over and over, and it always sounded so genuine and sincere—because it was!—but Bella hadn't reacted the way Easton had hoped. She'd apologized, yes. She seemed to accept Easton's apology, yes. But that was the extent of it.

"What, did you think she was going to jump up and throw herself into your arms, Evans? God, you're pathetic."

Yes, she'd also taken to talking to herself again. A lot. This was what it had come to.

"You blew it. You had something that could've been great, but you blew it because you unloaded on her. You gave her no chance to explain anything. You let your anger take over…" She stopped talking, wishing she could go back to that moment in Bella's office, wishing she'd handled it differently. She had every right to be angry, but she should've listened more instead of just beating Bella up over it.

Which was exactly the kind of behavior high school Bella—Izzy—knew from her.

Easton's eyes welled up again. Thank God Emma wasn't there tonight. She was a mess, and the last thing she wanted to do was explain her state of mind to a seven-year-old.

But she needed to talk to someone. She knew that beyond

a shadow of a doubt now. It was something she'd toyed with since Olivia had happened, but she'd never pulled the trigger, always had some reason to delay it another day, another week, another month, until another year went by. The irony was not lost on her that Bella was a therapist.

Easton snorted, which morphed into a quiet sob, and she swore as she reached to snag another tissue from the box just as the doorbell rang.

She sat up quickly, confused. It was seven in the evening, a light rain was falling, and she was expecting nobody. She grabbed her phone and gave it a quick glance in case she'd missed a call or a text while she'd been crying like a five-year-old.

Nothing.

"Shit," she muttered as she stood.

Easton blew her nose, took a deep breath, and hoped she looked halfway presentable as she crossed the living room to the front door, which she pulled open.

"Hi," Bella said, standing on the front stoop looking damp, a little windblown, and absolutely beautiful. Her dark hair was tousled and wavy, her hazel eyes were wide and hopeful. In her hands were a bouquet of purple daisies, a paper bag, and a bottle of wine.

Easton blinked at her. Dabbed the tissue under her eyes. Blinked some more.

Bella didn't wait for an invitation. She stepped through the door and set the wine and bag down on the table near the coat closet. "Listen," she said, standing tall—or as tall as somebody as petite as Bella could. "I saw you at the park earlier and—this is going to sound weird—but I think we know each other. In fact, I think we went to school together. Are you from around here?"

Easton blinked again, felt suddenly like she was having trouble keeping up. She took a moment to stare into those eyes. Eyes that were now saying so very much, showing so very much: hope, certainty, happiness, and more. Way more. Easton cleared her throat as she began to understand what was happening. "Is this…is this a do-over?" she asked quietly.

One corner of Bella's mouth lifted as she leaned forward and said, her tone conspiratorial, "I thought we could use one." Then she stood back up and asked again, "So, are you from around here or…?"

Easton shook her head with a hesitant smile. "No. A town a few hours east. Framerton."

"No way!" Bella's face lit up with excitement. "Me too!" She stuck out a hand. "Bella Hunt. It's nice to meet you."

Easton slowly put her hand in Bella's and felt the warmth radiate around her as Bella held on. "Easton. Evans."

Bella gasped loudly, brought her fingers to her lips in a lovely display of overacting. "Easton Evans, you say? Wow, this is strange, but…I don't think you were my favorite in school."

"No?" Easton played along, beyond interested to see where this was going.

"Oh, no. See, I had a major, *major* crush on you." Bella scooped up the flowers, paper bag—which Easton now realized smelled delicious—and bottle of wine and headed into the kitchen as she talked. "I was dealing with my sexuality, which I didn't know at the time, of course, because hello? Seventeen years old."

Easton followed her, let her talk. Once in the kitchen, Bella held up the bottle and Easton dutifully retrieved a corkscrew and two glasses.

"Every time I saw you, I got all weird and tingly inside." Bella shook her head as she chuckled and went to work with the corkscrew. "I was pathetic. No idea how to deal with what was going on in my head. I think I would have loved to talk to you." The cork popped, and she poured the deep crimson wine. "I also think that would've been a nightmare for both of us, so it's probably better that I didn't. Plus, you were always with that other girl who loved to make other people's lives as miserable as possible."

"Tara Carlson," Easton supplied.

Bella tipped her glass toward Easton and wrinkled her nose. "Her." She handed Easton a glass. "I wonder why she was so unhappy." That line was said in a quieter, more pensive tone, and Easton was amused that as adults, she and Bella had wondered the same thing about Tara. Then Bella seemed to shake herself as she looked back up.

"Can I add to this?" Easton asked quietly. She had the sudden urge to unload, but this time, in a good way. Maybe "unburden" was a better word choice. When Bella raised her eyebrows, Easton continued. "I want to be completely honest with you." She paused. Swallowed. "It's important to me."

Bella gave one nod.

Easton pulled out a chair, feeling the sudden need to sit during this conversation. She took a large sip of her wine, hoping to gain some courage from it. Bella followed suit with the sitting and once they were both settled, Easton set her glass down, folded her hands on the table, and held eye contact with Bella, those hazel eyes still full of so many things. They gave Easton strength. She took a deep breath.

"I'm so sorry, but I didn't remember you." She swallowed again, took another sip of her wine to help move things in her throat, to help the words come out. "I hate saying that, but it's true. And that's because I was going through the same thing you were."

Bella's brow furrowed in confusion.

"I was struggling as well. And I also had a crush. On a girl."

"You did?" Bella's voice was soft, tinged with surprise.

Easton nodded. "I did. Do you remember Kristin Harrington?"

Bella squinted in thought. "Redhead? Super nice to everybody?"

"That's her."

"You were crushing on her? But you were with Connor."

"I was. So, you can see my dilemma." A bitter chuckle followed.

"Wow. I had no idea. You were just so…" Bella met her eyes. "Put together. Perfect. You were perfect to me. I couldn't get you out of my head."

A scoff escaped Easton's lips. "I'm sure my perfection ended up pretty tainted."

Bella tipped her head to one side, then the other. "Yeah…"

Easton felt a gentle laugh bubble up. "Yeah."

"Did you ever tell Kristin? Or anybody?"

"That I thought I liked girls? Hell, no. I come from a family of successful medical professionals. We were well-known in the community. My mother, in addition to being a surgeon, was on every committee known to man. There was a path I was supposed to follow, just as my siblings did. Get straight As. Go to medical school. Marry a man with ambition who comes from a successful family. Have children. Be a pillar of the community. Nowhere was there anything about falling for a girl." She brought her gaze to Bella's, saw the wheels turning, and pointed at her. "Hey. Stop analyzing me, Ms. Therapist." She smiled to make sure there was no sting in her words.

Bella blinked. "Sorry. Occupational hazard."

"It's okay."

They sat quietly, and while Easton felt like she was waiting for something she couldn't identify, it was still companionable. Comfortable. In that moment, there was no place else she wanted to be than sitting in a room with Bella.

"I have an idea. Kind of." Bella's expression was uncertain, but hopeful.

"Okay. Tell me your kind of idea."

"I'd like to try to leave our past behind us. I mean, it's there, of course. It always will be. But we were kids."

"That's what Connor said," Easton told her with a sad smile.

"You told him about us?" Bella didn't seem angry or freaked out. Just mildly surprised.

"I did. I needed to know what he remembered, if he felt as horrible as I did."

"And?"

"He knew we'd been assholes a lot of the time. He felt pretty awful about it. But he also reminded me that we were kids, still figuring ourselves out, and that we're different people now. Not an excuse. Just a fact."

"That's true." Bella studied her hands, then looked up at Easton. "I'll make a deal with you."

"Okay." Easton drew the word out, not knowing what to expect.

"I'll let go of my blame if you let go of your guilt."

Easton could almost feel the weight of the words, the importance of the steady eye contact Bella gave her now. "I'm so sorry, Bella," Easton whispered, her eyes welling up. "I'm so sorry I made things hard for you. Then and now."

Bella's watery smile was everything in that moment as she reached across the table and grasped Easton's hand. "I know you are. And I forgive you. Okay? I forgive you."

A small almost-sob pushed itself from Easton as she felt her heart expand, fill with warmth. They stayed like that for a long time, just holding hands across the kitchen table, enjoying the silence of being together, the silence of forgiveness, of a possible future and what might come.

After a long while, Easton cleared her throat and finally spoke.

"What's in the bag?" she asked as her gaze landed on the paper sack Bella had brought with her.

Bella's eyes widened as if she'd completely forgotten about it. "Oh, my God. Dinner. It's dinner. Chinese. Probably cold now."

"Good thing I have this newfangled contraption called a microwave. It heats up food in a matter of minutes! Shall I demonstrate how it works?"

Easton was pretty sure Bella's smile lit up the entire room. "Yes, please."

"One condition."

Bella's dark brows raised. "What's that?"

"We eat it upstairs. In my bed. How does that sound?" Easton wanted nothing more than to spend time with Bella, to be close to her.

"Nothing has ever sounded more perfect."

Focus on the Chinese food hadn't lasted long. Two bites? Three, maybe? Bella hadn't been able to pay much attention before Easton's mouth was on hers, the lo mein and the cashew chicken moved to a dresser and instantly forgotten. Which, of course, was totally expected the second it was suggested that they eat in the bedroom.

"A bed instead of a couch, huh?" Bella had asked teasingly. "I'm moving up in the world."

"Hey, you're the one who was all about the couch that night," Easton teased back.

That night. That night had been amazing. It had been a cure, though. It had filled a void for Bella.

Tonight, though? Yeah, tonight was different.

Bella knew that immediately. From the first kiss, which Easton had initiated, and Bella was grateful for that. The last time they were together hadn't been as much about them as it had about connection in general. About feeling enmeshed with somebody. About feeling not alone.

This time, it was about them.

Easton was everywhere. It was the only clear sentence Bella could manage to form in her brain as she lay on her back in Easton's bed, trying to pinpoint where the indescribable pleasure her body felt was coming from. Easton was everywhere. Her hands. Her mouth. Her tongue. Her body. Her voice. All of her. Every inch of her surrounded Bella, touched her, loved her, lifted her higher and higher until she felt as if she was floating.

With no recollection of her clothes having come off, Bella lay naked beneath the most beautiful woman she'd ever laid eyes on. Easton's mouth on hers, Easton's tongue pushing in deeply, Bella gave back as much as she could, though she wanted more. Always more. She couldn't touch Easton enough, couldn't feel enough of her skin, couldn't smell enough of her scent, couldn't push her own tongue deeply enough into Easton's mouth. She managed to fumble Easton's bra off and capture both breasts in her hands, pulling a moan from Easton's throat. But Bella wanted more. So much more of everything.

"God, can't get enough of you," Easton whispered, as if reading Bella's mind. "You're so damn sexy."

"Yeah? Right back atcha," Bella told her, then tightened her grip and groaned as Easton's knee, tucked between Bella's legs, pushed up into her, pressed against her, rocked gently. Bella gasped at the contact.

"Yeah?" Easton asked. "You like that?"

"Very much." Bella was surprised she was able to form words at all, even two small ones, but that talent left her altogether when Easton slid a hand down her stomach and into her wetness, replacing her knee with alarmingly skilled fingers that seemed to know just what Bella needed.

It was too much. Was it too much? It was definitely too much. Bella tightened her grip on Easton, picked up Easton's rhythm as they moved together, gently at first, then more insistently. Her orgasm was hurtling toward her as Easton wrenched their mouths apart.

"Look at me," she whispered, and Bella had to force her eyes open. Easton didn't stop moving, didn't stop rocking. Just held Bella's gaze. And what Bella saw in Easton's eyes was something she'd never seen before. Never felt. She felt her own eyes tear as the words she knew were coming tumbled softly from Easton's lips. "I love you, Bella. I know it's too soon to say that, but I can't help it. It's true. I'm so in love with you."

Though she'd had plenty of warning it was on its way, Bella's orgasm dropped her off a cliff then, sent her rocketing through space on a stream of color and sensation as every muscle in her body tightened and she pulled Easton down to her, wrapped her arms around her, held on with everything she had.

Time was impossible. It meant nothing. Bella had zero idea of how long she lay there, catching her breath, eyes closed, the delicious weight of Easton's body pressing hers to the mattress. Might have been a lifetime. She had no idea. She didn't care. All she knew was that she was perfectly happy to stay just like that and never move.

Easton was the first to shift. She lifted her head from Bella's shoulder, pushed herself off to the side slightly, and Bella immediately missed the feel of her, the warmth. After a moment, Bella opened her eyes and focused on the gorgeous female form next to her.

Easton's face seemed…pensive. Uncertain. Her eyes darted a bit.

"Hey," Bella said softly. She smiled, reached for Easton's chin, turned her head so she could look her in the eye. "Don't you know?"

Easton's dark brows formed a V above her nose. "Don't I know what?"

Bella's smile grew wide; she could feel it. Her heart warmed in her chest and she had the strangest sense that her soul…settled. It was the only way to describe it. She felt settled. Like she was exactly where she was supposed to be. Finally. It was almost weird, almost fantastical that things would've ended up this way, that she would *feel* this way. How was it even possible? Fifteen years had gone by. Bella had done everything she could to scrub Easton from her memory and for the most part, she'd succeeded. But now? This? Looking into those big blue eyes, eyes that had drawn her for so long, eyes that held such love and kindness, eyes that were waiting for her response, Bella spoke the truth that suddenly filled her heart to overflowing, a truth so deep she didn't understand how she'd ever missed it. She let the words out. "Don't you know it's always been you? For the past fifteen years? I've tucked you away, but you never left. You've always been hanging out in the background somewhere, just waiting…waiting."

Easton's eyes widened, then filled, and a tear spilled over as she blinked at Bella. Bella caught the tear with her thumb, stroked Easton's cheek, and said it again, because nothing had ever felt so completely right.

"It's always been you."

About the Author

Georgia Beers is the award-winning author of more than twenty lesbian romances. She resides in upstate New York, where she was born and raised. When not writing, she enjoys way too much TV, not nearly enough wine, spin class at the gym, and walks with her dog. She is currently hard at work on her next book. You can visit her and find out more at www.georgiabeers.com.

Books Available From Bold Strokes Books

Comrade Cowgirl by Yolanda Wallace. When cattle rancher Laramie Bowman accepts a lucrative job offer far from home, will her heart end up getting lost in translation? (978-1-63555-375-8)

Double Vision by Ellie Hart. When her cell phone rings, Giselle Cutler answers it—and finds herself speaking to a dead woman. (978-1-63555-385-7)

Inheritors of Chaos by Barbara Ann Wright. As factions splinter and reunite, will anyone survive the final showdown between gods and mortals on an alien world? (978-1-63555-294-2)

Love on Lavender Lane by Karis Walsh. Accompanied by the buzz of honeybees and the scent of lavender, Paige and Kassidy must find a way to compromise on their approach to business if they want to save Lavender Lane Farm—and find a way to make room for love along the way. (978-1-63555-286-7)

Spinning Tales by Brey Willows. When the fairy tale begins to unravel and villains are on the loose, will Maggie and Kody be able to spin a new tale? (978-1-63555-314-7)

The Do-Over by Georgia Beers. Bella Hunt has made a good life for herself and put the past behind her. But when the bane of her high school existence shows up for Bella's class on conflict resolution, the last thing they expect is to fall in love. (978-1-63555-393-2)

What Happens When by Samantha Boyette. For Molly Kennan, senior year is already an epic disaster, and falling for mysterious waitress Zia is about to make life a whole lot worse. (978-1-63555-408-3)

Wooing the Farmer by Jenny Frame. When fiercely independent modern socialite Penelope Huntingdon-Stewart and traditional country farmer Sam McQuade meet, trusting their hearts is harder than it looks. (978-1-63555-381-9)

Shut Up and Kiss Me by Julie Cannon. What better way to spend two weeks of hell in paradise than in the company of a hot, sexy woman? (978-1-163555-343-7)

Spencer's Cove by Missouri Vaun. When Foster Owen and Abigail Spencer meet, they uncover a story of lives adrift, loves lost, and true love found. (978-1-163555-171-6)

Unexpected Lightning by Cass Sellars. Lightning strikes once more when Sydney and Parker fight a dangerous stranger who threatens the peace they both desperately want. (978-1-163555-276-8)

Without Pretense by TJ Thomas. After living for decades hiding from the truth, can Ava learn to trust Bianca with her secrets and her heart? (978-1-163555-173-0)

Emily's Art and Soul by Joy Argento. When Emily meets Andi Marino she thinks she's found a new best friend, but Emily doesn't know that Andi is fast falling in love with her. Caught up in exploring her sexuality, will Emily see the only woman she needs is right in front of her? (978-1-163555-355-0)

Escape to Pleasure: Lesbian Travel Erotica, edited by Sandy Lowe and Victoria Villaseñor. Join these award-winning authors as they explore the sensual side of erotic lesbian travel. (978-1-163555-339-0)

Ordinary is Perfect by D. Jackson Leigh. Atlanta marketing superstar Autumn Swan's life derails when she inherits a country home, a child, and a very interesting neighbor. (978-1-163555-280-5)

Royal Court by Jenny Frame. When royal dresser Holly Weaver's passionate personality begins to melt Royal Marine Captain Quincy's icy heart, will Holly be ready for what she exposes beneath? (978-1-163555-290-4)

Strings Attached by Holly Stratimore. Rock star Nikki Razer always gets what she wants, but when she falls for Drew McNally, a music teacher who won't date celebrities, can she convince Drew she's worth the risk? (978-1-163555-347-5)

Answering the Call by Ali Vali. Detective Sept Savoie returns to the streets of New Orleans, as do the dead bodies from ritualistic killings, and she does everything in her power to bring their killers to justice while trying to keep her partner, Keegan Blanchard, safe. (978-1-163555-050-4)